FIRE MOON

URBAN FANTASY ROMANCE

ANN GIMPEL

Edited by
ANGELA KELLY
Illustrated by
FIONA JAYDE

CONTENTS

FIRE MOON

ALPHAS IN THE WILD, BOOK FOUR

Urban Fantasy Romance Laced With Myth and Magic

Dark. Daunting. Unforgettable.
Survival adds a demanding edge to love in the wilds.

Fire Moon is dedicated to my friend, Sue Bolich. Sue was one of my first writing mentors, and we grew close over the last several years. She's the one who talked me into going to my first science fiction-fantasy convention, and she roomed with me at many more beyond that first World Con. Sue lost an eleven-year fight with breast cancer on October 4, 2016. The world is a dimmer place without her in it, and I will miss her. If you enjoy high fantasy, be sure to check out S.A. Bolich's books. You won't be disappointed.

BOOK DESCRIPTION:

Cara, a mountain guide with a hard luck past and John, a doctor running as hard as he can from his own demons, become unlikely allies. Fire raging through the Sierras forces them away from their planned route and makes escape a dicey proposition.

Cara struggles to outwit the inferno before it's too late. John's long-denied psychic side escapes its bonds, refusing to be ignored any longer. He recognizes the fire for what it is: magical creatures bearing the worst news of all. Fire dragons want Earth for themselves, and they'll stop at nothing to make it theirs. Protecting Cara from the destiny that's finally hunted him down turns into John's top priority, but spirit guides shanghai him, forcing his hand.

He never wanted a woman in his life. Too many complications —but something about Cara touches his heart.

She was burned out on men and vowed she'd spend the rest of her life in the mountains, guiding clients—but something about John sings to her soul.

If they can survive the dragons that set the earth ablaze, a different kind of heat just might bind them to each other.

CHAPTER 1

"*D*amn!" Cara Carlisle coughed and pulled the moistened bandana up over her nose again. It didn't help much, but anything was better than nothing. Squinting against the ever-present smoke, she wriggled to make her position on the narrow ledge more comfortable and checked her single piece of climbing hardware. It didn't budge when she tugged on it. Sweat dribbled from beneath her snug-fitting helmet and stung her eyes.

Piton's secure. What happens when I run out of water? Will the smoke do me in before thirst drives me mad?

"Climbing!" John's voice echoed off the canyon walls.

"Take your time. Be careful," she yelled. "I've only got a single pin in. It's okay for me, but…" As soon as the words were out, she rapidly hammered in another piton a few inches farther up, looping the rope through a second locking carabiner. The clatter of aluminum hanging off John's gear rack told her he was getting closer. More to kill time than anything else, she examined the rock face. The crack she'd chosen to defeat the thousand-foot wall zigged upward as far as she could see, but she couldn't see all the way to the top, not even close.

Fire raging through Kings Canyon National Park spread below them and made this route irreversible. They couldn't retreat, so she crossed her fingers and breathed a silent prayer she'd chosen well.

Fires weren't all that unusual. They rampaged through the Sierra Nevada Mountains every summer, especially as run-off from the last season's snow diminished to a trickle, but some idiot of a work crew boss must have brought in explosives to finish needed trail repairs. One of the fires had likely gotten too close, a stash of dynamite detonated, and the autumn-dry forest went up like a torch.

Cara had been high on the eastern escarpment of Dragon Peak watching it happen. To escape, she'd led her clients—there'd been three of them then—over an unknown, and as far as she knew previously unclimbed, route down toward Rae Lakes. They'd ended up miles from their camp on the wrong side of a thirteen-thousand-foot ridge. Wind had thwarted her, fanning the fire with breakneck speed, and narrowing retreat possibilities.

"Ah shit," she muttered through clenched teeth as memory jabbed her mercilessly.

Her next route choice had been a mistake, forcing them high onto this rock wall. So many other mistakes peppered her slightly less than thirty-five years, she winced. Having kicked the door-to-looking-back wide open, she stood at the lintel, an unwilling witness to her travesty of a girlhood. About the only thing she hadn't done wrong back then was running away from her drug-addled mother and Betty, her mom's bitch of a partner, the second she finished high school.

She still remembered that afternoon, saw herself as a gangly seventeen-year-old, ratty valise clutched in one hand, trying to rouse her mother enough to tell her goodbye. She'd finally given up. It didn't matter much one way or the other since her mother wouldn't remember. Goodbyes were for the living, and drugs had killed her mother's humanity.

Betty's words slammed against her as she headed out the door. "You'll never amount to nothing. Nope, nothing but trouble from you. Your ma'd be better off if you was dead."

Cara shivered, swallowing around a lump that formed in her smoke-sore throat. Once the memories wakened, it was pointless to stem their tide.

Might as well let 'em roll.

In rapid succession, she shuffled through her years of waitressing and a brief stint with a cruise line she'd left the minute it became clear *other* things were expected of their hostess staff. After that, she'd found Leif—or he found her. She'd never been sure quite which. Crack climber, ace skier, Leif had been a mountain man to the core. He was also a drunk and a womanizer and nasty as all get out, but he had taught her about the mountains. It had been Leif—nagging, pushing, and criticizing— who'd seen she got her certification as a guide. If it wouldn't have been for the avalanche that obliterated the entire group he'd been leading up Annapurna, she supposed she'd still be with him. Miserable, but at least not alone.

After Leif's death, she'd pretty much shunned men. She snorted under her breath, and her face contorted into a scowl.

No matter how far I run, I can't get away from Ma and Betty.

Cara squeezed her eyes shut tight and forced herself to focus. Wallowing in the past was an indulgence. She tucked her raggedy black braids more firmly into her bright red windbreaker. Hair caught fire fast. Her helmet protected most of it, but it was best if she kept the rest covered. Looking at the flames raging five hundred feet below, she felt an almost unbearable urge to just let go and finish things off.

"Bad call, sister!" she hissed. "I have to stay in the moment. I lost the other two. I owe it to John to hold it together." A flash of pain tugged at her attention and she realized she'd bitten through her lower lip. The jangle of John's hardware grew louder, and movement intensified on the rope.

"Easy, now," she called down. "You're close. Here, let me just scoot up to the next ledge."

"Not yet," he rasped. She heard an odd undernote in his voice, and he was panting. Not good. "I just have to—"

"It's all right, John. Take all the time you need." Cara tried to infuse confidence she wasn't feeling into her voice. She was good at what she did, had been leading and training climbers for over ten years, but this was one of the worst situations she'd ever landed in.

If you're so good, an inner voice—Betty's voice—mocked, *why aren't Ruth and Christopher still here?*

"Because," Cara snarled, "they didn't follow my instructions. They panicked and ran for the ranger station, right into the heart of the fire."

You didn't follow them. The implacable voice continued. *You were their guide. They paid you to take care of them.*

"I may have been their guide, but I didn't sign up to follow them into Hell." Control fraying dangerously, Cara tightened her hold on the rope until her hands hurt. "What the fuck am I doing talking to myself?" she muttered.

"Cara? Who are you talking to?" John's sooty face appeared out of nowhere at the level of her boots; his blue eyes were red-rimmed and bloodshot from the smoke. He sounded even more uncertain—or maybe concerned—than he had earlier.

Of course he's concerned. He just heard me talking to myself, sounding like a crazy person.

"It's okay, John. I'm okay." She stretched out a hand and helped him onto the ledge. "Ready to settle in? I'll get us up the next pitch."

"How many more do you think?" He coughed, choking on the smoky air. His flame-colored hair fanned around his gaunt face and stuck out at odd angles beneath his orange climbing helmet.

"Pitches?"

He nodded, licking his dry, chapped lips. "Yeah, can't quite see the whole crack from here."

"Uh, maybe half a dozen. I can't see the top from here, either."

"Around the corner—" he jerked his thumb behind him "—I thought I saw a way off here in, maybe, only a couple hundred feet." He hesitated. "You probably didn't see it because you were just looking at this crack."

"There's a different one?" she asked, nonplussed. How could she possibly have missed it? She *had* looked. In fact, she remembered looking. Leif had taught her to *always* look. It wasn't that his lessons were wrong, but they'd turned brutal fast if she didn't respond immediately to all his directives.

John nodded again and then croaked out, "Yes."

"Did you see a way from this crack to that one?"

"Not exactly. But I don't see things the way you might. It's worth the time for you to take a look, though."

"Okay." She blew out her breath. "Can't hurt. Belay me. I'll rap down a little and see if I can't pendulum over to it."

"What happens if you like it better? We need a plan while we're close enough to talk without yelling. Don't know about you, but my throat is trashed from the smoke."

"Mine is too. If there's a better crack, I'll position myself above where we are. Once I'm there, I'll swing my second rope over and top rope you up to me." Struggling to keep exasperation out of her voice—because she was certain there wasn't another way off this wall—she added, "Look, John, we have to move fast here. I don't know about you, but the smoke's really getting to me. My eyes feel gritty, and I'm nearly out of water. We've got at least a few hundred feet to go yet. If we can just get over the shoulder of Mount Rixford, there's an easy way down the other side to the Kearsarge Pass trail. We can get out from there."

Maybe. If Onion Valley's not on fire too.

"Okay, I'm good here," he said, his voice carefully neutral, as if he sensed she didn't believe him and didn't want to push things.

She watched as he went through the same wasted motions she had trying to carve something approximating comfort from their slender ledge. A rustling noise caught her attention. She sought its source and watched a small group of kites rise out of the smoke, their long graceful wings spread as they tried to escape the inferno.

"Too bad we can't fly," she said wryly, pointing at the raptors.

"Do you suppose they're coming for us?" The question was casual, but John stared at the birds through eyes narrowed to slits.

His question was so off-the-wall, she twisted to look at him. "Why would you even say that?"

Color flooded his sharp-boned face. "There's an old Indian legend about kites being spirit guides. About them showing up to cull the warriors from the cowards." He looked away, obviously embarrassed. "I know I don't look it—" he tugged at a coppery chunk of hair "—but my dad and grandmother are Lakota Sioux. She told me lots of stories growing up, because she said a man without history is like wind on the buffalo grass."

Cara forced out a laugh to cover sudden discomfiture. John's words creeped her out, and the last thing she needed right now was one more impediment. Something else standing between them and escape.

"John. I need you to focus." She infused a stern, no-nonsense note into her voice. "Those birds don't mean a thing. They're trying to get out of here, just like us."

Taking a deep breath, she pounded in another piece of hardware, pulled up the rope, and threaded it through a breaker bar into a figure eight. Double-checking everything, she moved one hand behind her and rappelled down about twenty feet to where she could see something. Breath whistled loudly through her teeth when she located John's crack.

"Jesus, how could I have missed that? It's practically a chimney," she snapped, furious with herself.

"Tension!" she yelled, as she began swinging the rope back and forth. Cara reached, lunged, extended her fingertips, but the crack remained stubbornly out of reach. She squeezed her eyes shut tight, sure the smoke was playing tricks on her. The crack seemed like it was moving away. Just when she was certain she'd have it this time, she missed by centimeters.

Panting and sweating, she let herself hang in her harness and stared at the elusive crack. Damn if it didn't look close enough to touch—except she knew better. She rapped down a few more feet to give herself more rope and a longer reach. She'd be worse than a fool if she let herself get caught up in believing the crack held some sort of supernatural power. This was a granite face. Solid granite. And that was just one more crack, although it was a damned promising one.

If she could just reach the fucking thing.

She pushed her body from side to side, using her feet against the rock to establish momentum. Each arc back and forth widened her reach. Penduluming could be a risky maneuver, and she hoped to hell it wouldn't place her square in the path of rocks falling from above. Reaching with the fingers of the hand that wasn't holding her rappel position, she flattened her body, stretching, making herself as long as she could.

Please, she sent up a prayer to the mountain gods. *All I need is a couple more feet.*

Aha!

The tips of her fingers grazed the edge of the crack. So much for her moronic occult theories about the damned thing teasing her by moving away. Next swing, she'd have it. Sending every second of her years of experience into her fingertips, she felt them connect with the edge and clung to it like a limpet. Triumph soared, but she didn't let herself relax until she'd jammed a foot into the crack.

She was getting ready to call over to John when she heard wings rustle again and felt a stab of pain in her rappel arm.

Surprised more than anything, thinking a rock must have fallen, hitting her in the forearm, Cara looked over—and froze.

One of the birds had landed on her. Its sharp black beak was firmly buried in the folds of her jacket, and the pain was excruciating. Shocked and sickened, she put her other foot atop the first one to stabilize her stance and tried to shake the bird off, but its talons only tightened.

"Okay," she said in measured tones. "Take that you son of a bitch."

Cara flung her arm hard against the wall. The bird's head cracked open on the granite, and it dropped like a stone. Red bloody pulp and black feathers joining the deeper red of the hungry flames.

Examining her jacket, Cara found bloody tracks where the kite's talons had dug deep into her flesh. John's words about the birds coming for them slapped her hard.

Aw shit, we don't need any more problems. It's not like there aren't enough of them already.

Stop it. Just stop right now. Those birds aren't any weirder than this crack was. Get a grip for Christ fucking sake.

"Cara?" John shouted. "The rope's slack. You okay?"

"It's good. The crack's going to work," she shouted, controlling her sense of outrage and anxiety about her latest assailant—and kicking herself for not alerting John as soon as she no longer needed his help. "Off belay. Coil the rope. Give me a couple minutes to shinny up this crack and I'll get my rope down to you. This will sound bizarre, but watch out for the birds."

"What?" He sounded wary, but not surprised. "The ones near me flew away."

Cara took a deep breath. Warning him was the right thing to do, no matter what kind of nut-job it made her sound like. "Watch out for the goddamned birds. Either you might've been onto something with your Native American legend stuff, or the smoke's made them feral. Put on an extra jacket if you have one. Do it before you rescue the rope."

She worked her way up the crack, which widened slightly as she climbed. Unfortunately, it was angling away from where she'd left John. If she went much higher, the rope wouldn't reach.

"Okay," she called out. "I'm going to snake the rope your way. Be ready."

"'Kay. Hurry, Cara. Those fucking birds are back, and they're dive-bombing me."

"Why didn't you say anything?"

"Just hurry."

A flat, dead tone underscored those two words. It chilled her and she swung the rope, gratified he caught it on the first try. "Got you," she shouted. "Give me a minute to secure you to this piton. I'll tell you when to come. Double check your knots."

There was a brief pause and she heard him call, "Now?"

"Not yet. Wait for me to tell you."

"Got it."

He sounded like he was holding on by the thinnest of margins, but covering it with bravado. She got set up for him as fast as she could. The sooner they got to the other side of Mount Rixford, the better she'd like it.

CHAPTER 2

"Now," she hollered. "Remember, nice and slow. There will be more rope movement since I'm not directly above you. Don't let it bother you."

"I'm not a neophyte climber," he yelled back. "Be there in a flash."

When he came into view five minutes later, climbing like a spider, her eyes widened in disbelief. Birds perched on his arms and his helmet. Blood dribbled from over fifty flesh wounds, and she developed a whole new level of respect for John. He wasn't screaming or trying to dislodge the bastards. His entire focus was climbing.

As soon as he came within reach, she batted at the kites, swinging her gear rack at their heads. Some flew away, but most clung tenaciously.

"Thanks," he gasped, tucking his lanky frame into the chimney right below her. "I was okay until I had to use my arms to climb, and then they were all over me."

As if they understood what John's hands being free meant, the remaining birds squawked at one another. They let go as a unit and spread their wings. Soon they floated lazily across from the chimney, staring speculatively at the two humans with their beady avian eyes.

Cara scanned the air below them and felt as if someone had booted her in the stomach. Air whooshed from her in a rush. More birds, at least fifty of the black-winged fuckers, circled up from the hellhole below.

"I haven't spent that much time in the Sierras, but I've never seen kites here before," John said in a voice devoid of intonation. "Have you?"

"No," she growled. "But we can't worry about that now. Climbing is our top priority." She shortened the length of rope between them. "We have to get out of here." Turning, she slithered easily up the chimney. For a brief moment, the joy she'd always found in ascents filled her, but it didn't last. John's question about the birds nagged at her. She'd never seen a kite anywhere in the High Sierra, either. What the hell did that mean? Where had they come from? Had the blast from the dynamite altered the ecosystem in some unnamed way?

Impossible. Things like that change slowly over time. Not in one fell swoop.

Wonderfully chilly air wafted from somewhere. Curious, Cara shifted her attention toward it. "Follow me," she instructed. "There's a cave just above me. And water I think. I can smell dampness."

"What about the top?" John asked. "I vote for us to keep moving."

"We can always get there. It's only a couple hundred feet above us, and the route is clear. Easy low Class Five. We could free climb it if we had to, but we need to at least check if there's water in this cave to refill our bottles. There won't be any on top of this peak, and not for a long way down the other side."

And I need to think about what to do next if Onion Valley is on fire. After we get to the top and I can see something.

Pulling her body through a rounded opening, Cara entered a rough cavern. Just as she'd suspected, a pool huddled against one wall fed by a small cascade of water running down the granite. John stepped beside her and glanced around the dimly lit cavern.

"Here," he said, and thrust his water bottle toward her. "You're closest to the water, but this place feels wrong to me. Sooner we get back outside, better I'll like it."

Cara dropped her pack and pulled out a headlamp. Clipping it to her helmet, she fired it. She retrieved her water bottle and John's and covered the few feet to the pool, trying to keep her elation in line while replaying the events of the past couple days. First the fire, then her clients making a suicidal run for false shelter, then this climb out of hell, and now water. Blessed water. Exactly what they needed most.

"Are you sure it's okay to drink?" John's tense query intruded into her thoughts like a raggedy, louse-ridden guest.

"Yes, I'm sure. No humans or animals to contaminate it." Hearing frustration in her voice, she aimed for a more conciliatory tone and added, "We're tired. We need a break. Let's have a little water and an energy bar..."

Her voice faltered, and a small yelp escaped. Grinning maniacally at them, a gleaming white human skeleton balanced precariously between boulders in an alcove in the rock.

"Wonder how he ended up here," John muttered. He donned his headlamp and twisted from side to side, examining the cave, "Shit! There's more. I knew this cave felt bad, but— Hang on." His voice faltered on the last part of *hang on*. "There's something on that wall. I'm going to have a look."

Cara followed his light and saw other bodies. Methodically, dully, she counted ten, some just bones, while others had stringy bits of flesh still clinging to them. The scraps of clothing scattered about looked modern, but there wasn't enough left to tell for sure. Hurriedly filling their water bottles, she dropped John's near the opening to the cave and moved to stand next to her client. Written in dull dusky red that looked like blood, repetitive words inscribed on the granite walls made her head spin crazily. Nausea rose so fast, she was sure she was about to puke.

Birds blazoned across the rock. Announcement as well as warning.

Birds. Birds. Birds.

Another word she couldn't interpret showed up too. "Can you read that?" She pointed to the unrecognizable group of letters.

"Yeah. It's one of the Sioux expressions for birds."

"Oh my God," she moaned and choked back bile as her imagination leapt off the edge of a cliff into crazyland. "No wonder I didn't see this chimney the first time. I didn't see it because maybe it wasn't there. Aw, Jesus. It's beyond farfetched, but that inviting crack only formed *after* something sensed our presence. The chimney is macabre bait and we're the—" She tried to stem the torrent spewing out her mouth, but it kept right on churning.

Cara was babbling; she couldn't stop herself. "This whole thing's nothing but a trap, like something out of a grade B horror movie." Twirling abruptly, she flung on her pack, stuffing her headlamp into a pocket. "We've got our water," she gritted out and had trouble breathing around the knot in her chest. "You were right. We need to go. Now."

Goddammit. I'd been planning to settle in here. Take a break.

Mistakes. More mistakes.

"I don't figure it will be that easy." John's voice broke on every other word. He spun away from her. She heard the zipper of his pants and then smelled urine, acrid and pungent, as it spattered against the stones littering the floor.

"What did you mean about it not being easy?" she asked once he'd turned back to face her. "The birds are still a huge threat, but why would you think we couldn't get out the same way we got in?"

"They—" he flung his arm in a semi-circle "—didn't get away. Someone—or something—lures people in here and…and…"

"Maybe that was a long time ago," she interrupted sharply. "These bones have been here for a while."

"If something's eating them, there'd be no way to tell how long they've been here."

"My, aren't you the cheery one," she muttered as she bent to ease herself through the rounded opening leading to freedom back in the outside world. Having overcome her descent into paranoia, she was back in full guide mode. "Come on. We'll be fine. Pick up your water and follow me."

The deafening sound of granite grinding against itself filled the cavern. Tasting dust, Cara threw her body through the opening, turning an ankle as stone jaws very nearly closed on it. John's screams followed her from the other side—the wrong side —of what had nearly become her prison.

Guilt threatened to obliterate her. She tore at the rock until her fingers were abraded and bleeding. Birds circled cawing, but none of them landed.

It's as if they're mocking my efforts. Telling me how futile and trivial they are.

The next thought, when it surfaced, was so outrageous she pushed it aside as soon as it formed.

Maybe they're not really birds.

Defeat settled about Cara like a shroud. She didn't know how long she'd been digging at the rock, only that her hands were bruised and aching from the effort. At first, she'd tried talking with John, but he hadn't answered, and she'd long since given up. Either he was dead, or he'd retreated deep within himself to a place she knew well. A place where the only one you communed with was yourself.

You've gone and lost another one, her nasty inner critic noted. *Cara, the great mountain guide. Bet if you told the truth, you'd never find another client.*

"Shut up!" she shrieked. "Just shut up." Twisting to re-establish her body in the chimney, she looked down. Flames still dissolved every living thing they came into contact with. Then she looked up and saw the kites. They'd settled on each outcropping, as far up the chimney as she could see.

It's like they're waiting. Waiting for me.

CHAPTER 3

John Cassavettes had followed Cara into the cave against staunch misgivings. It held a stench that made him want to vomit. Couldn't she smell the same thing?

Apparently not, but then she's not psychic.

He flinched. Of all the times for him to finally reach out and own his paranormal abilities—something he'd held at arm's length his entire thirty years.

He would have refused her cave idea entirely, but they did need water. Cara hadn't said much, but he wasn't all that certain the other side of Mount Rixford would lead them to safety. It was well above timberline, so there wasn't much that could burn, but the fire could effectively trap them. Keep them from descending. He'd done a credible job memorizing the topographic map of this section of the Sierras before leaving on this trip, but he'd be damned if he could recall the slightest detail now that he needed it.

Two days without water and they'd be done for, so he'd swallowed his qualms and piled into the cave after her. That unearthly smell—a cross between grave dirt and rotting carcasses

—had grown worse. A whole hell of a lot worse. That was when he'd voiced his opinion they needed to leave and handed his water bottle to Cara.

Because he couldn't not look, he'd located the skull…

No. He corrected himself. The putrid energy emanating from it had drawn him like a lodestone. He didn't have to stretch his paranormal ability very far to hear the dying screams of the cave's unwilling occupants. And he had no doubt if he dropped into trance state, he'd see how each of them died in bright, living technicolor detail.

John shuddered, grateful for the dim light inside the cave. Men weren't supposed to give in to fear, and he'd sounded petrified outside on the ledge. Cara had enough on her shoulders without him turning into a basket case. He drew the cave's dank air deep into his lungs, hoping it would steady him, but it just made things worse. It was so filled with hopeless terror from the poor sods who'd died in here, it made him want to slice open his veins and join them.

John settled for shallow mouth breathing. And hoped he wouldn't hyperventilate and maybe pass out. While he dug through the cave's grisly remains, something his grandmother told him blasted out of a pit deep in his subconscious.

He'd been slated to be the tribe's next shaman. Magic flowed strong in him, but he hadn't wanted anything to do with it. He'd run off to college, and then medical school. And then a family medicine residency in a poor section of Las Vegas where he could actually save lives no one else cared about. One of his few trips home, his grandmother caught him up and invited him to walk with her. She hadn't said much, but her words from that day had never left him.

"You can run away, Johnny-man, but your destiny will find you. No matter how hard it has to hunt."

He swallowed a snort as a spate of uncomfortable questions taunted him. It appeared that destiny was front and center—and there wasn't a damned thing he could do to change it. His medical training was done. He'd signed on with Doctors Without Borders and was due to leave for a desperately underserved area in equatorial Africa next month.

Would he still be alive to make that trip? Or would he end up stuck here in this cave?

Another shudder racked him. Cara wasn't doing very well either. Fear had loosened her tongue. He wondered what she'd be saying if she knew what he did. If she could smell the sour tang of magic that made his skin prickle and the fine hairs rise on the back of his neck.

Twirling abruptly, she flung on her pack, stuffing her headlamp into a pocket. "We've got our water," she gritted out. "You were right. We need to go. Now."

"I don't figure it will be that easy." John tried for matter-of-fact, but his voice broke on every other word and a sudden need to empty his bladder overwhelmed everything. He spun away from her and dragged his cock out. The stench of urine, acrid and pungent, almost covered up the reek of magic and death.

Almost, but not quite.

"What did you mean about it not being easy?" Cara asked once he'd turned back to face her. "The birds are still a huge threat, but why would you think we couldn't get out the same way we got in?"

"They—" he flung his arm in a semi-circle to encompass the cave's macabre occupants "—didn't get away. Someone—or something—lures people in here and…and…"

"Maybe that was a long time ago," she interrupted sharply. "These bones have been here for a while."

"If something's eating them, there'd be no way to tell how long they've been here."

"My, aren't you the cheery one," she muttered and bent to ease herself through the rounded opening that led to freedom back in the outside world. "Come on. We'll be fine. Pick up your water and follow me."

Listening to Cara, he had a whopping ten seconds of believing maybe they'd trounce the odds—make it out unscathed—before a harsh grinding beat against his eardrums. He dove for Cara's retreating form, knowing the trap was snapping shut and equally certain he'd never make it through. Hell, she barely did, and she must've wrenched her ankle all to crap since it disappeared through the crack a split moment before rock grated against itself, leaving him in darkness. A scream rocketed from his throat, followed by one more before he got a handle on his panic.

Not panic, he instructed himself firmly.

More a howl of frustration and defeat. If he lost it now, he was done for, and he knew it.

Outside, Cara yelled his name, but he ignored her. Nothing she could do for him. Maybe if he kept quiet, she'd do the smart thing, climb to the top of the chimney, and work on saving herself.

He still had his headlamp attached to the front of his climbing helmet, and he flicked it on. The sense of wrongness that had attacked him outside the cave ratcheted up tenfold, and he killed the light. Whoever was running this show clearly preferred darkness.

His heart hammered against his ribs, and his mouth went dry. Adrenaline left a harsh, metallic taste in the back of his throat. He sank to a crouch and wrapped his arms around his legs. At least he finally understood why he'd signed on for this climbing trip. Sure, he'd had time between finishing his training and his stint with Doctors Without Borders, and he'd always enjoyed climbing. But he'd preferred solo trips into Nevada's many mountain ranges. When this Sierra trip showed up on one of his online climbers' groups, he'd thought long and hard before signing up for it.

Cara's picture had drawn him. Something about her. Vulnerable and competent wrapped into one package was hard to resist, but he wasn't looking for a woman to tie him down. He'd be out of the country for the next year. Maybe longer if things worked out.

He'd still been waging internal arguments about the advisability of the trip when he filled out the liability waiver and sent in his deposit…

Slowly, as if he moved through thick mud, he rose to his feet and squared his shoulders. If this was some backhanded, sneaky, slimy way for the destiny his grandmother had threatened to find him, he'd meet it head on, goddammit. Not hunkered into a cowardly mess on the rock-strewn floor.

He breathed deep, ignoring the taint in the air, and used the extra oxygen to unlock the hidden place in his mind. The one where his power dwelt. It raced to his summons with giddying speed, obviously delighted to finally be free.

Three spirits flowed into the cave on the heels of his magic, surrounding him with crackling, blue-white light. The rotten stench gave way to ozone and the antiseptic scents he associated with the lab.

He thrust out his chest and narrowed his eyes. Maybe it was his magic at work, but the cave was illuminated enough to see the dead scattered through it. "I am Dancing Wolf, shaman apparent to my tribe," he said in the Sioux language. "What is your purpose in trapping me?"

"At least he owns his heritage," one of the spirit guides muttered.

"Indeed. We assumed he would not," another chimed in.

"The birds told us who you were," yet a third added. "Once they'd tasted your blood."

"What? You're spirit guides and you couldn't figure that out on your own?" John scoffed. Maybe if he could get this crew on the defensive, rattle them a bit, they'd let him go.

"It is not your place to question us." The first spirit slid right in front of John.

John reached for the thing intent on binding it with magic—

assuming he could recall the incantation—but his hand slid through icy, empty air.

"Uh-uh. None of that." The spirit had moved a couple of feet away. "We have a task for you."

"Not one you can sidestep—as you've sidestepped your duties to your kin and your tribe," the second spirit cut in.

"Each man is born for a purpose." The third spirit's voice was whispery, like wind rustling a pile of bone-dry leaves.

"I suppose you're going to tell me what mine is?" Though he tried to modulate his sarcasm, John didn't do a very good job. He forged ahead anyway. "While we're at it, let the woman leave unharmed. She's had a hard enough life—I've caught glimpses of it in her mind. She doesn't deserve to end up trapped in this cave."

His three hosts broke into brittle laughter that jangled John's nerves. He wanted to ask what was so funny, but held silence. Whatever this crew wanted, they'd tell him eventually. It was obvious they needed him alive—at least for now—or he'd be as dead as the cave's other occupants. The knowledge settled him, and the fear that had twisted his guts into knots began to retreat. If he could ensure Cara's safety, all would be well. Or as well as it could be for now.

He held himself ready. For anything.

Voices spoke into his mind, sketching out what they expected him to do. Incredulity vied with outrage. One man couldn't possibly accomplish all the things they'd just piled on his plate. Not in ten lifetimes. The only good part was they agreed to let Cara leave. Apparently this cave only trapped and held men and women the spirit guides wanted to test.

Culling the warriors from the cowards, just like he'd told Cara earlier.

"So the ones in here didn't make it out?" John tried for clarification.

"Does it appear they did?" one of the guides replied.

"You waste your time as well as our own," another said.

John switched tactics and opened his mouth to protest the rest of what they'd laid out, bargain it down to something manageable.

The first spirit shook his head. "I had you pegged for a braver man than that, Singing Wolf."

"It's Dancing Wolf," John gritted through clenched teeth.

"Doesn't matter. You'd give up before you even begin," the second guide muttered, sounding disgusted.

"Maybe we should sacrifice him now and be done with things." The third guide grinned, displaying the elongated roots of teeth set into bony gums. "Like I wanted to do in the first place."

Breath whistled through John's teeth. He was the only warm, living thing in the cave, and he didn't care for the odds. "What happens if I fail? Will I ever get my normal life back?"

"Your first task is to find your way out of this cave," one of the spirits said. "If you can't do that, none of the rest will matter."

Tell me something I don't know.

John shuttered his mind before anything else sarcastic leaked out.

The first guide glided within inches of his face. When he spoke, his chill breath coated John with miniature ice chips. "Hear me, *shaman apparent*. If you succeed, you may get your *normal life* back. By then, you'll no longer want it."

Before he could ask what the hell that meant, the spirits flickered and faded, leaving him alone in the dark with his magic. He tried to stuff it back under wraps, but it refused to go. Maybe it knew a hell of a lot more than he did about the hours and days to come.

Grim laughter bubbled out of his throat. "Okay, Destiny," he mumbled. "Bring it on. I may not be ready, but I know when I'm stuck with something."

Medicine had been a good proving ground. Many things had lodged unpleasantly in his craw, but he kept going anyway by focusing on the good parts and relegating the rest to a back burner. This wasn't any different. He moved to the boulder blocking the entrance and focused a beam of power to move it aside, not surprised when it didn't yield quite the way he'd hoped. It rocked, but didn't move.

Maybe everything the spirits had tasked him with would require a combination of his rusty magical skills and brute force. He bit his lower lip hard enough to draw blood. Whatever it took, he'd do his damnedest. It wasn't part of his makeup to give any less.

And he refused to join the lineup of bodies littering this cavern.

CHAPTER 4

*H*ours passed. Greasy, black smoke wafting up from the canyon thickened, and her lungs and eyes stung worse than ever. Cara was certain John had to be dead, but she hadn't been able to force herself to leave the chimney in front of the cave. She'd dozed off and on, waking because coughing racked her sore throat. Every time she looked up the chimney, more birds lined its sides. Even though she thought she should've been terrified, she had a hard time ginning up anything beyond indifference.

The screech of granite grating on itself had her on her knees in an instant. "John! You're alive!"

"More or less."

His voice sounded dry, dusty, unused, and for the barest instant she wondered what would crawl out of the cave. Cara put the kibosh on that train of thought fast. It had to be John. Nothing else in there had been alive.

Amid more grating, he managed to pry whatever was blocking the entrance to the cave back an inch or two. Noise and motion broke through the inertia that had gripped her ever since she'd escaped, leaving him a prisoner.

27

"I'll help you," she shouted. "On my count of three…"

She counted and pulled so many times she lost track. Her hands, already sore and abraded from grappling with the rock, bled so profusely she dug out her gloves. Sputtering and panting, she fought with the intransigent boulder as if it were a living assailant. From time to time, she talked to John, but he was back to not answering. She could hear him grunting, though, from inside the cave.

Snuffling snorts that sounded inhuman.

Her earlier fear rushed back, chilling her, but she swept it aside. John was in there, trapped because of her poor judgment. He needed help. Her help.

"Put your feet against it," she exhorted. "Brace yourself against something and push while I pull. Your legs are much stronger than your arms."

That last bit of advice did it. After a shuddering moan from the rock, a sibilant echo hung in the air. John stuck his boots through the hole, first one, and then the other. She thought about telling him to start with his shoulders since they were the broadest part of his body, but was so exhausted she couldn't find words.

Wriggling his slim body back and forth like a snake, he gradually emerged. Cara tried to pull on his clothing to help, but didn't get much purchase until she grabbed his climbing harness once his upper thighs came into view.

A grueling whimper escaped him, and she stopped yanking on the harness long enough to ask, "Are you hurt? Damn it, John, talk to me."

"Leave me alone. I've got this figured out."

"What?" She started to say more, to demand what the fuck he meant, but shut her mouth. A part deep inside her—the same intuitive part that understood she had to leave Mom and Betty—was so terrified her tongue stuck to the roof of her dry-as-dust mouth.

What in God's name is going to come out of that cave? It looks like

John, but it doesn't feel like him. If I leave now, I can out climb him. And outrun him once I hit the top.

I can't do that. I have to stay. He's my client for chrissakes. His welfare is my job.

Scrunching her eyes shut, she reinforced her shaky decision to wait for John. No matter what. Cara shouldered her pack and coiled her ropes for travel. That done, she scooted about five feet up the chimney and watched, mesmerized, as John continued to lash his body from side to side, grunting and heaving. Dust peppered the smoky air, and displaced rocks rolled off the ledge in front of the cave.

It was slow work. John's shoulders did get stuck, just like she'd thought they would. A sudden cracking noise battered her, and she knew he'd broken a collarbone exiting the viselike opening. It had to be a collarbone since that was the thinnest of the bones in the shoulder array, always first to snap under pressure.

Jesus, did he do that on purpose?

She felt momentarily dizzy, but bit down hard on a gloved knuckle to give herself something to think about besides her fear.

John jackknifed his body around after crawling through the crack. He grinned, baring teeth that looked as if he'd been eating dirt. "Told you I had this nailed."

"But your shoulder—" she began, and then gathered herself together.

"I'm a doctor," he interrupted. "I know exactly which bone broke and where. I'm working to fix it."

She swallowed hard. Doctor or not, how the hell could he possibly repair his own broken bone? Because she really didn't want to go there, she asked, "Do you think you can climb?"

"'Course I can. Lead on." He swept his gaze over her. "Do you have any idea what a fine looking woman you are?"

Normally, she put clients who came on to her in their place fast, but she couldn't quite find the words. Something had happened to John in that cave. He wasn't the same man, but she didn't want to rip the lid off that can of worms, either.

"L-let me toss you the rope," she stammered. "I can come down to tie—"

"Nah," he interrupted, a strange undertone in his voice. "Told you, I'm taking care of my problem. Nothing for you to worry about."

She thought about telling him he needed something to stabilize his broken collarbone, but something in his response curdled the words in her throat.

Cara dropped her gaze to her boot tops. Something was terribly, wretchedly wrong here, except she didn't know what it was. When she looked up, the birds that had been clinging to the chimney, eyeing her with vulturesque greed, were nowhere to be seen.

What the hell? When did they leave?

"Are you ready?" she called because she sure as fuck didn't want to talk about the birds.

"Ready," echoed back to her, the first normal-sounding thing he'd said.

Cara grabbed a convenient handhold and pulled herself up.

Climb, dammit. I can think later.

The chimney was just as simple an affair as she'd believed it would be, requiring neither rope nor hardware. In very little time, she hauled herself onto a ridge top where she could look down the easy side of Mount Rixford.

John was still about twenty feet from the top. He climbed using both hands, which meant he was putting pressure on a bone she knew had broken. Why wasn't he screaming when the bone ends jammed against one another? She'd broken bones; they burned like liquid fire.

I could still leave, her inner voice suggested silkily. *I know the way down, he doesn't.*

No. I'm not losing any more clients. This is about me taking care of him, like I'm supposed to.

Part of her wondered if maybe, just maybe, John wasn't already beyond her reach. Since she didn't understand why she would think that—or why the fine hairs on the back of her neck stood on end—she forced herself to stand quietly and wait for her client. She ferreted a water bottle out of one of her pack's side pockets and took a long drink, followed by another.

She took advantage of those few minutes to test the ankle she'd injured escaping from the cave. It was tender, likely bruised, but she didn't have any trouble standing on it. Next she scanned the flanks of Mount Rixford down to Bullfrog Lake. No fire. Would it be smarter to hole up next to the lake or to make a run for it over Kearsarge Pass?

She was still pondering their route when something latched onto her arm. Her heart ramped into overdrive, and she whirled to find John only inches away, an unreadable expression on his face. "How did... I didn't hear you..." she stammered and yanked her arm out of his grasp.

"You wouldn't have. Not now." His blue eyes scanned the same vista she'd been staring at.

She eyed his right arm, hanging at an unnatural angle. "You should let me tape that shoulder."

Before he could answer, a whooshing sound filled the air and the kites, conspicuously absent for the past hour, rose from both sides of the high ridge. The air above her turned black with their bodies, and warm little globs of bird shit fell like raindrops. Wing beats rose and fell in the same stiff breeze that tugged at hair escaping from her braids.

"I don't have much time," John said, sounding more like himself again. "Not right now, anyway. I made a deal with them back in the cave. Remember I told you about sorting the warriors from the cowards?" At her terse nod, he continued. "They told me if I could get myself out of there, they'd consider me a warrior and would take me somewhere. A place of honor where they'd tell me more about what they need me to do. Hells bells, Cara, they already told me enough, I'll be an old, old man before I finish all their tasks." Resignation edged his voice.

"I'm sorry, but this is nine kinds of weird. Way too much to take on faith. What the fuck happened in there?" She gestured back toward the chimney.

He shook his head. "It's too long a story to tell, but they hunted me and finally found me. I'm just sorry you were involved."

Cara wanted to ask who *they* were—and why they'd been hunting him. Instead, she grabbed his left wrist, probing for a pulse, needing to reassure herself he wasn't something out of a nightmare. She felt his gaze on her as she repositioned her fingers, and then moved them a third time, finally picking up a strong, steady heartbeat. Meeting his eyes, she nodded. A hint of a smile curved her badly chapped lips.

"I knew I was still alive." Understated humor ran beneath his words.

"And now I know the same thing. With everything else that's happened and those bodies in the cave, I wasn't sure."

Cara grasped his hand. "Maybe you don't have to do what they said," she began. Something in his eyes stopped her rush of words.

"I do. A bargain is a bargain. They let me live. You too. That was part of it. I said they had to let you go."

"You did that for me?" Her heart clenched, and she grappled with his sacrifice, not feeling worthy.

He nodded. "Yeah, but they'd have done that anyway—even if I hadn't asked. That cave was a testing chamber for Native Americans, not for you. You're a decent sort, Cara, and a gifted climber. You just need to believe in yourself. It's not your fault Ruth and Chris were idiots and ran right into that inferno."

The reverberation from the wing beats escalated, almost as if the kites were becoming impatient. John extricated his wrist from her fingers. Moving close, he gave her a quick kiss on one cheek and then turned to wend his way down the talus-littered mountainside. "Thanks," he called back over one shoulder, sounding almost cheerful as he picked his way along a route marked by kites that had landed in groups of twos and threes. "I'll find you when this is over if I can."

Cara raised a hand in farewell as she watched him go. Tears welled in her eyes and tracked down her sooty face. "He's right," she said to whatever mountain spirits might be listening. "I am a good guide, but I need to shuck all that baggage. It's been like a millstone mired to my soul for way too long." Latching onto the power in her words, she felt lighter than she had in years.

She had plenty of daylight to make the top of Kearsarge and set off at a brisk pace across the talus to intersect the well-worn trail. A scant half hour later, she stood atop the pass. "I can see," she exulted, looking down toward Onion Valley. It was clear, not obliterated by smoke. The fire must have swept north and missed the trailhead. She could get out.

Whistling softly, giddy from her unexpected reprieve, she pulled her headlamp out of the pocket she'd stuffed it into earlier. Settling it into grooves in her helmet so she'd be ready when night fell, she trotted down the trail. As she hurried along, she considered what to tell the authorities. Ruth and Christopher would be simple. Sad, but easy. She was less sure what to tell them about John and finally settled on a variant of the truth. He'd insisted on finding his own way down.

Cara felt strangely at peace for the first time in years.

I can move beyond my past. I know I can. It was me who gave it so much power. From now on, I'll be finding my own way too. Just like John.

She mouthed a silent prayer of thanks to her client and hoped the kites had guided him to a Sioux Valhalla where someone was tending his shoulder. Cara quickened her pace. For a time she worried whether the Sheriff would believe her about John, but she couldn't do much about that one way or the other.

She'd just passed Flower Lake, only a couple of miles from her car in the Onion Valley parking lot when she heard steps behind her. It had seemed odd she was the only one on a highly used trail, but Cara figured everyone else had scurried from the high country in the wake of the fire. Since it sounded as if whoever was behind her was running, she stepped to one side to give them plenty of room to pass.

It was getting dark, and she flipped on her headlamp. Once stopped, she realized how bone-weary she was. Her ankle bothered her, and she was hacking black phlegm from all the smoke she'd sucked down. She considered taking off her helmet, but then she'd have to carry it—or take extra time to remove her pack and secure it.

Soon, she promised herself. *I can drive a few miles, pull off, and sack out in the back of my car.*

"Cara! Wait up."

"John?"

She turned and stared up the trail, incredulous when his unmistakable, long-legged figure loped toward her. "But, how?" She flicked off her headlamp so she wouldn't blind him and started back up the trail, sweeping him into a hug. "I am *so* glad to see you," she cried, holding on tight. "Oh my God, your shoulder. Did I make it worse?" Backing away, she bit her lip in consternation.

"No, you didn't hurt me." He grinned. "Told 'em you'd get into trouble if I wasn't there to back your story about what happened to Ruth and Chris. They understand about White Man's law." He grimaced and spat. "So they helped me catch up to you, after they fixed my shoulder. And fleshed out what they need me to do."

"Who are *they*? I wanted to ask before, but—" She would have asked more, but he shook his head.

"Uh-uh." He laid a finger across her lips. "I'm not sure how much of it I can talk about. Not yet, anyway. Come on. Maybe we could cook something after we get to your car. I'm famished." He draped an arm around her and faced her back down the trail.

Questions rose and fell as she walked, the yellow pool from her headlamp illuminating the trail ahead. She kept them to herself.

It's one of the mysteries. Same as the mountain gods who protect climbers and fools. I've always believed in them, so why not this?

Finally, she looked over at him. "I know they let you go to bail me out, but can you stay afterward?"

He laughed. "Yeah, Cara. I think so."

"But what about being an old, old man before you're done with whatever they tasked you with?"

"I didn't totally understand it. I know more now."

Her heart squeezed painfully after doing a funny little flip-flop in her chest. She told herself not to care that he wasn't going anywhere. It wasn't wise. It would make her vulnerable. "Sorry," she mumbled. "That wasn't the best question. Forget I asked it."

"Which one? You asked two."

"The one about staying. It was too personal."

"Yes, but I liked that particular question." He smiled and reached for her hand, grasping it firmly.

No one was more surprised than she was when she didn't pull hers back.

CHAPTER 5

*J*ohn enjoyed the feel of Cara's strong, tapering fingers encased in his hand. She had the build of an athlete, with lean, rippling muscle coating her five-foot-ten-inch frame. Straight black hair had mostly escaped from her braids, and strands hung nearly to the center of her back. She had the most amazing eyes. Sometimes green, sometimes almost golden, with crinkles in the corners from a life he suspected she'd led mostly out of doors.

They came around a corner, hips bumping against each other as they walked side-by-side down the narrow trail. He narrowed his eyes against the encroaching night, realizing the magic he'd awakened was sharpening his senses. He felt it spilling through him, but rather than fighting it like he'd always done, he welcomed the bright, prickly warmth.

"Why didn't you tell me you were a doctor when you filled out the paperwork for this trip?" Cara's question came out of left field. Out of all the things she might've said, he hadn't expected that.

He shrugged, not letting go of her hand. "Would it have made a difference?"

"Sure." Cara laughed. "I guess you missed the fine print about not having to pay for the trip if you agreed to be the team doctor."

"Guess I did." He paused, gathering his thoughts. "Do you get many physicians who take you up on that?"

"Not on trips like these," she replied. "But on the big mountain expeditions, like ones to the Himalayas, I do. Those are expensive enough, people are always looking for a break. And those are the ones where we really need specially trained personnel who know something about high altitude medicine."

"I'll keep it in mind." He chuckled softly. "For next time."

"Will there be a next time?" she asked and then shook her head. "I didn't exactly mean that the way it sounded. I wasn't talking about trips with me. You're a good climber, but I got the sense at the front end of the trip that you've mostly climbed by yourself."

John was impressed. "How'd you figure that out?"

"Wasn't hard." She flashed him half a smile. "We'll be at the car soon."

"Yeah. I know. I can see the parking lot a few hundred feet below us."

Cara ground to a halt and faced him. "How?" she demanded. "It's dark."

Oops.

John scrambled for a credible response. "When we left your car here to set up our shuttle, I looked up this canyon, and I recognized the terrain."

"In the dark? For a place you've only been once before?" Cara screwed her face into a puzzled expression tinged with suspicion and tugged her hand back. "Either you've got the best memory ever, or there's something you're not telling me."

"We're even then," he said smoothly and started walking downhill again, figuring she'd follow him, which she did.

"What do you mean, even?" she asked.

"You never told me how you figured out I've mostly climbed solo."

"That one's easy," she retorted. "You solved your own problems. Never waited for me to suggest anything." Cara hesitated. "Never mind how that crack system we used to escape showed up, you're the one who found it. Not me. A novice climber would've been so freaked out by our situation, they wouldn't even have been looking."

"All good points," he agreed. "You've honed your observational skills. Why would you find it odd I've done the same thing with my own? Part of medicine is taking a good enough look the first time—and remembering what you saw."

John took a deep breath and held it a hair too long. Would she buy his logic?

"Guess you're right," she mumbled. "What happened to us was just so odd, I'm seeing bogeymen behind every bush."

He exhaled long and slow, wanting to reach for her again. Touching her had wakened another part of him he kept under wraps. Maybe because his power was online, it was harder to keep the other parts of him corralled. The steady beat of her boots behind him, and the feel of her energy would have to be enough —for now.

"How'd you end up a mountain guide?" he asked.

"I had a partner who guided. He trained me at first, and then I got my own certifications about ten years ago. They're not static," she hurried on. "I have to retest every few years for most things, including my EMT certification."

Something lay beneath her words. Something guarded, carefully crafted, as if he'd received a canned answer. She'd said she had a partner. Past tense. John took a chance. "What happened to him?"

"He died on an expedition to Annapurna a long time ago. Got avalanched off the mountain." This time, a bitter note underscored her words.

"I'm sorry. Didn't mean to pick the scabs off an old wound."

"I'm not sorry. Look. It's okay. Leif was a risk-taker. He knew the odds and tossed the dice over and over. This time he didn't come back. Only bummer was all his clients died too. Plus a couple of Sherpas. They trusted him, and he should've been more careful with their lives."

"It sounds as if you're still angry with him."

They'd reached the parking lot, and John fell into step next to Cara. He made a grab for her hand again, and she squeezed his fingers in return.

She stopped next to her car and extracted her hand, but the movement didn't feel abrupt. More like she needed it to shuck her pack and her helmet. Dark hair streamed down her back and shoulders, and she groaned. "Jesus, but I'm glad we're here. I'm beat."

John thought maybe he shouldn't push the topic, but his need to know trumped caution. "You didn't exactly answer me about Leif."

Cara narrowed her eyes to slits as she dug for her car keys. "I'm not angry about him dying on me. I am pissed he didn't do the things he always taught me to do, which was to prioritize safety."

"Maybe he did. You're still alive, which means you weren't on that particular trip."

Cara hit the clicker and the car beeped. John went to the back of the older model green Subaru and opened the hatch. He removed his pack and helmet, rotating his shoulders and stretching. He figured she wasn't going to answer, but she started talking as she stowed her gear next to his.

"There are ways to predict how unstable a snow slope is. They were the only group to die in that avalanche. That tells me Leif cut a few corners he shouldn't have."

He wanted to ask more questions. Like had she been in love with him? Had she mourned? Had there been other men since?

And the most important question of all: Did she have a boyfriend now? Instead, he said, "What do you want to do about supper?"

"We need to drive out of here." She gestured to the parking lot where they were the only car. "It looks like the Forest Service evacuated this place. Hope if they put up a road closure, we can drive around it. Once we're closer to Independence, we can either stop and cook something, or we can find a restaurant in town."

"Good enough for me." His fingers itched to draw her against him. He wanted to tangle his hands in her long, thick hair and explore her mouth with his own.

Almost as if she'd read his thoughts—and didn't want him to go there—she reached up and slammed the hatch shut. "I need to retrieve the bear cans I left in the storage lockers, and then we'll be good to go."

"I'll get them." He loped to the series of brown metal storage bins sitting side-by-side next to the outside johns. Recalling where she'd left her food stash, he stooped and pulled out the two plastic canisters with Carlisle scrawled across the top. Lots of people had abandoned food in the locker, which meant they'd left in a god-awful hurry. Fire had that effect, but having survived today, he wasn't frightened of it anymore. Not in the same, primal way that affected most people.

He secured the locker and tucked a canister under each arm, returning to the car and tossing them inside. "Got 'em."

"Thanks." She trotted to the driver's side and got in.

Once he was settled in the passenger seat and had his seat belt engaged, she picked up the thread of their earlier conversation. "I never get involved with my clients. Leif had other gal pals. Lots of them. One was on the Annapurna trip. I always figured he was in a hurry to hole up in a tent with her."

The Subaru's engine caught on the second try, and Cara maneuvered the car around the edge of the large parking lot and down the steep, zigzag road leading to the Owens Valley five thousand feet below.

John wasn't quite sure what to say, but Cara saved him the trouble.

"Pretty awful, huh?" She glanced sidelong at him. "But not unusual. The mountains make for some odd bedfellows. When you put your life on the line, sex is how you celebrate still being alive."

"For him, but not you?"

"Yeah. He'd have hurt anyone I took up with. Besides, I'm smarter than that." She drove around a placard suspended on an A-frame wooden base that said the road was closed to all but emergency vehicles.

Protectiveness for the woman sitting next to him surged, along with anger and incredulity at how Leif had treated her. "You deserved better than that. Good God, I'm shocked the old double standard is alive and well." He paused a beat, still furious. "By hurt someone, do you mean he'd have actually fought them?"

"That's exactly what I mean. Look. I'm sorry I answered the first bunch of questions that got us here. Can we talk about something else?"

"Of course." John threaded his fingers together to avoid the temptation to reach across the console. "About supper. What do we have in the car?"

"Freeze-dried glop and my stove. This road parallels a creek soon enough, and we're about to pass the upper of two campgrounds. Both of them front the creek, and they'll have drinking water too."

"That sounds great to me. I'll even cook. Glop is one of my specialties."

Cara laughed, and it both lightened the mood and warmed him. "You're on. I can get the tent up—unless you want me to run you back to town tonight where we left your car."

"Nope. I'm good with us staying here. I don't have much of anything to go back to right now. I'm between jobs."

She pulled the car down a steep grade. The campground was

as deserted as the parking lot had been, and she guided them into a level spot next to the creek and killed the engine. "How can a doctor be between jobs? Isn't there a shortage of you guys?"

"Yeah, but I just finished the last of my training. I was slated to go to Africa in a month with a group that provides medical care to places people really need us."

She turned to face him. "Was? Did whatever happened today change that?"

He shut his eyes for a moment. When he opened them he said, "You're quick on the uptake."

"Have to be." A corner of her mouth turned down. "It's part of the job not to miss anything."

He slumped against the seatback. "I'm still getting my mind around exactly what today means, but that's likely part of it. I've always been a planner. Planned my life out to the nth degree."

"And today blows those plans out of the water?" She quirked a brow his way.

"You might say that. Lead me to that freeze-dried glop, so I can get our dinner going."

He opened his door, needing something to do so he didn't splatter his mental unrest in front of Cara. He wanted her to respect him, maybe even view him in a romantic light, but that would never happen once he told her the truth about his shamanistic roots. About his grandmother who had precognitive visions, or about his father who was a weather-worker. Never mind the panoply of aunts, uncles, and cousins with varying degrees of paranormal abilities. He'd been an only child, and he'd cursed that fate more than once. If he'd had siblings—and they'd had power—he'd have been out from under the eight-ball. Someone else could've picked up the shaman banner and—

"Dinner's back this way." Her voice drew him to his feet, and he walked to the open hatch of the Subaru. He'd been so lost in feeling sorry for himself, he hadn't heard her exit the car or open the hatch.

"Sure you're all right?" she asked, handing him a bear canister and a stove that ran on butane cartridges.

John shrugged. He was a long way from *all right*, but he wasn't about to admit it. "I'm together enough to cook for us." He tapped the clear plastic bin. "Any preferences?"

"Surprise me." She flashed him a grin before digging out her pack and dragging things out of it. "If you hand over your sleeping bag and pad, I'll get our home for the night set up."

Nodding, he put the dinner items down and dug in his own pack for his bedding before heading for a nearby picnic table with the cook kit. He set up the stove, filled the integrated pan with water from a spigot, and returned for the food.

As an afterthought, he scooped his headlamp off his helmet. He didn't need it, but Cara had commented about his unusual night vision on the trail, and he didn't want to give her any further reasons to see him as anything other than normal, whatever *normal* meant.

Back at the picnic table, he screwed the lid off the bear-proof plastic container and glanced through the possibilities, settling on a sausage and mashed potato mix with onion gravy. Freeze-dried food had come a long way these past twenty years or so. It actually tasted pretty good now, not like the chili mac and shrimp creole he recalled from his teenage years.

As he worked, his internal penchant for planning out his life raced to the fore. He'd have to return to his parents' home outside Bakersfield. And he'd need to include at least his grandmother and father in his plans. The spirit guides had been quite clear about the power of shared blood—and about the ritual that would initiate the cascade of magic they claimed was essential to Native Americans not being totally assimilated by White Men's demons.

To hear them tell it, the fate of his kin lay in his hands. John had a hard time believing that. He was only half Indian. His mother had been Irish. She was where his red hair and blue eyes came from. When he thought about the genetics and his paranormal ability, it made a certain kind of sense. Ireland was nothing if not a haven for old magics. From the days of the Sidhe and Tuatha de Dannan, the hills and barrows of the Old Country had housed potent spirits.

Perhaps his combined bloodlines were more powerful than if he'd been one hundred percent Native…

The fragrant mixture in the pot didn't require more heat, so he turned off the stove and settled the lid in place, waiting for the boiling water to fully rehydrate their dinner.

"Smells good." Cara joined him. "I've always loved bangers and mash."

"Me too." He smiled. "Maybe five minutes more and we can eat."

"Did you pick out a dessert?"

"Nope. Why don't you do that?"

Cara bent over the bear can, rooting through it. She'd changed into a black long-sleeved stretchy top, zip-off cargo pants, and sandals.

"No fair," he said. "You've got clean clothes on, and I still reek of smoke."

She lifted her head from her perusal of their food stocks. "Do you have anything else with you?"

He nodded and pushed himself upright. "Yeah. I'll change while we're waiting for dinner." Turning he walked toward the car.

"I rinsed off in the creek," she called after him.

He laughed. "I know a hint when I hear one," he called back.

John dug shorts and a T-shirt out of his pack, along with an old, cracked pair of Crocs. Making his way down a short embankment, he knelt shy of the water to remove his boots and socks. The rest of his clothing joined them in an untidy heap. The water was cool when he stepped into it, almost cold enough to have a bite, but he welcomed its refreshing aspect as he sluiced grime, ashy soot, and dirt off his body. It wasn't deep enough to immerse himself, so he settled for the climbers' version of a sponge bath.

He used his dirty clothing as a towel and slipped into cleaner clothes. They still smelled like smoke, but at least they didn't stink of days' old sweat. His mind returned to planning mode, but he shut it off before it could churn through what happened in the cave—and afterward—again.

Tonight would be him and Cara. He'd be damned if he'd cut into the simple enjoyment of being with her by worrying about something he had no control over.

"Food's ready," she called.

He grinned. In addition to everything else he enjoyed about Cara, she had a low, musical voice. "Be right there."

By the time tonight was over with, he'd know a whole lot more about Cara Carlisle. He wanted to sleep with her, but indulging his body could wait. Far deeper than that, he aimed to lay the groundwork for a relationship. Maybe altering his plans to leave the country wasn't such a disaster after all.

He made his way to the picnic table where he'd set up their dinner items. Water dripped off his wet curls, but he felt rejuvenated and shook his head one more time to help his hair dry.

She handed him a spoon and patted the wooden bench next to her. "Five more minutes, and I'd have started without you."

"Hell, Cara, you could've eaten the whole thing. There's lots more in that food stash of yours." He settled beside her.

"Yeah, I don't like to be hungry."

As it had earlier, something raw rode beneath her words. Something that made his heart hurt.

He waited for her to take the first few bites before digging into their dinner. Both of them were obviously starving, and the pot was nearly empty before he came up for air long enough to ask, "That Visalia address where I sent the forms and money, is that where you live?"

She nodded. "Why?"

"Because I'll be headed to Bakersfield when we leave here, and it's right next door. We could hit the western slopes and do some climbing—when you're not guiding, that is."

"What happened to Las Vegas?"

"Told you, I'm done there. No more job. I let my apartment go, and put what I wanted to hang onto into storage. Planned to visit family this last month and live in motels."

"Storage? Oh yeah. I'd forgotten." She licked droplets of gravy off her spoon. "You're leaving for Africa. Except now you might not be going. Convenient about Bakersfield, huh?" Cara glanced at the empty cookpot and rolled her eyes. "Want me to mix up another batch of this same stuff? Don't know about you, but I'm still hungry."

"Sure. While you're at it, tell me about yourself."

He set his spoon on the table's scarred wooden top and gazed expectantly at her, willing her to want to share her life with him. He could push her with magic, but that felt like cheating.

CHAPTER 6

"Not much to tell," she mumbled and pried open the plastic bin to extract another freeze-dried dinner. His comment about heading for Bakersfield had rattled her. She'd felt a whole lot safer with him in Las Vegas and the spine of the Sierra Nevada Mountains between them. While not exactly "next door," Visalia was a straight shot, eighty miles north of Bakersfield along a major highway.

"Try me. Did you grow up in Visalia?" He trained his blue eyes on her.

"No. Portland."

"Maine or Oregon?"

"Oregon," she said crisply, mixing water into the powdered mix and slicing sausage to add to the pot.

John sucked in an audible breath. "I just want to get to know you, Cara. I don't bite. I promise."

She dumped sausage slivers into the cookpot and stirred while the mixture came to a boil, her mind a jumble of conflicting thoughts. Part of her wanted to talk with John, but another, well-trained part had years of practice keeping everyone at arm's length.

"It's not that so much," she said after turning off the small stove and settling the lid firmly on the pot.

"What is it, then?" His voice was gentle.

Cara turned to straddle the bench so she faced him. "I guess I got out of the habit of talking about anything personal—with anyone."

He drew his brows together as if her answer concerned him and reached to lay a hand on her thigh. It felt warm and soothing. She thought she should move it away, but couldn't bring herself to. He was offering emotional support—or that's what it felt like. She'd had so little in her life, it was hard to recognize compassion directed her way.

And even harder to resist it.

"What do you want from me?" she blurted, embarrassed by her words, but it was better to know than not.

His lips curved into half a smile. "I already told you. I want to get to know you. Usually people begin by trading histories."

"And you know this how?" Cara cringed at her bluntness. "I'm sorry," she mumbled. "Trusting anyone is hard for me."

"It's okay." He squeezed her thigh lightly. "I'll begin while we're waiting for what's in the pot to rehydrate. I was born on a reservation in Bakersfield. My father's side have been our tribal shamans for at least the last hundred years. Even though Sioux aren't native to that part of California, that's my tribe."

Something coiled deep inside Cara began to relax. "Is your mother Native too?" she asked.

John nodded encouragingly. "See, that wasn't hard. Please. Ask anything you want. Nope. Mom was Irish as they come, brogue and all. Dad did a stint in the Air Force and met her in the U.K. I'm their only child."

Cara couldn't help herself. She smiled. "Were you that difficult, they stopped with you?"

"Nah. Mom was past forty when she had me. I figure they

thought they were doing good to get one baby." He lifted his hand from her leg and bent over the pot, removing the lid to test its contents.

The place his hand had been felt empty, and she wished he'd touch her again. Instead, she asked, "Is it ready?"

He nodded and placed the pot on the bench between them before swinging his leg over so he faced her squarely. "Sure is. Dig in."

"I'm guessing you stayed in Bakersfield," she said between chewing and swallowing, "because your kin are still there."

"We did. Grandma had a big part in raising me because Mom and Dad both worked."

The conversation was non-threatening enough, Cara relaxed into the velvet of the night and the warm food in her belly. "What'd they do?"

"Dad was a heavy equipment operator for the county. He still flies helicopters for Search and Rescue, kind of a carryover from his military days. Mom was a physician's assistant, but she died last year. Cancer got her." John reached for a water bottle and drank deep. "I finished high school in Bakersfield and went to UCLA for college and medical school. Did my family medicine residency in Las Vegas. Along the way, I did an extra year and picked up a master's degree in public health."

"And now you're ready to use that career you trained for. I'm sorry about your mother." The pot was closing on empty again, but the half-starved feeling—the one that made her panic because it reminded her of too many nights without food growing up— had receded.

"It's okay about Mom. She packed a whole lot of living into seventy years." He paused and skewered her with his sea blue eyes again. "You didn't ask, but I've steered clear of anything like a steady girlfriend. I knew I wanted to practice medicine outside the country—at least for a while."

Cara sifted through what he'd said, and what he hadn't. "Do you want anything for dessert?"

"Sure. I saw some raspberry crumble in there. Might be a good chaser to dinner."

She worked in silence, weighing her next words as she got up to rinse the remains of their supper out of the pot so she could use it to mix the dessert. So far their conversation had skimmed the surface. If she asked what he wanted out of his life, it would open the door to deeper disclosures, and she wasn't sure she wanted to invite quite that level of closeness.

"You're quiet," he observed after she sat back down, got the dessert ready to go, and moved the pot aside so it could set up.

"Thinking," she replied. "What happened to that multi-generational shaman thing in your family after you left?"

He tilted his head to one side, his gaze never leaving her. "My family saw that as a problem too, but it's one that appears to have vanished. My grandmother told me I couldn't escape my destiny. Damn if she wasn't right."

"Mmph." Cara placed the pot between them again. "It'll still be a little runny—"

"Don't apologize." He laid his hand on her thigh again. "Your turn."

Cara straightened her back. She hadn't taken the quid pro quo aspect of his disclosures into consideration. Or maybe she had, but had enjoyed listening to him so much, she'd conveniently forgotten his earlier comments about getting to know her.

"I'm afraid my life hasn't been anything like yours," she mumbled and took a large spoonful of vanilla pudding laced with graham cracker crumbs and dried raspberries. For a moment, she wondered if the gelatinous mixture would choke her going down and made a grab for her water.

"Doesn't mean I don't want to hear about it," he said.

Cara set her spoon on the table. Her stomach twisted into an uncomfortable knot, and she didn't want to eat anything else, afraid she'd heave it back up. Because she was looking at her lap, she didn't see him move his hands. They landed on her upper arms.

"It's all right, Cara. Look at me. I'll never judge you. Besides," he went on, "you were a child. Whatever went wrong couldn't possibly have been your fault."

Her throat thickened with emotion, and she felt the quick, hot bite of tears behind her eyelids. Wrenching herself away from him, she stumbled to her feet. "You don't have to be kind," she gritted out. "I got past everything a long time ago."

"Really?" He stood and moved behind her, close but not touching. "If you were over whatever all this is about, you wouldn't be on the verge of crying. You went through hell herding us through that fire, and you never gave in to your emotions. What is it about your past that hurt you so much?"

"I am not on the verge of anything," she protested, horrified when a tear slid down one cheek. At least she was faced away from him, so he couldn't see. Another tear joined the first, and then a few more joined the party.

"Talk to me, Cara," he urged. "Even if we never see each other after tonight—and I hope that's not the case—you can't keep all that bottled inside. It's poisoning you. Every closet full of skeletons needs to see daylight. It will make them a whole lot less terrifying."

Maybe he's right, an inner voice piped up.

Even if he's not, I never have to see him after tomorrow, so what's the harm in trying?

She was intensely aware of him standing behind her. Of his warmth, his gentleness, his scent. He smelled like pine forests and the outside world she'd adopted as her home. Maybe it was his scent that decided things, but Cara began talking. At first her words were hesitant, but soon they came in a torrent she couldn't have held back if she tried.

"Not that it matters," she started, "but I was born in Portland.

No idea who my father was. Mom was an alcoholic and a drug addict. Mostly heroin after I got older, but she'd take whatever she could get. Mostly we didn't have enough money, but what addict's home does?"

Bitterness filled her, mixed with anger, but Cara kept talking. "Somewhere along the line, Ma decided she liked women. Her last partner hated me. I never could figure out why, except Betty was insanely jealous of anything or anyone else Ma paid attention to.

"I tried to keep a low profile, stay out of everyone's way." She took a deep, shuddering breath, just wanting to get through with things. "I loved school. It was the only place anyone was ever kind to me."

"Did you ever talk with anyone? A school counselor, maybe?" John's question surprised her. For some reason, she'd figured he would be so disgusted by her sick family life, he wouldn't mine for details.

"No. I was afraid they'd toss Ma in jail again, and move me to another foster home. They were worse than living with Ma and Betty. I finished high school when I was seventeen and left home —for good. I've never been back. Ma's likely dead by now, but I don't know that for sure."

"That explains why you'd tolerate a man who abused you."

The anger that bubbled just below the surface drove her, and she spun to face him, hands balled into fists at her side. "You have no fucking idea—"

"Maybe I do." Compassion carved lines into his forehead. "Remember, I grew up on a reservation. Many families looked a whole lot like what you just described. I may not have lived your life, but I saw a lot of it up close and personal. What happened after you left home?"

The sudden burst of fury bled out of her, and she flexed her fingers. "What happens to anyone? I went to work. Had a bunch of jobs. Managed to finish a couple years in community college.

Met Leif—" she held up a hand "—and before you jump to conclusions, he did good things for me too. If it hadn't been for him, I'd never have ended up guiding."

Cara took a deep breath and blew it out, and then did it again. "Thanks to him, I finally found not just a vocation, but something I truly loved. It was a huge amount of work, but I hold all the top guiding certificates from the International Federation of Mountain Guides. I've guided clients all over the world, and the mountains have become my home and made up for the family I never had."

He closed the distance between them and wrapped his arms around her. After a quick, hard hug, he stepped away. "Thank you for trusting me."

Cara swiped at her wet cheeks. "Doesn't come easy."

"After today it will be easier."

"How do you know that?"

He tilted her chin with his forefinger so she had to look at him. "Because you've lived with shame and guilt for a long time when you had nothing to be ashamed of or feel guilty about. Today—or tonight—changes all that. You had nothing to do with your mother's addiction or her neglect. I'm sorry you had to live through those things, but they've made you who you are today."

"Who's that? Some days I don't have clue one, so I strap on my pack and go climb something."

"I'll let you tell me once you're done figuring it out. Want to finish that dessert now? I felt bad when my prodding made you lose your appetite."

What she wanted to do was wind her arms around him, feel the length of his body against hers, but it wasn't wise. Why would a man like him ever be interested in someone like her? He needed someone more like himself. Sex would just complicate things between them. Besides, he was still her client and crossing that line was wrong.

Despite all her reasoning, she still ached for him.

No, I want comfort, pure and simple.

She angled her head away from the finger beneath her chin. "Sure, we can finish what's in the pot. I still have a hard time throwing food away. Can't make myself do it." She smiled weakly, grateful the worst of her emotional storm had blown itself out.

He smiled back. "Perfect. Then we should get some sleep."

SLEEP MIGHT'VE BEEN his suggestion, but it proved elusive. John's body was beyond exhausted, but his mind wouldn't shut off. He'd wanted to hold Cara, draw her against him and stroke her long, silky black hair, but she'd zipped into her bag and turned onto her side, facing away from him. Moments later, the cadence of her breathing suggested she'd slipped into sleep.

Before that, though, she'd thanked him for listening and said it went a long way toward helping her accept everything she'd lived through. He started to caution her to give herself time to heal, but hadn't wanted to erode her newfound confidence.

The more time he spent with Cara, the more he wanted her as a permanent part of his life. She was brave, bright, and inventive. He'd seen her in the toughest of situations, and she kept right on slugging. Despite an upbringing that would've sent most people deep into chemical abuse, she'd powered through her broken places and carved out a life for herself. Africa had mountains. She could lead expeditions on Kilimanjaro or Mount Kenya or Mount Meru.

He made a grab for his runaway thoughts. Africa was a stretch. Just because he was drawn to its remoteness and mystery was no reason she'd feel the same. Besides, it wasn't as if he was even still going. The responsible thing to do, once he arrived in Bakersfield, would be to contact Doctors Without Borders, apologize profusely, and cancel his contract.

He could always go to work for Indian Health Services and remain close enough to his family to carry out the spirit guides' assignment. Maybe once it was well underway, his father and grandmother could take over...

Bad call. It's my job. Maybe the guides targeted me because I shined tradition and left, but I made a commitment in that cave. One I can't conveniently shuck now that I'm loose.

The spirits would track him down again if he welched. This time, they'd kill him. Not offer a reprieve.

Cara sighed in her sleep and rolled against him. The warm length of her body pressed against his side was alluring, and he leaned toward her and softly kissed her forehead.

The patter of water over rocks trilled from the nearby creek. At first, the musical rhythm was soothing, but it reminded him of the problem the spirits had tasked him with.

Monsters he didn't have a name for flashed through his mind. Monsters forged in fire who wanted Earth to dry up so they could take over and rule it. His Sioux was rusty, and he hadn't understood what the spirit guides meant until they sent an image into his mind. The creature had looked like a cross between a sea monster and a dragon with brilliant red scales, short forelegs, and a long, forked tail. Fire spewed from the thing's mouth.

Many places on Earth were becoming parched wastelands. Animal species were dying right and left. Others were mutating— or migrating toward the poles—to survive. Somehow, the spirit guides expected him to stem the tide. He'd tried to explain it was beyond what one man could do. That global warming—and its consequences—were a done deal.

They'd laughed at him, told him what he'd been trained to view as climate alterations from mankind's meddling was really the dragonkind's doing. The monsters wanted Earth, but they couldn't live in a place with so many people—or any people at all. So they'd began to systematically stage events—like the fire raging in the Sierra and droughts in Africa and Australia—to alter

Earth's ecosystems. If the guides were correct, every cataclysmic episode over the past century was attributable to the dragons. They were actually lords over some distant world. Who knew if their subjects were dragons too?

John had been trying to wrap his mind around their farfetched theory when the spirit guides instructed him to leverage his magic, leaving out details about exactly how his link to the mysteries hiding in the earth could add water to dried up canals and disappearing lakebeds.

Never mind whatever it might take to defeat the scaled abominations. If what the guides said was true, dragonkind would fight back—and John would be their first target. Maybe he'd address the drought aspect of things first since it felt more manageable. His father was a weather-worker. He might have some ideas…

Maybe that's not such a good idea. It'll place Dad square in the creatures' gunsights—right along with me. Misery might love company, but I'll be damned if I put him at risk too.

Cara pressed tighter against him, murmuring in her sleep.

This time, he gathered her close, folding her into his arms. She nested her head in the crook of his shoulder, fitting against him as if their bodies were made for one another. At least it quieted his overheated mental processes, trading one sort of heat for another far more pleasurable one. He was starting to feel like a rat trapped in a maze where every tunnel led to something worse. Concentrating on the woman in his arms helped—a lot.

The growl of motors rumbled from outside, likely trucks delivering personnel to fight the fire. He sniffed, scenting the air, and thought he could smell smoke. The campground air had been clear when they arrived, so either the fire was spreading or the wind had changed direction.

Cara wriggled against him. "Sorry," she mumbled and tried to draw away.

"No sorries. You're right where you belong. Did the trucks wake you?"

She nodded against his shoulder. "Must be fire crews. They'd have seen my car and stopped long enough to tell us to leave if the campground wasn't safe. Have you gotten any sleep?"

"Not much," he admitted, "but it's okay. First thing after we get back to the west side of the mountains, we'll go into a Forest Service office so we can alert the authorities about Ruth and Christopher. I'll retrieve my car in Independence and follow you. I want to see that part settled before I head for Bakersfield."

And you go home to Visalia.

John tightened his hold on her. If he had his way, she'd never leave his side again, but it was premature to give voice to something that held a Neanderthal *you're my woman* edge. That might be enough to send her scrambling to get as far away from him as she could.

"We won't have to wait that long for a Ranger Station." Cara sounded much more awake. "There's an office outside Lone Pine about a mile down the Death Valley highway."

"Well, I'm following you back across the mountains anyway. Just to make sure you get there safe."

Cara giggled, but at least she'd stopped struggling to escape his arms. "For a minute there, you sounded suspiciously like a parent. Or like I always assumed one might sound."

He positioned himself so he faced her. "The last thing I want is to be your parent," he murmured just before he closed his mouth over hers. Maybe it was a stupid move on his part, but he wanted to taste her lips, explore the inside of her mouth with his tongue. Lose himself in her wildflower scent, firm curves, and thick hair.

He didn't know what to expect. Would she jerk away? Haul off and slap him?

For a moment, she froze, but then she opened her mouth to him and kissed him back, her lips petal soft. Even better, she threaded her arms around him and tangled her fingers in his hair.

Where it was sandwiched between their bodies, his cock sprang to attention, straining against his shorts and the layers of feathers and nylon between them. He teased and nibbled her lips and opened his mouth to her tongue. His heart accelerated and breath hitched in his throat. He wanted to tell her he'd take care of her, protect her, make sure nothing bad ever happened to her, but he didn't want to stop kissing her long enough for the words to happen.

As quickly as she'd accepted his kiss, she drew back, scooting a few inches away. "That was lovely," she said, sounding breathless, "but—"

"But nothing," he growled, his voice harsh with wanting her. "Come back here." He reached for her.

"Nope." She shook her head. "You're still my client until I deliver you to your car. I don't sleep with my clients."

"Once I'm officially off the books?" He winked broadly, hoping she'd suggest they rent a room at the first motel they came to after reporting in at the Forest Service office.

"Then we can regroup." Her voice grew serious. "Don't get your hopes up. I'm not that great a bet, and I've spent the last ten years alone for just that reason."

He opened his mouth to protest, but she started talking again. "Sleep. Or at least try. We'll be up at dawn. I'll feel better once I'm done filing my official report with the authorities."

John held out his arms, but she didn't move toward him. "It's better this way," she said. "My willpower's not strong enough to say no to you twice."

He laughed. "And we've already established I have none at all."

"Get some rest," she repeated, but she was laughing when she turned away from him.

He settled deeper into his down bag. Cara might not be locked in his arms, but she hadn't shut him out, and he took it as a good omen.

Yeah, all I have to do is slay a few dragons, restore water to a parched Earth, and I can claim the maiden and ride off into the sunset.

All in a day's work for a Knight Errant.

While I'm at it, a second wry voice cut in, *how about finding the Holy Grail?*

CHAPTER 7

Cara trudged out of the Forest Service office and glanced at the sky. She'd ended up spending hours there, and it was closing on late afternoon. The Inyo County Sheriff had taken a statement from her, and she'd drawn endless diagrams detailing their route, decisions she'd made, and the fateful spot where Ruth and Christopher had broken away and made a run up the side trail leading to the Rae Lakes ranger cabin. John had been more than a godsend, adding credibility through staunch support of every detail of her story. As she thought about it—not that her tired brain was doing much beyond pedaling in circles—him being an M.D. likely helped too.

John, who'd stayed back to answer a few more questions, caught up to her as she reached her car. Dark smudges sat beneath his eyes, and he looked as trashed as she felt. "Damn, that was brutal," he muttered.

"I knew they'd be thorough," she countered, "but we were in there for close to seven hours. It was almost like they thought my story might change if they asked the same thing enough times."

He narrowed his eyes to slits. "Maybe so. I'm not that familiar with police procedure. I assumed they wanted all those details for Ruth and Christopher's families."

Cara leaned against the car. "You might be right about that. I'm just relieved I don't have to be the bearer of bad news. I've done that enough times. It's always a bitch, and it never gets any easier. I suppose it was good there at the end when the chief ranger said he'd hire me if I ever considered working for the government."

"Yeah, I took that as a good sign too." John grinned at her, and it lightened the gaunt planes of his face.

Cara thought about what would happen next. John had gone well above and beyond for her. Even though she was drawn to him, wanted to spend more time together, it wasn't fair to put those kinds of demands on him. Just because he'd been her client —and they'd gone through hell together—wasn't a reason for them to be joined at the hip forever. Besides, he needed to address whatever he wouldn't tell her about that had happened with the kites and the Indian spirit guides.

That would happen with his kinfolk back in Bakersfield, not here in Lone Pine. He was such a decent man, he probably wouldn't leave her side if she didn't kick that door wide open. It cost her, but she made a decision.

Tugging her car door open, she pasted a smile on her face— wondering just how false it looked—and tried for an upbeat note. "It's kind of late for a long drive, especially after not getting much sleep last night. Never mind those nights we were trapped on the fire's side of Mount Rixford. I'm going to get something to eat in town and drive to Walker Pass. I know a few places well off the road where I can pitch my tent and sleep tonight."

She forged ahead not waiting for him to answer. "You've been wonderful, and I truly appreciate you putting your life on hold for me, but I can take things from here."

His jaunty aspect fell away. "Is that what you want? For me to leave?"

Cara swallowed hard. "I don't want to hold you up. Don't you have things you need to attend to?"

He closed her car door and gripped her shoulder. "I do, but that's not what I asked."

She flinched and tried to pull away, but he held on tight. "Let me try this from another angle. I like you, Cara. If you're going into Lone Pine for supper, I'd like to come along. And I want to camp another night with you—if that's what you're doing."

She opened her mouth, but he shook his head. "I'm not finished. If you don't feel the same way, I'll get in my car and leave you be. You don't have to worry about me bothering you. I don't do things like that."

Her mouth was still hanging open and she clacked it shut. "Jesus," she muttered. "You're pretty damned direct."

An expression she couldn't name flitted across his face. "No point in not stating things clearly. Avoids misunderstandings." He sucked in a tight breath. "I learned early on in my medical training, it was best to be straight with people about their disease and the odds. Some of the other docs preferred to sugarcoat things, but I felt like I did dying patients a disservice if I pretended they might have more than a few months."

"Sometimes miracles happen."

A ghost of a smile curved his mouth. "Yes, but they're few and far between. You never did answer me."

She squared her tired shoulders. "All that time you've worked on being a straight-shooter, I've buried my feelings. Worse than that, I pretended they didn't exist."

"So?" He quirked a brow.

"So maybe this is harder for me."

"I doubt it. I just laid my heart at your feet, and I'm waiting to see if you're going to accept my gift or stomp all over it."

"Ouch." She winced.

"Yeah. Ouch. Look. We may not have a future together like I hope we might, but if we don't keep trying, we'll never find out."

"Fair enough." She looked at the ground because she couldn't meet his unwavering gaze. "Yes, I'd like to stay together for dinner and tonight." She swallowed a snort. "I can hardly believe I said that."

"Well you did, and the earth didn't open and swallow you up. Do you have a favorite place to eat in Lone Pine?"

"Not really. How about if you follow me into town, and we'll take a walk and see what looks good to both of us."

John did a credible rendition of a low, sweeping bow before pulling her car door open. "You're on."

A laugh bubbled from somewhere deep inside her, a place she'd almost forgotten existed. "And you're impossible."

"You have no idea, sweetheart. See you in a few." He loped across the almost empty parking lot to his white Toyota 4Runner. Unlike her older model Subaru, his car looked almost new. She enjoyed watching his long, effortless stride and how his body moved, all sinuous muscle and graceful motion. Something tightened deep in her belly, and her nipples hardened beneath her sports bra.

My body responding is the easy part, she reminded herself. It remained to be seen whether she had a heart left to share with anyone.

THE SKY over the Sierras held a gray pall tinged with red as John drove south out of Lone Pine after an excellent dinner at a small steakhouse. The local news had blared from a flat screen television, and according to it the fire was spreading fast. He and Cara had been fortunate to escape. Although as he thought about it, the spirit guides probably had something to do with that. They needed him alive, not turned into cinders blowing across Rae Lakes Basin.

They'd made certain he found the crack that led to freedom,

and confined him in the cave long enough to chivvy him into doing their bidding. It wasn't accidental they'd allowed Cara to exit the cave before closing him inside. They didn't want any witnesses. He wasn't certain if she would've been able to sense the spirits as anything other than a mild electric aspect to the air, but watching him hold a heated conversation in the Sioux language would have held an unnerving aspect.

How long would she have kept quiet before asking who the fuck he was talking with? Or worse, demanded that he focus his attention on their escape. The spirit guides might have killed her for something like that. Truth washed through him that he'd escaped because the guides needed him free. They wouldn't have lifted a finger if he hadn't made a good faith effort to exit the cavern. Once he went to work with elbow grease and magic, they made certain he found his way back to the chimney and the world they wanted him to save.

As he drove, he took inventory of the changes—subtle and otherwise—from awakening his power. Because he'd never been interested in learning about it, he had no idea the extent of what he could do. His only use for it in recent years had been to reinforce his intuitions about which patients would survive.

He hadn't been totally honest with Cara when the topic surfaced earlier. His well-honed instincts were why he felt it was both duty and obligation to help his patients prepare for what he saw in their futures.

How much should he tell her? Would she chalk him off as one more nut job if he said too much? Somehow he didn't think so. She hadn't raced up the chimney away from him when he'd emerged from the cave. That was a good sign. She hadn't broken and run when the kites had marked his way down the mountain, either.

He tried out various approaches about exactly what to tell Cara, while keeping her car in sight and turning off the highway when she did. They weren't on 395 anymore. The road had split a few miles back, and they were traveling south on 14. Neither of them expected the road across the Southern Sierra would go all the way through because of the fire, but they'd agreed to travel to the first decent turnout and stop for the night. In case they didn't get as far as the creeks Cara knew about, they'd picked up a couple gallons of water from a convenience store to tide them over.

It was almost dark, and the air blowing through his open window held a smoky tinge. He picked up his cell to tell Cara stopping sooner rather than later would be best, but *No Service* lit on his phone when he tried to activate it.

She must've read his mind because she put on a flasher and pulled down a sandy road, following it as it grew progressively narrower. The clatter of rushing water reached him, and he smiled. Cara must've known about this place. The odds of picking a road and having it yield a creek were thin. Sure enough, she pulled off to the side and killed her engine. He slid his Toyota next to her and did the same.

When he got out of his car, she was faced away from him, looking up at a blood-red moon, elbows akimbo. "Smoke did that." She pointed skyward. "Even though I know what causes it, it still creeps me out. The moon isn't supposed to be that color."

He walked up behind her fighting an impulse to wrap her in his arms. It sounded hokier than hell, but he said, "It's a fire moon. It'll be all right. I'll take care of you."

She turned until she faced him, only inches away. "Protect me from red moons and other weird shit, huh? My own personal Sir Galahad?"

His face grew warm despite the cooling night air, and he shrugged uncomfortably. "Problem with being a modern man is that whole damsel in distress thing went out of fashion a hundred years back."

Cara captured her full lower lip between her teeth. "Would you really want me to be helpless like that? Where I turned to a man for everything."

"Of course not, but if I had my way, nothing would ever hurt you." He almost lurched into a stumbling explanation of her having suffered plenty. Thank God he had enough sense not to give voice to that. She'd opened up to him. He'd do well not to remind her of the chance she'd taken doing that. She was aware enough of it without him saying anything.

"That's the thing about how I grew up," she said so slowly, it seemed she was weighing her words. "When no one believes in you, it's hard to believe in yourself."

He cupped the side of her face in one hand. "I believe in you. I've seen you keep going when you had to be scared shitless."

"Oh, I've got brass balls to spare when it comes to mountaineering." She narrowed her eyes. "It's the out of the mountains part that needs shoring up."

Not so different from me.

John inhaled raggedly. "Funny, but I have the same problem."

"What do you mean?" She frowned. "You haven't used the backcountry as a shield against having to face your inner demons."

"No. My drug of choice was medicine. I'm hell on wheels in the hospital or the clinic. Outside of a medical environment, everything shifts and I sometimes struggle to find a comfort zone." He snorted. "You've bewitched me. Men aren't ever supposed to admit to any weaknesses. Let's get that tent set up, so we can get prone."

"We have that in common too," she murmured.

"What? Wanting to lie down? It's been a long day on top of a whole bunch of other long days."

Cara went around to the Subaru's hatch, clicking it open. "No. I was referring to your weakness comment. Mountain climbers aren't supposed to have any flaws, either. At least not when it comes to our skills. The ones who don't keep plugging away—no matter if the world's imploding—don't last as guides. Leif used to say that the mountains were full of surprises, and occasionally they were even pleasant."

"Makes sense. I've done enough climbing to know that most of the unexpected shit slams my adrenaline-junkie side into high gear. Here. I'll take that off your hands." He grinned crookedly, reached for the tent, and made his way to a level spot near a rushing creek. The water glowed pink in the moon's reflection, lending it a macabre appearance.

She brought bedding, piling it near him, and then helped him stake out the tent once he'd suspended it from its aluminum frame. Tent up and sleeping bags spread out, he draped an arm around her shoulders. "Feel like a quick dip? There's a pool between us and the far bank."

"It's getting cold. If we're going to do that, we'll have to be in and out fast." She glanced at him, her expression unreadable.

"I can give you privacy if you want." He waited and felt her body stiffen beneath his touch before she moved in front of him and placed her hands on his shoulders.

"What do you want?" she asked, a husky catch in her voice.

"You. I want you."

He cradled her head between his hands and brought his mouth down on hers. She tasted sweet like the brandy they'd shared over dessert. She slid her arms beneath his and splayed her hands across his back. Digging her strong fingers into him, she held on as if he were a lifeline.

He snaked his tongue along the seam of her lips and she opened her mouth, kissing him back. He licked, sucked, bit, nibbled, never wanting the kiss to end. Her nipples hardened into fine points pressing against his chest, and his cock charged to attention.

She writhed against him, butted her hips against his erection, and straddled one of his legs, pressing the heat of her core against his thigh. A low, needy moan rose from her, and she tore her mouth from his, breathing hard.

"If we're going to do this, can we at least lie down? Stand-up sex has its merits, but—" Her green-gold eyes twinkled, and she moved a hand between them and curved it around his ridged flesh.

John growled, guttural, feral, and bucked against her hand. "We can do anything you want, sweetheart. Are you sure you don't want that dip in the creek first?"

"I'm sure. The water's not more than forty degrees." She squeezed his cock. "I'm into heat right now, not cold."

His heart thudded against his ears and he wanted nothing more than to strip Cara's clothing off a piece at a time, but taking her in the pool beneath the red globe of the moon would be wonderful.

He dipped a hand under her top, cupping a breast. She pushed into him as he reached inside her bra to twirl her nipple between two fingers. "I can make it warm."

A low, throaty laugh bubbled from her. "You make me more than warm. Now about those clothes?"

"Cara. I can make the water warm for us."

She drew back and stared at him. "What am I missing? It would take forever to warm enough water on the stove for baths. We're not that dirty."

He hunted for words to explain how his magic could warm the pool for them, but his brain was mush with her so close, and his throat dry with wanting her.

Giving up, he settled for, "Hush. Ssht. Not important."

He drew her top over her head, followed by her sports bra. For long moments, he just looked at her, admiring her breasts. Full and firm, they were tipped with copper colored nipples. Her skin pebbled in the cool night air, and he bent to take a nipple in his mouth. She arched against him and threaded her fingers into his hair.

He moved from one breast to the next before inserting a hand between her legs and pressing the vee in her crotch. His cock was on fire with wanting her. If he got any harder, he'd shatter into a million pieces. Letting go of her breasts, he knelt before her and undid her boots, helping her slither out of them.

He unlaced his own before he straightened, and held onto a tree to toe them off. Cara tugged his shirt over his head, and traced the lines of his upper body with her fingertips and mouth. She'd unlatched his belt and began on his zipper when the unmistakable beat of wings surrounded them.

Kites.

A whole flock of them if he was any judge, and they weren't trying for stealth. They lit up the night with their caws and screeching.

Lust pierced him. He wanted the woman in his arms, needed to bury himself inside her, claim her, make her his own… It made no sense. He'd never felt as if he'd die if he didn't have sex before. And where the hell had that atavistic thought about claiming her come from?

With a great deal of difficulty, he got his breathing under control and held tight to Cara, trading desire for a savage protectiveness. If even one bird tried to harm her, he'd kill the fucking thing.

"What the hell? Why are they here?" Cara dug her fingers into his back.

The birds fluttered to nearby trees and the ground, until they formed a circle with himself and Cara inside.

"I suspect we're about to find out." He glanced at the birds. "If we get lucky, they'll leave soon and we can pick up where we left off."

In his heart, he knew better. The birds presaged the spirit guides. Either things had turned to shit faster than they'd anticipated, or they were pissed he hadn't followed their instructions and made a beeline for his father and grandmother.

"Cara." He swallowed hard, but forced himself to keep talking. "You'll see and hear things that seem impossible. Keep an open mind, and don't talk with the guides unless they address you directly."

"Guides? What guides?"

"Spirit guides."

Her voice cracked. "How could anything be more off-the-wall than those kites attacking us on Mount Rixford?"

"You've seen birds before. You've never seen spirits. And you may not see these. Depends if they're willing to show themselves to you."

He kicked himself for keeping his mouth shut earlier after a tremor tracked down her body. He wanted to tell her everything would be all right, but he wasn't sure about that, and he wouldn't lie to her.

Cara was too important to him to offer her anything less than the truth.

CHAPTER 8

*S*pirit guides? What the fuck is he actually talking about?

When he'd mentioned them while they were climbing out of the fire's reach, she'd assumed they were some sort of abstract concept. Not something real.

Cara forced herself to breathe, slow and steady, her desire from moments before fading. Breath control was the same tactic she'd cultivated to deal with her fear when the mountain gods turned on her. She would've sought the safety of her car, but she was half-naked, and she didn't trust the birds as far as she could throw them. She remembered how they'd attacked in the Sierra. Her forearm still bore gouges from the one who'd made it his personal mission to destroy her.

An image of all the dead bodies in that cave formed in her mind. She suspected the kites had something to do with picking the flesh off those skeletons. A tremor passed from her bare shoulders to her feet and she refocused on breathing. Just breathing. It worked for less than a minute.

"What exactly are you?" she asked, working hard to keep her voice from turning shrill.

"I told you. If I'd stayed around, I'd have been the tribe's next shaman."

"But what does being an Indian shaman actually mean?" she persisted, dragging her head back far enough to look at him.

"I wish I had a decent answer for you. I have magical ability, but I have no idea how deep it runs—or exactly what I can do—because I'd never called on it or tested it to any extent before I ended up trapped in the cave."

She unclenched fingers that she'd dug deep into his shoulder muscles. He hadn't complained, but she had to be hurting him.

"You picked a hell of a time to do a test run on unproven skills. It would be like me tackling a class six aid climb if the best I'd managed before was class three scrambling."

"I deserve that." He let go of her long enough to pluck her top off the ground, slipping it over her head. "It's about the same thing my grandmother would've said."

"Great," Cara sputtered, tugging her stretchy shirt into place. No bra, but it was better than being naked. "If I ever meet her, maybe we'll get along."

"No doubt about it." He ducked into his shirt.

The birds chittered after being silent, and the air developed a glowing quality off to one side.

"What's that?" she pointed.

"Guides. You can wait in the car if you're more comfortable." John stood straight and turned so he faced the place she'd pointed at.

Despite having wanted to lock herself in the car before, Cara was curious. What would walk out of that light? If she hid, she'd never know. Besides, whatever this was, it was linked to John, and she wanted to know everything she could about the man standing next to her. If she threw in her lot with him, she had to know what she was signing up for.

All of it. The good and the bad.

And the impossible.

She'd been young when she met Leif. Too young to question their attraction. Being in a one down position was something she was used to because it mirrored what she'd had at home. No more. She had enough years under her belt to demand a partner where they shared everything as equals.

"If you're going to get in the car, do it now." He broke into her thoughts.

"Nope. I'm staying."

He glanced her way. Respect and approval flashed across his face, warming her. She wanted both those things from him. Leif had never offered her either.

He shifted his attention to the light that had grown so intense she had to squint against it, and bowed. After a pause, he spoke a few words in a language she didn't recognize, and nodded once, sharply.

John turned to her. "I'll be gone, but not far and not for long. No matter what, remain here. It's not safe for you to do anything else."

Questions bumped around in her head. What did he mean by *not safe?* Surely she could get in her Subaru and return to the main highway. The light pulsed, prickling against her skin. The birds formed the same groups of twos and threes as they had before, and John walked through them, vanishing behind the curtain of light.

Cara started forward, intent on remaining with him, but stopped when a sharp rock cut into her bare foot. He hadn't specifically told her not to follow him, but maybe it wasn't a good idea. She hadn't quite reached the first clump of kites yet, and they snapped their beaks in what sounded like a warning. Feathers rustled as they fluffed themselves so they appeared larger, more menacing.

She retrieved her socks and boots and got back into them, waiting. Chanting competed with the creek, the odd combination of vowels and consonants rising and falling around her. In any other situation, the lyrical quality might have soothed her, but there was nothing soothing about tonight.

She shut her eyes to ease the glare from the pulsing light. When she opened them, she glanced toward the southern tip of the Sierras, wondering if the illumination would extend that high. Breath slammed out of her in a *whoosh*. The red glow she'd seen earlier had intensified tenfold, which was odd since the smoke smell wasn't any worse.

"When the fuck did that happen?" she muttered.

Was the fire spreading? It sure looked as if it was.

If her senses told the truth—and who knew what was true anymore, between sentient kites and glowing spirit guides—she and John needed to get out of here. And damned fast. She bolted toward the tent, dove inside it, and gathered the sleeping bags and pads. Once she'd stowed them in the back of her car, she went to work taking the tent down. Soon nothing remained but to drive east into the desert, out of the rampaging path of the fire.

Where was John?

Would calling him make any difference?

A kite cawed, almost as if warning her against disturbing whatever its masters were doing with John. She dragged her keys out of her pants pocket and stared at them. She could leave. Nothing was stopping her.

He said not to.

Yes, but he didn't give me any real reasons. My life hasn't been "safe" since I took up guiding.

She licked her chapped lips and moved farther from the glowing light so she could see the encroaching fire better. She'd been in hard situations before, and she needed more information to decide what to do. She could leave a note in his car and go, but that didn't feel right. Like leaving him to fight something huge and terrible on his own.

Something I don't understand.

She shielded her eyes with one hand and squinted, willing

herself to see better across distance. What the fuck was going on with the Sierra Crest? That red glow had moved down its eastern flanks, but she couldn't hear the characteristic crackle of flames and the air was still breathable. Normally, this close to a major fire, she'd have the same trouble breathing she'd had in Rae Lakes Basin.

Something red and shimmery detached itself from the mountains and moved toward her, followed by two more crimson blobs. She couldn't have torn her gaze away if she tried. What the hell were they?

"Holy shit!"

Her stomach twisted into a mass of fiery snakes. If she didn't know better, three dinosaurs were flying toward her.

Cara clapped a hand over her mouth and instructed her dinner to stay put. She needed the calories. "Can't be dinosaurs," she muttered. "They're extinct."

Extinct or not, the three things flew closer. Close enough for her to see huge red wings and fire spewing from their mouths.

"Oh Jesus. God," she gasped. "Not dinosaurs. Dragons. It's not possible." Her head spun crazily, and she ripped her attention away from the dreadful things. Whatever they were—and they sure as shit couldn't be what they appeared—they were headed right for her.

Swallowing back a shriek, she bolted for her car. Adrenaline pounded through her, and the only thing she could think about was escape from those horrific creatures bearing down on her from above. Smells buffeted her—rot, decay, death—and the air temperature shot up so fast she began to sweat.

Arms closed around her from behind, and she lost it, shrieking, "No! Stop it! Let me go." She flailed like a mad thing, desperate to lock herself into her car and drive like a banshee—as far away from this nightmare as she could get.

"Cara. Get hold of yourself." John's voice finally penetrated the panicked fog around her brain. He shook her, but not hard.

"You can fall apart later. Right now, you have to do exactly as I say."

"Leave," she moaned and turned to face him. "We have to leave right now. Everything's in the car—"

"Not an option." His voice was harsh, and he didn't sound anything like himself. "This fight came to me. The guides and birds will help, but I need your energy too."

She stared hard at him. Had he lost his mind? Though the words had been in English, they may as well have been Swahili for all the sense they made. "What fight? Why do you need me?"

"It'll take too long to explain." He wound a hand into her hair and tilted her head until she had to look at him. "I trusted you to get us out of a tough spot in the mountains. Now I'm asking you to trust me. Can you do that?"

"No. Yes. Shit, I have no idea. I don't know you well enough to trust you."

The harsh planes of his face softened. "Yeah, you do. Besides, you don't have a choice. If you started down the road in your car, the dragons would blow it to smithereens. They'd set the fuel on fire. Even if you got away from the inferno, which is doubtful, you'd be stranded."

Dragons. He called them dragons. Holy mother of fucking God.

He tightened his grip on her. "I want you to be safe more than anything in the world, and right now that safe place is next to me. You'll have to take that on faith. Can you do that?"

She never understood why she didn't slap him and make a run for her car, but she didn't. Instead, she nodded.

"Good. I told the guides, the guardians, you'd help."

"Who are they?"

"I'll tell you everything, but not right now." He let go of her hair and took her hand in his. "Turn like this. Face the sky—and the dragons. Be strong. They feed off fear."

"What happens next?" It took an act of God to keep her voice steady.

"We blow those fuckers out of the sky. And then we drive out of here."

"What happens if they torch us first?"

The rustle of kites' wings almost cut off her words, and the flock of black birds took to the air in a rush, forming a barrier between them and the dragon like things.

"Not going to happen," John retorted. "Not on my watch."

JOHN HAD BROKEN A CARDINAL RULE. He'd severed his mind link to the guides when he sensed Cara's panicked dash for her car. He'd felt torn, but hadn't had any choice. Not really. The guides could've killed him for disobedience, but they let him go.

Yeah, because they need me right now.

He gritted his teeth together. This was one of the reasons he hadn't wanted jack shit to do with being a shaman. He'd never taken direction particularly well, especially when his absolute compliance was assumed.

He caught Cara from behind and held her against him while she tried to reach back and gouge his eyes out. When it wasn't going well—or fast enough, given what they faced—he cheated and sent a calming spell into her mind. He needed her front and center, not telling him to go fuck himself and peeling rubber away from him.

He breathed a sigh of relief once she was by his side and the only thing he had to do was take out three dragon lords.

Only thing. Yeah, right.

John felt woefully ill equipped. Nothing in his almost thirty-one years had prepared him for today, but focusing on his lack of knowledge was a sure recipe for disaster. The guides made it sound simple enough. Earth trumped fire every time, smothering its essence. All he had to do was surround each dragon with earth power, and it should vanish, drawn back to its home world.

Cara's energy would boost his, since female power complemented male.

"Listen to this chant," he told Cara. "It's a simple three-line refrain. Once you have it, say the same thing with me."

"Got it. Hurry. They're almost here." Panic crackled beneath her words, and she squeezed his hand hard enough to crack his bones together.

He inhaled raggedly—thinking too much would only make things worse—and began to chant, gratified when she picked up the repeated phrases almost instantly. They'd direct her energy into his spell.

Sweat poured down his body. The dragons were near enough their smell gagged him, and they heated the air until it must've been close to a hundred degrees. He settled for shallow, panting breaths, but it didn't cut the stench much.

The kites screeched, but held their ground. White light bloomed near them, and he knew the guides had joined the fight. They'd told him they would, but he'd been afraid his hasty egress had angered them, and they might not keep their word.

The dragons were blasting everything in their path with fire. Bushes near him blazed like small torches. Two of the kites turned into pyres and plunged to the earth. John said a quick prayer that one of the guides could save the fallen birds. Despite masquerading as enemies on Mount Rixford, they'd turned into brave and resourceful allies.

John stopped thinking and focused everything he had on the middle dragon. The creatures drew energy from one another, and taking out the middle one would weaken the other two—at least according to the spirit guides.

Crazed laughter wanted out, but he choked it back. Maybe this was all a bizarre hallucination. One where he could make it go away by not believing it existed. Sweat pouring down his face and stinging his eyes reinforced how far off base he was—and how real the dragons were.

This is just the tip of the iceberg. He reminded himself how high the stakes were in this game.

Cool power closed from his other side, the one opposite from where Cara stood. "Focus," one of the guides exhorted in Sioux. "We do this on my count of three."

If Cara heard the spirit guide, she didn't give any indication. Her voice rose and fell alongside John's without a break.

He opened himself to the power of the earth, thrumming beneath his bare feet. Not having shoes on was a huge boon. When the guide reached three, he turned his body into a conduit and sent power spiraling upward, drawing on the earth and Cara.

A huge boom nearly deafened him, but the middle dragon exploded, leaving trails of fire across the sky. The other two bugled their rage and rained fire on the birds. Some of the flames made it through the barrier, and Cara's hair caught fire, right along with his own. He let go of her hand long enough to tug a hood over her head. The guide placed an ice-cold hand on John's smoldering mane.

He raked the sky again, to make certain the third dragon was well and truly gone, before nodding at the one on the right.

"Good choice," the guide said. "Let's knock it back to the hell it came from."

Fires smoked, blackening everything that would burn around them. The other two guides raced from one conflagration to the next, focusing magic to put them out before neighboring brush turned the whole meadow into an inferno. A barrier formed around the birds—likely the work of a guide who'd decided it was easier to protect them than to save them once they caught fire— and they cawed indignantly at the dragons.

John repeated what had worked with the middle dragon. Maybe he was tired, but it took a hell of a lot more out of him this time. In the dim reaches of his memory, he remembered his grandmother lecturing him about magic having a steep price, which was why he needed to practice.

"More!" the guide next to him exhorted. "More earth power. Now. Before the dragon realizes how pathetically weak you are."

John was too exhausted to be outraged by the spirit guide's criticism. Besides, it was accurate. His power was a joke.

Not after tonight, he vowed. *If I get out of this in one piece, I'll work my ass off before I face these abominations the next time.*

The thought shook him to his core. For there would be a next time. Lots of next times. Until they either wrested Earth back for their own—or lost it entirely.

"I said more," the guide shouted. "Now."

John didn't think it wise to stop chanting long enough to protest how tired he was, so he reached deep into the bones of the earth and the bones of his soul, gratified beyond words when power flowed through him. He'd have shaken a fist skyward, but he needed every iota of energy to power his magic.

Die, you bastard.

Die.

Another enormous boom shook the earth beneath his feet, and the second dragon joined the first. Exploding into nothingness that left red contrails across John's visual field. He stared blearily at the last dragon, knowing he didn't have enough of anything left to take it on.

What would that mean?

"I-I'm sorry," he broke off chanting to stammer. "I can't do any more."

"Tell whoever you've been talking to to use me," Cara screamed. "We're almost there, goddammit."

The words were no sooner out than cool, white light surrounded her, and a guide wrenched her hand out of his.

"You're not done," the guide next to him said. "Give me access to your mind so I can boost the woman's essence."

John wanted to ask exactly what that meant. Spirit guides were notorious for playing fast and loose with human lives. "Don't hurt her," he cried.

"Open your mind and watch over her," the guide challenged.

John felt the spirit augur into him. The world tilted until he saw things unfold from many angles. From all three spirit guides, from Cara, and from his own perspective—all at the same time. The collage was dizzying, and events took off at breakneck speed. The guides used Cara as a lightning rod, burning earth power through her. Finding power he didn't know he had, John reached inside her mind to cushion their intrusion.

He was so focused on Cara that the boom presaging the dragon's destruction shocked him. Everything happened at once after that. The dragon shattered, leaving the sky awash in red contrails. Water exploded from above, dousing the last of the smoking fires, and the guides and birds vanished.

Cara swayed on her feet, a shell-shocked look stamped into a face with all the color drained out of it. The unnatural rainstorm plastered her dark hair against her head.

"Cara! Jesus, Cara. Talk to me." He gathered her into his arms with water running down his face and body. He'd done his best to shield her. What if his best hadn't been good enough?

"Yeah. I'm still here," she said just before she slumped against him, unconscious.

CHAPTER 9

John dropped to the sodden ground with Cara in his arms. Her heartbeat was strong and steady, and she'd spoken to him before she passed out. Those had to be good signs.

"Think like a doctor," he admonished himself, and checked her pulse, respiration, and her pupillary reaction to the beam of a headlamp he dug out of a pocket. Not finding anything seriously wrong, he switched to magic and probed her mind.

Resting. Thank fucking God. She's treading the surface of consciousness, and it wouldn't take much for her to break through.

He'd been frightened the shock of the power flowing through her had driven her into a coma. One she might never come out of.

"Cara." He put his mouth next to her ear and repeated her name twice more.

Her eyes fluttered open. She stiffened and tried to bolt out of his arms. "Are they gone?" She twisted her head from side to side, her gaze raking the sky.

"Yes. For now. Hush. You've had a shock and you need rest."

"Bullshit." She wriggled out of his lap and sat across from him, skirting puddles that had formed. Water had to be soaking through her outdoor pants. Cara wrapped her arms around herself. "Jesus! I never thought I'd be cold again, but I'm freezing. Wish I'd left the tent up."

"You're wet, probably all the way to your skin. Let's get into my car, and I'll turn on the heat and find you something dry to put on."

She smacked her forehead with a hand. "Cars. I'm not thinking. We need to get out of here."

John shook his head. "Not anymore. We're safe enough for now."

Her eyes rounded into small moons. "What does *for now* mean? Those things. They're coming back?"

He nodded, wondering where to begin. Or if he should begin at all. She could leave now, with minimal collateral damage.

Cara stumbled to her feet. "Let's fire up one of the cars. While it's getting warm, we can brew up some coffee on the cook stove. You're going to tell me enough so I understand what happened here tonight."

"I can do that, but once you know, you'll be stuck. The knowledge isn't something you can turn your back on once you know about it."

She screwed her face into a grimace. "So is it one of those deals where you have to lobotomize me once you've told me?"

"Not exactly." Breath whistled through his teeth, and he shivered. "Coffee's a great idea. The deal is this, Cara. You can get in your car and drive away from this place and me. I actually recommend you do that. Before you go, I'll alter your memories so nothing about tonight remains. You'll go back to your guiding business and forget all about me. And the dragons. And the war."

"War? What war? What will you do if I leave?"

He shrugged. "What do you think? This is my war. I didn't pick it, but I can't run from it, either."

"What happens if we lose?" Her voice was low.

"The dragons will make Earth uninhabitable for humans."

"Why?" She choked on the word.

"Because they want it for themselves."

Cara wobbled from side to side looking stunned. He jumped up to put an arm around her. "You really should be sitting down, and you're shivering."

"So are you," she countered. "Plus you're nine kinds of nuts if you think I could just walk away and let you face this all by yourself." She tilted her chin upward. "I'm in, but I need information."

He swept her into a hug, so overcome with emotion, he couldn't talk. "Better watch it," he said after he got himself under control. "It wouldn't take much for me to fall in love with you."

"Maybe the feeling's mutual." She swatted his ass. "Get that engine going. I'll make coffee, and then I want to know everything you do about what the hell is happening."

"Shouldn't take all that long," he muttered. "Since I don't know all that much myself."

"If not you, then whom?"

"Maybe my grandmother. She's the one with psychic ability who foretells the future."

Cara rolled her eyes. "See. Told you that you should've gone straight to Bakersfield. Do not pass go. Do not collect two hundred dollars—"

"If I'd done that, they might have attacked you here by yourself." Truth in his words made him never want to leave her side—ever. But he kept that thought to himself.

She narrowed her eyes. "I'm not so sure about that. You seem to be the one they want."

"No. I'm who the spirit guides want. The dragons are equal opportunity destroyers. I liked your coffee idea. Do you want me to get it going while you warm up in my car?"

"Nah. I'm on it." She trotted to her car, opened the hatch, and emerged with the butane stove and a pot that she filled from one of the gallon water jugs they'd picked up in Lone Pine. Once the water was heating, she poured instant coffee mix into two titanium mugs.

The hiss of the stove got him moving toward his Toyota. Snagging his keys out of a pocket, he reached inside long enough to turn the engine over, and then went to get his cup from Cara. The rain had departed as precipitously as it arrived, but the dry desert air stank of charred vegetation, burned human hair, burned feathers, and the charnel stench of the dragons. A thick cloud of soot obscured the sky, but it was settling out.

A star or two winked through. Even though it made no sense, that small bit of normalcy gave him hope.

"Here." Cara thrust a metal mug into his hands.

"Thanks. Car should be about ready for us." He walked to the passenger side, opening the door for her. Once she was inside, he took a tentative sip of the scalding coffee before making his way to his side of the car and getting in.

Cara wrapped her long fingers around the mug and leaned against her well-padded tan leather seat. "Jeez, I was tired before all this, but now I feel like a train ran over me."

"The guides borrowed your energy, your essence. I helped where I could, but I was tapped out."

"Are you saying I killed the last dragon?" She shot him a look that said he was a candidate for the psych ward.

"They're not dead. They're back where they began."

She sipped from her cup. "Damn! Here I was hoping there were three less of those bastards. How about if you start at the beginning? I'll try not to ask questions, but I won't guarantee that."

John tucked his coffee into the cup holder in the console between the seats. "This story has two distinct threads. The first is about me. The second is about the dragons. I didn't know anything about them until yesterday when I was trapped in the cave." He shook his head slowly. "Seems like that was forever ago."

"Go on." Cara crooked two fingers his way.

"The part about me is easy. Like every other human attribute, magic has genetic roots. I was born into a magical family, so I had magic too. Turns out earth power was my forte. There are others for whom fire, air, or water are primary."

"I know I said I'd keep quiet, but what would've happened tonight if fire had been your strength?"

He reached for her hand, and she grasped his. "I have no idea. Since I can't imagine being as strong in that element as the dragons, I assume we'd be dead."

"What elements do those guides control?"

"All of them, but none with great effectiveness. They need to borrow from humans to leverage their ability." He chuckled. "Would you rather just ask questions? That works too."

"No. Tell me in the order that makes sense for you. Why didn't you want your magical heritage? Seems like something most kids would kill for."

John considered her words before he answered. "Kids don't want to be different. I wanted to be just like everyone else. Magic got in the way. When I was small, it escaped my control all the time, and I felt like an ass. I didn't want to stay on the reservation. Growing my life beyond that part of my tradition became an all-consuming focus. I worked extra hard in school and did well in sports."

"You could've had both your magic and leaving the reservation." Her words were gentle, thoughtful.

"I see that now, but I didn't see it when I was ten or fifteen or eighteen. My grandmother told me it wouldn't work, but I didn't listen."

"What wouldn't work?"

"Running away from my destiny. She said it would hunt me mercilessly and force me to accept it."

A strangled sound emerged from Cara, and she coughed. "You said she was psychic. Do you suppose she foresaw this?"

He shrugged. "Hard to say. It wouldn't be her way to chase me down if she did see it, but I bet I get a piece of her mind when I get home. Anyway, the crux of things here is since I didn't want my magic, I never devoted much time to learning about it. Some of leveraging power is intuitive, but mostly it's like any other skill."

"Gets better with practice?" Cara inserted and arched a brow.

"That's right. I suspect I have some of my grandmother's precognitive ability since I've known which of my patients wouldn't survive, and I know my affinity lies with earth magic, but that's about as far as things go for me and magic."

Cara drank deep. Letting go of her hand, John retrieved his mug and did the same, welcoming the jolt from the caffeine as it hit his bloodstream.

"Are you still planning to go to Africa?"

Cara's question came out of left field, but it slapped him with a dose of reality as chilly as the rain that had cascaded down on them earlier.

"Probably not. At least not next month, which was when I was scheduled."

She reached across the console and curved a hand around his arm. "Probably not? Does that mean you're hunting for a work-around?"

"Do you hold everyone's feet to the fire? Or just mine?"

She skewered him with her direct green-gold eyes. "After all that's happened, *probably* surprised me."

Defensiveness surged, but he bit back the flow of excuses about how he'd planned for years to be able to doctor the needy in Africa. Of course he wouldn't abandon his dream without a struggle… Even his thoughts held a whiny, sullen note that made him wince.

When he scraped down to bedrock, if he couldn't find a way to defeat the dragon lords and their quest to make Earth uninhabitable for humans, the plight of the poor in Africa wouldn't matter. They'd be just as dead as everyone else.

He attempted to recoup a few scraps of dignity by muttering, "Told you I was a planner. We don't surrender our strategies easily."

"I'm a planner too," she countered, "but the thing about the mountains is they teach you flexibility. Plans are good, but knowing when to jettison them in favor of something else, beats flogging a dead horse. It's one of the reasons I'm still alive."

"Touché." He drained his cup and set it down. "Africa is off the table for now. Maybe saying that out loud will help. I'd actually been thinking earlier about seeing if you wanted to come with me."

"Me? To Africa? What would I do there?"

"Climb mountains. Relocate your guide service..."

WARMTH FLUTTERED behind Cara's breastbone, and her heart did a painful little flip-flop. Despite not knowing her very well, he'd wanted her to come to Africa with him.

A snort blew past her lips. "That pretty much negates your assertion about being a planner," she countered. "You'd want to bring a woman you've only known for a week halfway across the globe? What if I turned out to have some really hideous habits?"

He cradled the side of her head in his hand. "I'll take my chances. I couldn't stand the thought of not seeing you for the months I'd have been gone."

She wanted to ask what he would've done if she said no, but they were getting far afield, and she understood why. Talking about the dragons would solidify their existence, anchor them as a threat. Something that had to be dealt with.

She swallowed hard, wishing she had more coffee. "Dragons," she prodded. "I'd love to know why you wanted me to come to Africa, but I need to know about what we face more than hearing sweet nothings."

He stroked her cheek and moved her still-wet hair behind her shoulders. "Not sweet nothings. My feelings for you are way more than that."

She angled her head. Kissing him would've been the easiest thing in the world, but she resisted tangling her hands in his wonderful hair. "Dragons," she repeated.

"Kind of been avoiding them, haven't we?"

She nodded and made come-along motions with two fingers.

"Like I said earlier, I don't know much. Apparently they're rulers on another world, one that's running out of resources and the ability to support life. So they began hunting for a replacement. Earth was close and met most of their requirements, except it has too many people and too much water. They've hastened the damage to our ecosystems to shape our world to meet their needs."

"But we'll have more water as Earth warms and the polar ice caps melt. Are they aquatic? What will they eat after the planet can't support life anymore?"

"I don't know the answers to either of those questions. I have no idea about their reasoning process. It might be totally flawed, but that's not important. They could be dumb as dirt, but they've still targeted our home. We have to make things so miserable for them they pick someone else's planet to pillage."

"Humph. It would be better to destroy them, or at least weaken them enough they never bother anyone again." She caught her lip between her upper teeth. "Moving on. Who exactly are the spirit guides? And what role do the birds play?"

"The birds aren't really birds—"

"No shit," she broke in. "What are they?"

"Another type of spirit guide, but a subservient one that obeys the others."

"That tells me less than nothing. Where do the master guides come from? Why do the birds put up with being bossed around? Can you see the guides as something other than light? Can—?"

"Whoa." He placed a hand lightly over her mouth. "Too many questions. I see the guides as they choose to appear to me. Sometimes they look like old-fashioned Indian braves with headdresses and loincloths. Sometimes they look more modern. They're not human and never were. Legends say they're made from the four elements and four directions, and that each tribe has their own."

"Do you believe that?"

John shook his head. "Not exactly. I believe they're part of seeing the world through magical eyes. We all have some amount of magic, whether we have Native American blood or not. It's like the analogy of looking through your third eye and seeing the world differently. Anyone can cultivate that by learning to meditate."

Cara rolled his words around in her mind. At least it answered one of her questions. "So that's why I sensed them today."

"Yes. It is. Fear is a powerful motivator to rip off the blinders. You'd already been blasted by the reality of dragons plunging from the sky, so why not believe in spirit guides? Plus, when you yelled at me to use you, the guides took it as invitation. You have to invite them in, or they can't access your mind."

"Is that true for you too."

John nodded. "It's true for everyone."

Cara stifled a laugh.

"What's so funny?"

"Vampires. You have to invite them in too, at least according to urban myths." Her eyes snapped open wide and she stared hard at him. "Are they real too?"

"In theory, but they're rare, and I've never seen one."

Crap. Just crap.

She drew away from him and buried her face in one hand. John let her be while she sorted and reorganized the world she thought she'd always known. Her heart thudded dully inside her chest, and her muscles tightened into rocks.

When she finally looked up, she said, "It's overwhelming."

"Yeah. And one of the many reasons I left the res. Magic would've turned into a fulltime career. I'd never have followed my dream to become a healer. Not a Western one, anyway." He took a measured breath. "In retrospect, I blended my magic into my medical training. It wasn't conscious, but it happened in spite of me willing it to leave me be." A sheepish expression flitted across his face. "I didn't end up all that far from the path everyone was convinced belonged to me."

Intuition struck hard and she captured his gaze. "You probably didn't realize that before these last couple of days, huh?"

"Nope. Mostly because I wasn't looking at the picture from the right angle."

"Funny how that works." She blew out a tight breath. "My take home message from the fire and the dragons is that there are worse things out there than my mom and her bitch of a partner. They were nothing compared with what we just lived through." She choked back the sadness that rose whenever she thought of her childhood, but relegating it to something manageable was easier this time. Much easier.

"Perspective is everything," she mumbled.

"And sometimes perspective sucks." His deep voice rumbled near her ear.

He reached across the console and drew her awkwardly against him. "I'd have given a whole lot to spare you this. All of it. The knowledge. The battles that are sure to come."

"But then I wouldn't have met you." Her voice was muffled against his chest, and her throat grew thick with emotion. "Bitter with the sweet."

"I hope you still see me as an asset worth suffering for once this is over."

She pressed as much of herself against him as the confines of the car allowed. Her head pounded and her lungs were raw from smoke. Her eyes felt as if they were lined with ground glass. She'd been in this place before. Beyond exhausted, but so keyed up, she didn't know what to do with herself.

A shudder wracked her, followed by another. "Aw shit. I'm not going to let myself cry. Not after everything that's happened."

"It's okay if you do. We need to sleep." He rubbed her back and shoulder blades, kneading the tension out of her, and she leaned into his touch. Time dribbled past until she felt a little more like herself.

"I can set the tent back up," she murmured.

John shook his head. She felt the movement against her shoulder. "Plenty of room in the back of this car. You just sit tight. I'll spread out our pads and bags and let you know when I have a nest ready for us."

She wanted to tell him she'd help, but her tongue wouldn't cooperate. The adrenaline rush from earlier had vanished along with the coffee's mild jolt, leaving her so exhausted she couldn't keep her eyes open. He kissed her forehead and slipped from the car. Her consciousness ebbed and flowed as he opened the back of the 4Runner and rustled about. She must've fallen asleep because him lifting her into his arms and carrying her into the back of the car roused her.

She tried to thank him as he tucked her into her down bag, zipping it to her chin, but he cut off her words with a quick kiss.

"No thanks needed, Cara. I'll watch over you. Come morning, we'll get moving."

CHAPTER 10

*L*ight streaming through the car's windows woke John. Cara lay next to him, eyes open, watching him. Her full mouth stretched into a soft smile. "Morning, sleepyhead."

"Morning, yourself," he retorted and drew her into his arms. "Nothing like a fresh day to dig into."

"Things never look quite as grim once the sun's up," she agreed, melting into his embrace.

Her firmly muscled body felt intensely right against his. Joy filled him when she wrapped her arms around him. He was anxious to get moving, but he couldn't resist her full lips, and he brushed his thumb across them.

She flicked out her tongue, teasing his thumb. Heat blasted through him, and his cock swelled with wanting her. His arousal from the previous night hadn't fully receded, so his body hit Mach ten with very little prodding. It wasn't wise, but he wasn't strong enough to stop himself from closing his mouth over hers.

Just one kiss, and then they'd pack up and leave. His magic struck a warning gong deep inside, but he ignored it. What harm could one kiss do?

Cara tightened her arms around him and kissed him back,

99

opening her mouth to his tongue and sucking on his lower lip. He bit her lightly and strung kisses down her face and neck before returning to the allure of her mouth. Between them, the layers of nylon and down grew uncomfortably warm from the heat of their bodies, and he batted blindly with one hand, hunting for the sleeping bags' zippers.

An image of her mounded breasts with their pebbled, copper-colored nipples slammed into him. He wanted to suckle them, and then move his mouth lower to the mysteries between her legs. His cock jerked against his belly, perilously close to release. He might have an agenda of what he'd like to do with Cara, but the odds of him lasting long enough to accomplish any of it was thin. He hadn't made love for months, and his body reminded him of that with urgent desperation.

Cara panted, her breath warm atop his mouth, and ground her pelvis against him. Breaking the kiss, she gasped, "Got to get out of these bags."

He rolled on top of her, kissing her again. He'd never wanted a woman with such ferocity; letting go of her was out of the question. If he ever got done kissing her, then he'd worry about the sleeping bag problem.

What about leaving? An inner voice nagged.

Later.

A blast of disapproval cloaked him in cold so intense it stole what little breath he still had. The sensation ebbed immediately, but it had been damned unpleasant for a few seconds. His magical side was clearly triggered. Was that what just rebuked his choice of priorities? The thought was so ludicrous, his mind rebelled, but he did draw his mouth away from Cara's.

"Did you feel that?" he asked, still shocked by the warnings pouring through him. They weren't cold anymore, but they were just as clear. Armageddon was on its way, and he needed to do something besides lose himself in the wonder of the woman beside him.

She jammed her pelvis against his painfully hard cock. "Of course I feel it. Did you finally come to your senses about getting these bags out of the way?"

"Aw, sweetheart. I'd like nothing better, but we can't."

"Why not? Did you decide you don't like me?" she teased.

"That's not it, and you know it. Something's activated my magic, and I got really cold for a moment."

She moved a hand to the side of his face, frowning. "Are you feeling all right? It's anything but cold in here." She jerked her chin at the car's steamy windows.

"Yeah, I feel fine. I'd feel better if we were in a nice motel somewhere, and no one could bother us. I don't want to let go of you—ever—but we've got to leave."

A low rumble hit the pit of his stomach just before a series of muted booms shook the earth beneath the car.

Cara bolted upright, her eyes wide. "Earthquakes. Shit." She scrambled out of her sleeping bag. "Thank God we're still dressed."

John unzipped his bag and handed her boots and socks to her. He stuffed his feet into his while the car rocked from side to side. He followed its trajectory, concerned it might tip with them in it, but it wasn't swaying that badly. The noise outside grew louder.

Crashing.

Ripping.

Tearing.

Thank Christ there weren't any trees tall enough to fall on them and crush the car.

"You don't suppose those dragon things came back?" Cara jammed her bag into a nylon sack and cinched it, then did the same with his sleeping bag.

"I don't think so. No guides or birds." He grabbed a towel and wiped the window nearest him clear. Dirt and grit flew through the air. Gaping holes spread outward like wagon spokes in the rocky ground, expanding as he watched. He'd been right about one thing. Not a kite anywhere. And the characteristic energy denoting the spirit guides was absent too.

She jammed her head next to his. "Aw shit! That's horrible. Your intuition—or your magic, or whatever—was right on. We should've left the moment we got up."

The same cold prickle ran down his spine, but not nearly as intense this time. It didn't need to be because his attention was directed at the problem.

At least it tried to warn me.

Yeah, and I didn't pay attention.

He moved to the other side of the car, the one facing west, and wiped the windows clear. The ground was heaving and rolling, but it lacked the fissures spreading on the other side.

"What happens if we follow this road west?" he asked. "I wasn't paying that close attention last night when I was following you, and I've forgotten some of what I used to know about the geography here."

"It goes past Lake Isabella and eventually comes out near Bakersfield. Or you can turn north at the far end of the lake and come out closer to where I live. I often take this route as a shortcut when I'm heading for the Eastern Sierra." She folded a hand around his upper arm, her grip like iron. "I'm sure both those roads are closed farther west because of the fire."

John angled his head and gave her a hard kiss before jackknifing his body into the front seat and making a grab for his stash of topo maps.

Cara joined him and tugged a different map than the one he'd opened out of the pile. "This one," she said, unfolded it, and pointed to a jagged series of lines denoting jeep roads that cut through the Sierras. "Lots of possibilities once we figure out exactly where the fire is—and how fast it's moving."

"We're better off staying on the paved roads. We can make faster time." He jabbed an index finger at Lake Isabella. "This is still a resort community, right?"

"Yes. Maybe twenty-five miles from us."

"All the people there must have evacuated to the west. A cavalcade of cars hasn't driven by since we got here, and the authorities probably moved all those people somewhere."

"Maybe it was already done before we got here last night."

"No way to find out. My cell doesn't work."

"It will when we get closer to Lake Isabella. Maybe. If the cell towers didn't burn down. Hey! The car stopped shaking." Cara pushed a door open and got out. "I'm going to take a look at the main road. Maybe it's just here things are so damaged."

John shoved his door open and bolted after her. "Cara. Hold up. I say we drive. Just because the current round of quakes is done, nowhere is it written there won't be more, and we're safer in a car."

She halted and spun to face him, shaking her head. "Damned fight or flight mode. It kicks in at the worst times."

He grasped her hand and hustled back to his car. "Are you good with us taking the Toyota and leaving your car here?"

"I guess so, but why?"

"If we have to talk our way past a roadblock, it might be easier with one car. I can play the doctor card if I have to. They've been known to let medical personnel through."

"Well, don't forget I'm an EMT."

Cara ran to her car and dragged the hatch open, gathering her pack and a food canister into her arms. He joined her, and took an armful of the climbing gear scattered in the back of her car. They dumped everything into the 4Runner and went back for another load. Once the back of her car was empty, Cara switched to the front and cleared out the console and glove box, handing a pile of papers to him.

"Is that everything?" he asked.

"Pretty much. I'll lock it up and we can get out of here." She patted the hood wistfully. "It's been a good car. First thing I actually bought for myself after Leif died. There was a little insurance money, and the car we had was a junker, so I bought this one."

John stacked the things from her console in a box in the back of the Toyota and turned to look at her. Her shoulders were slumped, and her face forlorn. "If it's important to you," he said, "we can transfer everything back and take the Subaru. If we move the cars right next to each other, it won't take but five minutes."

"Nah. I'm just being sentimental. Makes much more sense to stick with the newer car. If we run into trouble, yours is less likely to crap out on us." She hit the clicker, and her car chirped merrily.

"See." Cara grinned sheepishly. "Ruby's oblivious to the fact she's being abandoned. I've left her at so many trailheads, I'm sure she thinks this is just one more."

"You name your cars?"

"Yeah." Cara folded her arms beneath her breasts and furled her brows his way. "Doesn't everyone?"

Feelings for the woman in front of him swelled until he wasn't sure he could hold them all. He walked in front of Cara and placed his hands on her shoulders. "We will retrieve Ruby. And if something happens to her while we're gone, I'll buy you a replacement."

"Aw, that's really, really sweet, but I can't let you spend that kind of money on me. Besides, Ruby will be right here waiting. I'll get her back." Cara's eyes glistened with what might've been tears. "Let's get out of here. The sooner we hit Lake Isabella, the sooner we'll know if we can get through."

He helped her into the car and went around to the driver's side. The engine caught, and he backed around until he was headed toward the roadway before putting the car in four low. The dirt track they'd followed to the creek had cracked in multiple places, but nothing he couldn't drive across.

In short order, the empty roadway loomed before them. He glanced toward the east. "Do you think we should at least take a look that way?" He jerked a thumb out his open window.

"Probably not a bad idea. We made assumptions about the road being impassable, but they might not be correct."

Magic jabbed him with the same cold precision it had when Cara was wrapped tight against him. His psychic side—or sixth sense, or whatever it was—wanted them to turn right, not left. Was it because his power was herding him toward Bakersfield? Could it possibly be something that simple?

"What is it?" she asked.

He pounded a fist down on the steering wheel. "Damn it! I wish I knew more about how this magic crap worked." The ice pick sensation of being jabbed in his guts intensified.

He gave up and turned right, toward Lake Isabella. The stabbing sensation ceased as soon as the car rolled down the road.

"What happened to checking out the other direction, back toward Highway 14?" Cara asked, sounding mystified. "I thought we'd decided—"

"We did." His voice was harsher than he meant it to be. "Sorry. Let me back up. Earlier this morning, when making love with you was the most important thing in my world, even if it meant not leaving right away, I got this odd, deeply unpleasant, warning sensation." He stopped to suck in a tense breath. "The earthquakes began on its heels."

Cara narrowed her eyes to slits. "That was why you asked me if I'd felt something." A lovely rose color rose to her cheeks. "I was pretty caught up in wanting you too, and I wasn't tracking all that well."

He nodded. "Like I mentioned earlier, it was this intense cold. Anyway, I just felt it again when we were discussing which way to go. For whatever reason, my magic didn't like the idea of us heading east, so this time I thought I'd pay better attention."

CARA BIT down hard on her lower lip, only backing off when she tasted blood. This was getting stranger and stranger. She'd lived through lots of earthquakes—the entire Sierra chain sat on a branching network of faults—but none of them had just kept on rolling like the series this morning.

For a moment, she considered telling John to turn around and take her back to her car. She'd take her chances on her own. Her heart squeezed in her chest, and a dull ache spread through her. She didn't want to leave him. He was everything she respected in a man. Bright, resourceful, good climber, quick wits. Plus, he made her hotter than hell. She wanted to crawl all over his lanky body, licking, tasting, taking him deep within her. While not exactly a nun since Leif's death, she hadn't ever come close to wanting a relationship with anyone.

Until now.

Yeah, and he's also really, really weird. Maybe not him, exactly, but all the magic mumbo-jumbo.

"Is the paranormal stuff creeping you out?"

His question caught her by surprise because it mirrored her inner turmoil. "Do you read minds on the side?"

"Don't have to." He glanced askance at her. "Anyone would be freaked out coming face-to-face with something they've never believed in. Hell, I grew up with it, and it bothers me."

Cara didn't know what to say, so she rolled her window down a couple inches. The smoke smell was definitely worse, so she closed it again. She unlatched her seatbelt and crawled into the back of the car, rooting in the welter of packs, gear, and climbing paraphernalia.

"What are you looking for?" he asked.

"The instant coffee and water. It's better hot, but it'll mix okay if you can live with a few lumps. I was going to make you some too."

"Thanks, Cara. That would be great." He hesitated, as if he were considering his next words. "Are you sorry you didn't take me up on last night's offer to leave and forget everything that's happened?"

She pushed things aside so she could sit and make drinks for them.

Well, am I?

"Not really, but the supernatural stuff will take some getting used to. Here." She handed him a mug through the space between the front seats.

He took it and said, "Thanks. Give me yours too."

She did and clambered back into her seat. The powdered mix hadn't totally dissolved since the water wasn't hot, but the liquid soothed her smoke-scorched throat, and the sugar and caffeine gave her a nice lift.

"This was a good idea," he said and drank deep.

"Look!" She pointed. "First roadblock and we've got a long way to go."

John nodded. When she studied his profile, he looked exhausted. His face was smudged with soot. Tanned skin splashed with freckles stretched tightly over his high cheekbones and square chin. Week-old red stubble dotted his face.

"Could you dig my wallet out of the console, please?" he asked. "Better chase down the most recent registration and insurance docs too."

She found everything easily and waited while he rolled the car to a halt and opened his window before handing his wallet over.

A highway patrol officer got out of his car and strode toward them, a shocked look on his face. "Where in the blazes did the two of you come from?" he demanded. "Road's impassible between here and Highway 14. Quake destroyed it."

"We were camped this side of Walker Pass," John said and handed his driver's license and another plasticized square to the officer.

"We swept that area," the officer—Hemmet according to his badge—protested. "Late last night when we got word from the seismic guys we might be in for it." He scanned John's identification. "Doctor, huh?"

John nodded. "Yes. I'm trying to get to Bakersfield. Got word from my family that I'm needed on the res."

A resigned sounding breath whistled from between Officer Hemmet's teeth. "Let's see your insurance and registration."

Cara handed them across the car.

The officer bent and looked in the window. "Who are you?"

"Cara Carlisle." Since she'd anticipated him asking, she handed her driver's license to him.

"Carlisle. Carlisle," he muttered. "Cassavettes and Carlisle. You two remain here. I'll be right back." He plodded back to his cruiser with all their identification and the car's insurance verification and registration clutched in one hand.

"What do you think?" Cara kept her voice low. It didn't take a magical side to get the feeling the world was conspiring to keep them away from John's family.

John shrugged. "We spent most of yesterday closeted with California's finest. I'm sure your statement got some airtime. After all, you reported deceased climbers."

Cara drained the rest of her coffee. She'd just pushed her door open, planning to go into the back and make more, when the heavy tread of Officer Hemmet's boots drew her attention.

"Please remain in the car, Ms. Carlisle."

"Sorry." She tugged her door shut.

The officer closed the distance to John's side of the car. "Here you go, Dr. Cassavettes," he said and handed all their documentation back to him. "You're the ones who escaped the fire. Thought I recognized your names. Lucky you got over Kearsarge when you did. That fire's cut off the main trail you used to get out of there."

"It's been a hell of a few days," Cara muttered.

"From the sound of things, you did everything humanly possible," Officer Hemmet said, not sounding like a cop for the first time since they'd stopped for his roadblock. "What happened to your vehicle, Ms. Carlisle? You were driving a Subaru when you reported in at the Forest Service office in Lone Pine yesterday."

"It's parked back where we camped last night," she replied. "We were concerned about getting out of here—after the series of quakes—so we consolidated all our gear into one car."

"Smart. You locked the other one up, right?"

"Yes. Of course."

"Probably for the best," the officer went on. "Been some odd things folk reported last night, but it might've just been mirages from the fire. People see funny things when they're scared."

John cleared his throat. "Can we leave, Officer Hemmet? They need me on the res. Some kind of odd illness, and my aunt's never trusted anyone but me to treat our family. Not since I finished medical school."

"Yes. You can leave, but only because there's no other choice. The road behind you doesn't exist anymore, but fire could cut you off going this way. The air quality is extremely bad about five miles farther on. Do you have water?" He peered into the back of the Toyota.

"Yes, we do" John replied.

"Excellent. Keep your windows closed, and put wet bandanas over your nose and mouth if you have to. We evacuated everyone out of this area late last night. Stay on the road that veers west into Bakersfield. The one that cuts north heads right into the heart of the fire. You'll find a second roadblock there—if the smoke didn't get to them and they left to get gas masks."

"Got it. Thank you." John rolled his window up and engaged the engine. The Toyota rolled down the deserted roadway at a moderate pace.

Cara tucked the car's documents into the glovebox and John's ID into his wallet before putting her driver's license away.

"Maybe this won't be all that bad," she ventured.

"I wish I could believe that. Granted we got through the first gauntlet—because they don't want any civilians in this area—but we're far from safe."

She fought a sinking feeling. "It's your magic again, isn't it? What's it telling you?"

"You'd be right about that. It's kicking up an unholy fuss, but it's different from last time. To answer your second question, I have no idea how to interpret what it wants, and a mistake could cost us." He paused a beat. "The mistake I made earlier already came home to roost. If I hadn't wanted you so badly, we'd be safe on highway 14, headed for Tehachapi Pass."

"Well, you weren't exactly a lone player. I wanted you just as desperately." She laid a hand on his thigh. "And I still do. One of these days, we'll find a bed and finish what we began. Meantime, don't be so hard on yourself. You have no idea if Tehachapi is even open. It might be shut just like this pass."

He closed his mouth with an audible *clack*, and a muscle danced beneath one eye. Cara could almost hear his teeth grind against each other.

"Is there anyone you could consult?" she asked. "Your grandmother, maybe?"

"How? Have you looked at your phone lately?"

She dug it out of her jacket pocket and checked the screen.

At first the search icon lit, but soon it changed to *No Service*.

"How about telepathy?" She was grasping at straws, and both of them knew it, but giving up wasn't in her vocabulary. Besides, how could she launch a strategy against something she couldn't see and didn't understand?

"What makes you think I'd even know how to begin to use something like telepathic communication?" He shook his head. "Sorry to sound surly. I'm angry with myself for being such a stubborn ass when I had the opportunity to cultivate my power. Mostly what I did then was throw it back in grandma's face—or use it to try to trick her."

"I have a feeling that didn't work very well."

"You'd be right about that. Nana is one canny woman. You have to get up mighty early to pull one over on her."

Cara blew out a frustrated breath. They'd just passed a deserted town, and something flashed past her peripheral vision. "Hey! We just passed a phone booth. How about a nice, old-fashioned landline?"

He braked hard enough for the Toyota to fishtail before he made a U-Turn. "Worth a try," he said, bolting out of the car once it squealed to a stop in front of a dilapidated, gray phone booth.

Cara got out too and stretched her arms over her head, rotating her torso. John pushed coins into the phone and then a credit card. Good. Meant the line wasn't down.

She reached for their empty mugs and opened the back of the Toyota intent on making more coffee and finding something they could eat. Smoke thickened the air, but it was still breathable—barely. If she listened hard, she thought she heard the crackle of distant flames.

"Focus on now," she muttered.

A hard-earned lesson from her years in the mountains, and one that had served her well. Taking her own advice, she concentrated on mixing more coffee and pulling cheese and crackers out of one of the bear canisters. They'd be back in the thick of things all too soon, and they needed fuel to sustain themselves.

CHAPTER 11

*R*elief surged once John realized the landline was functional. His grandmother picked up on the first ring, obviously knowing it was him because she peppered him with a tirade in Sioux before he could say a word. John snorted. Nothing mundane like *hello* or *how are you* from his grandmother.

He pictured Rose Cassavettes with her tall, angular build and black hair shot with silver that fell to her knees when it wasn't braided. Sharp, sweeping cheekbones, a beak of a nose, and shrewd dark eyes completed the picture.

"You can stop now. You were right. I was wrong," he cut in when it appeared Rose wasn't going to interrupt her tirade for long enough to take a deep breath. "I called because I need help."

"You have help. You don't need me anymore." Her voice was dry, cracked, like wind rustling through parched grass.

"Nana. I'm missing something here. What the hell are you talking about?"

"Stop reacting long enough to think," his grandmother retorted acidly. "Be quiet and listen with your third ear and your heart."

He clutched the receiver tighter as words rolled through the phone lines. The Western part of him wanted to take notes, but a deeper, wiser part understood it wasn't necessary. Enough time elapsed, he had to authorize more money through his debit card twice.

Finally, his grandmother fell silent.

John's throat and chest constricted with apprehension. He'd always loved the old woman, even if he'd given her teachings a wide berth. "I'll do the best I can," he ground out.

"I know you will. Don't get lost in what you should have done in years past. Nothing you can do about those omissions now. Listen to the guides and the birds. They won't steer you wrong."

"I love you, Nana."

"And I never stopped believing in you. Remember what I said about not being able to run far enough or fast enough to escape your fate?"

"Yeah. I already told you that you were right."

"We're going to give that fate a boost. Your father left for the heliport about five minutes ago. Look for his chopper. He'll get you out of there."

Anxiety formed a knot beneath John's breastbone. Flying over fires was risky business. "Tell him not to."

"Too late. He's already on his way."

Another thought slammed into John. "Will he be flying a four-seater? I have someone with me."

"You think I don't know that? My ability to see past events is crystal clear. I know exactly where you've been, what you've done, and whom you're with—if I choose to look. Focus, grandson. You can't afford to get any of this wrong."

No. I can't.

"See you soon, Nana."

"Not that soon. At least one more challenge stands between you and me. My ability to scry the future isn't as accurate as my skills looking backward. All I see in the immediate future is darkness. I can't pin it down more specifically, but the fire dragons won't make it easy for you to escape. You know about them now, and they can't afford humans launching an all-out war to get rid of them. Not yet, anyway."

"Why not?"

"They haven't damaged Earth enough to make the jump and occupy it. If we launch a massive offensive, all the work they've done these past hundred years will be for nothing."

Breath whistled through John's clenched teeth. "Any other cheery news?"

"Better the truth, than not. Just make sure my son isn't injured. You need him to fly that bird."

The line went dead. Since the tinny, robotic voice hadn't piped up asking for another ten bucks, either his grandmother had hung up, or a pole supporting the phone line went down.

It was all right. He'd heard enough.

Cara sat in the shadow of the open hatch munching on something. She waited until he got close to hand him a mug of instant coffee and pat the area next to her.

"You were on the phone for almost an hour," she said. "That coffee's been cold for a while, but you must be parched."

The length of time surprised him. "That long? Probably means we need to get rolling. I can snack on whatever you're having." He slugged back half the coffee. "Thanks. I needed that."

"Would you like me to drive? That way you can eat and get more coffee on board."

"Sure, Cara. That would be great." Gratitude sluiced through him. They were both beyond exhausted, and the conversation with his grandmother hadn't helped much. Responsibility had fallen squarely on his shoulders, so much so he was surprised he didn't collapse under its weight.

Bullshit! I'm stronger than that.

He made his way around the car and got in. Once they were underway, he ate mindlessly, realizing how empty he was after half a box of crackers disappeared along with a quarter pound of cheddar.

"Thanks for not peppering me with questions," he said.

"You needed food. I ate while you were on the phone. What did your grandmother have to say?"

"Dad is on his way with a chopper to intercept us and fly us out of here, so I guess we'll have two abandoned cars."

"There's a good piece of data." Cara pulled to the side of the roadway.

"What are you doing?" he asked.

"We need to pack things to take with us once your father shows up. Right now, gear is strewn from one end of the car to the other. Let's at least get our packs together."

"I'm glad one of us is thinking." He got out of the car, walked to the back, and popped the hatch.

She joined him and gave him a quick, hard hug. "It would've occurred to you once your blood sugar got back to normal. You can tell me more about the conversation while we work."

Cara pulled both their backpacks out of the welter of equipment, handing his to him. She sorted items so his were in one stack, hers in another, and proceeded to stow her sleeping bag, clothing sack and other assorted gear.

He went to work arranging equipment in his backpack. "Nana said a whole lot of things. The abbreviated version is I'm the tribe's shaman now. It's what the spirit guides and birds mean. Apparently, they mainly show themselves to one of us, and they've abandoned her in favor of me."

Cara looked up from coiling two lengths of climbing rope. "Did they tell her they were doing that? Or did it just happen and she figured it out?"

Making a grab for their third rope, John went to work on it. "Worse than that, I'm afraid. She conferred with them and told them to pass the baton to me, that her time was drawing to a close, and the battle to come was too critical to leave it in the hands of an old woman."

"What exactly does being the shaman mean? How big is the tribe?" Cara clipped her pack closed and secured the ropes to the outside.

John shut his eyes for a moment. He hadn't let himself think about either of those things because they'd hammer home just how drastically his life had changed.

If I fuck things up, none of us will have lives to worry about.

"John?" She'd moved on to filling water bottles. She tucked two into her pack and handed two more to him.

"Yeah, I heard you. It's the whole Sioux nation. So maybe a hundred fifty thousand. Possibly more than that. The government keeps tabs on us, but we don't cooperate very well."

Cara's mouth fell open, but she recovered fast. "Jesus! How did your grandmother deal with so many people?"

"Not directly. That's for damned sure. It's not as if she was the only one with magical power. She provided oversight, leadership." He took a measured breath. "I know less than nothing about how to do any of it."

"Looks like you'll learn a whole lot on a fast track." She patted his arm reassuringly.

John laughed skeptically. "Thanks for the vote of confidence. You should be running the other way as hard and as fast as you can."

"Well I'm not." Cara opened both food canisters. "Take half and stow it in your pack. I'll get the other half."

He started to protest they wouldn't need a bunch of freeze-dried food since it was a short flight to Bakersfield, but something in her face stopped him. "You spent a lot of time hungry as a kid, huh?"

She bit her lower lip and looked away. "Is it that obvious?"

"It's all right. I don't mind hauling food out. When things settle out a bit, we'll plan something fun in the mountains and use it all up."

"I'll hold you to it. By then, you'll probably need a break from whatever crash course your grandmother lays out for you."

"No shit. You'll like Rose. She's got a can-do attitude that matches yours."

Cara quirked a brow. "That's a compliment, right?"

"You betcha!"

They worked in silence until the only things still loose in the back of his car were the stack of paperwork from her Subaru, the two empty bear canisters, and a large, black leather satchel. Everything else was either inside their packs or strapped to the outside.

"What's that?" Cara pointed at the satchel.

"My medical bag. It goes everywhere, and there's a scaled-down version inside my pack."

"Good to know. At some point, we should compare what we have. No point hauling duplicate materials when we do things together."

He moved close and kissed her forehead. "I love your practical side."

"Excellent, because so do I. It's how I stay on track." Cara dusted her hands together. "Now we won't hold your dad up."

John glanced at his watch and did a few calculations. Worry gnawed at him. "He should be here already. It's not that far as the crow flies from Bakersfield to us."

"Do you suppose they wouldn't give him clearance to take off?"

"I'm sure they wouldn't—if he told them the truth about where he was going. Dad's cagey that way, though. Let's get moving again. He'll show up. I can take over driving again."

The Toyota was rolling when Cara said, "I'm not being nosy—or maybe I am—but there has to be more to what your grandmother told you."

"There was. She had lots of suggestions for how to manage the guides and birds—"

"What'd she say about the dragons?"

"Yeah, the dragons," he muttered. It was harder than hell to talk about them, almost as if by remaining silent, they'd go away. "They're why she foisted the guides and birds off onto me."

"Is she frightened?"

The question gave him pause. He'd never known the old woman to fear anything. "I don't think so."

"What is it, then?" Cara prodded. She reached across the console and placed a hand on his shoulder.

"She believes my magic is stronger than hers—although she did say we might have an opportunity to face the threat together."

"Might?"

He glanced sidelong at her with an uncomfortable grin. "Not only don't I understand magic terribly well, my Sioux is rusty, and Nana's English has gaps in it. She was taken from her tribe and forced into a White Man's school as a youngster, but she never gave up the Sioux language like they wanted her to."

An exasperated look washed over Cara's face. "Spit whatever it is out."

"I suspect we'll see the dragons again soon. Between here and Bakersfield."

"Okay. Why? Don't make me drag this out of you."

John laid his hand over the one she had on his shoulder. "Psychic ability isn't precise. It's not like watching something unfold on a screen. Nana said she saw darkness between her and me and cautioned me to be careful."

"See." She shot a meaningful look his way. "Good thing we packed the food. We might need it."

Emotion raced through him, warming him. "Thanks for sticking by me, Cara. You didn't have to. This isn't your fight—"

"Are you fucking kidding me?" she cut in. "It's everybody's fight if I understand things right. None of us can sit back and twiddle our thumbs while our home goes up in floods and smoke.

Speaking of which—" she rolled her window down an inch and sniffed "—smoke's definitely worse, just like the highway patrol dude said it would be."

He inhaled too—and listened. "Open your window a little more," he instructed. "I think I hear a chopper."

~

Cara punched the window's electronic control and angled her head to listen. Sure enough, the characteristic *whump-whump-whump* of a helicopter's rotor met her ears.

"Might be aerial support to fight the fire," she said.

"Maybe so. We'll know very soon if it's Dad or not." John pulled the car a few feet down a side road and got out.

Cara joined him. The smoke was so bad, her eyes began to water and her throat, already sore from her stint marching through fires and facing dragons, ached all over again. She swallowed, trying to ease it, but it only grew worse. The distant crackle and whoosh of flames battered her hearing.

"It's looking like we wouldn't have been able to drive through these mountains," she muttered.

"I was just thinking the same thing," he said. "Since Nana gave me a swift kick in the backside, I've been experimenting."

Cara coughed and moved next to him, wrapping an arm around his waist. She liked having him close. He felt warm and solid and so many other things, it scared her. "Experimenting with what? Say more."

He draped an arm around her shoulders and drew her close. "There are ways to send magic outward. I'm not very good at it, but when I tried to extend my reach farther down the road than I can see or hear, it didn't look good. The road is still open, but everything on both sides is on fire, and debris is starting to pile up on the asphalt."

"One thing you don't have in this car is a shovel."

"True enough." He rubbed her shoulder. "You didn't have one in the Subaru, either."

"It's summer," she countered. "I always carry one in the winter. Not that that will do us any good right now."

Cara squinted through the smoke. She could still hear the chopper, but it hadn't come into view yet. "Good thing we got everything ready to load once he lands."

"If it's him."

"Don't you have some way of figuring that out?"

"You'd think so, but Dad has his own magic. He's always been an enigma. I've never been able to sense his energy." John shielded his eyes with a hand, peering upward. "There's the helicopter." He pointed behind them. "Must've circled around."

The silver bird with red markings came into view, dropping through a smoky layer toward the empty roadway dead ahead. "Guess that settles one thing. Whoever's in that chopper is coming for us." Cara ran around to the back of the Toyota and slid her pack onto her back."

She carted John's by its haul strap, hefting it his way. "Ooph. Here you go. We need to work on getting you lighter gear."

"It's Dad. I recognize the chopper, and lighter stuff has been on the list for a long time." He buckled his pack into place and reached through a side door to snap up his medical bag. "Do you have everything?"

Cara nodded. "I did a quick sort of the papers we took out of the Subaru while you were on the phone. The important ones are in my pack."

He sent a crooked grin her way and locked the car, pocketing the keys. "Maybe if I hang around you long enough, some of those organizational skills will rub off."

"I suspect there's nothing wrong with yours," she said, shielding her eyes against the prop wash as the bird's skids kissed the asphalt.

The helicopter's door popped open, and a tall, spare man with straight as a stick black hair that hung to his shoulders, dark eyes, and high cheekbones ran toward them bent low to avoid the spinning rotor. He wore faded chinos, well-worn work boots, and a white T-shirt with the Rolling Stones blazoned across its front. Straightening, he extended a hand toward Cara. "Mark Cassavettes. It's a pleasure."

Cara grasped his hand and squeezed hard. "Cara Carlisle. For me too. Thank you so much for risking yourself to come get us."

"Least I could do." He punched John's upper arm and pried the medical bag out of his hand. "Doofus finally came to his senses, and Ma would've had my hide if the two of you roasted to a crisp out here."

Cara snorted back laughter. "Doofus? What kind of pet name is that?"

"A very old one. That's the problem with meeting someone's family," John shot back. "We're ready, Dad. Before you blow any more secrets."

"I'll do my best to uphold your sterling image, son. Watch the rotors. You'll have a hard time getting in with those packs, so stop when you get to the door and hand them to me. I'll stow them, and then you can climb in." He took off at a lope for the chopper without waiting for them to answer.

"Go on." John let go of her.

Cara sprinted for the bird, careful of the blades. She'd traveled by helicopter in the mountains many times, so it felt familiar. The craft was an older model, but one known for its stamina at altitude. Unlatching her pack, she handed it to Mark. He moved to the back of the bird with it, and she climbed inside.

"Where do you want me?"

"How about left seat behind me? I've got the packs on the right, so your weight will counteract them." Mark hustled past her and grabbed John's pack, placing it next to hers behind the four seats. He looped webbing over them to hold them in place.

John popped inside. "Sure you don't want to sit up front?" he asked her.

"Nope. I'm good." She buckled into her seat.

John settled into the right seat and handed a set of headphones back to her. His Dad moved with an easy grace as he took the pilot's seat and slammed the door. He fiddled with the nav device, and dialed up a nearby flight service station, choosing their automated briefing option.

Cara looped her headphones around her head and listened. Before the briefing had cycled through, Mark fed power to the rotors and they headed skyward.

"Got to go around the mountains," he informed them. "It was dicey as hell getting here. I can't fly high enough in this to return the same way. The fire's dragging all the oxygen out of the air."

"How's our fuel?" John asked. Peering at the gauge, he snorted. "Never did get it fixed, huh?"

"Nope." Mark sent an annoyed looking glance across the space between the two front seats. "How about if you stick to what you know, and let me take care of this craft?"

"You got it, Dad. Cara thanked you for coming to get us, but I never did. So thanks. I don't think the car would have made it through."

"Accepted. It wouldn't have." Mark's voice was gruff, and Cara sensed the depth of feeling between the two men. The same sad place that stirred whenever she was faced with families where the people actually loved each other came to life, but it didn't hurt as much as it had in the past.

She angled her head and watched as they rose above the layer of smoke, gaining altitude. They'd have to cross Walker Pass, but it wasn't high enough to cause any problems since the fire hadn't reached it yet. Mark angled the craft southeast, following the roadway beneath them.

"Cara, right?" Mark's deep voice rumbled through her headsets.

"Yup, that's me," she agreed.

"What do you think of my son, so far?"

"Dad!" John's voice crackled loudly, right against her ears.

"Well, you're not getting any younger," Mark went on. "We figured you'd meet someone in medical school, or residency, but it never happened."

"It's all right," Cara broke in. "Your family cares about you. That's not a bad thing." She stopped shy of adding he was lucky he had a family to do that. "To answer your question, Mr. Cassavettes—"

"Mark," he cut in. "Call me Mark. Mr. Cassavettes sounds like my father, and he's been gone from this earth for a long time."

"Will do, Mark. To answer your question, I like your son a lot. We went through hell and then some getting out of the Sierras. He's a good climber and solid in the backcountry."

"That's important to you," Mark said.

It hadn't been a question, but Cara answered it anyway. "Yes. I guide for a living, and I value competence in the mountains."

"What else do you value?"

It was a deep question. One she had to think about. "Honesty, for one. You'd be surprised how many people sign up for my trips and lie about their climbing resumes. On bigger, international trips, I've taken to holding test weekends where I get everyone together. It lets me weed out the bad ones before we're halfway around the world, and everyone is depending on them for something they don't know how to do."

"Doesn't surprise me," Mark countered. "I've taught flying for years. Folk lie all the time. What else?" he prodded.

Cara had been staring out the window while they chatted, grateful they'd almost crested the pass. At first, a red haze across the mountaintops had looked like fire. As she scanned the skyline, the same red blobs that had formed the previous night, separated from the rest of the haze. Her heart leapt into triple time, and her sore throat grated against itself.

"John! Look out the left windows."

He craned his neck to look around his father. "Goddammit." He pounded a fist down on the instrument panel.

"Fascinating." Mark was looking that way too. "What are they?"

John barked a few words in Sioux.

"Even more intriguing. Maybe we can outrun them," his father suggested.

"Not going to happen. Put the bird down. Before they damage it, and we're all stuck back here."

"Ma warned me about something like this," Mark muttered and fiddled with the controls. The chopper lost altitude fast.

"Yeah, well she warned me too. Once we're down, stay out of harm's way."

"Not my style," his father retorted. The helicopter settled on the asphalt with a solid *thump*.

"Not your choice. Assuming those bastards don't kill us, we'll need you to fly us out of here. Shut the engine off. We'll be here for a while. No point blowing through our fuel."

Cara opened her mouth to say she knew the rudiments of how to fly a helicopter, but shut it. No reason for Mark to put himself in danger.

Hundreds of kites swarmed out of nowhere, with the characteristic blue-white light she'd come to associate with the spirit guides right behind them. If she'd had even a single doubt about the fire dragons coming for them, they frittered away like so much smoke.

I'm never getting out of this alive.

Snap out of it, girl. Another voice in her head cracked like a whip.

Believing you'd make it was half the battle. Cara had learned that lesson a long time ago. She narrowed her focus to the next few minutes and jostled her fear out of its center stage position. They'd bested the fuckers before, which meant they could do it again.

ark grumbled, but moved to the back of the bird so they could get out without crawling over him. Cara joined John next to the chopper and sucked in a deep breath. At least the air here was cleaner than what they'd left. The rotors were still spinning, but they'd stop eventually.

"What happens next?" she asked.

"This will be harder than last night," he cautioned. "They didn't expect us to win, so there are more of them today. I saw at least ten before Dad put the bird down. This bunch isn't all red. Some are black, and some gray. I'm not trying to frighten you, but today's odds are steeper."

"Why?" She choked out. "Why target us?"

"Fire feeds their hubris, makes them playful and cocky. They showed themselves to us last night because they were certain they'd destroy us. I'm sure it was a huge sore point when that didn't happen. They can't afford us alerting the authorities or anyone else. They have a few years yet before Earth is trashed enough to meet their needs."

"Was that one of the things your grandmother said?"

He nodded, his face set in grim lines. "She said they'd make it as hard as possible for us to escape these mountains. Probably the only reason Dad got through is they didn't realize he was coming to help us."

Bird shit rained down as the flock of kites formed a protective perimeter. Confusion rocked her. "I don't get how this works. Last night, you said we sent them back to where they came from. Where is that, exactly? How easy is it for them to travel back and forth? Are these even the same dragons?"

John glanced up at the birds. "Damn it. I can't see anything through them. Legends say there are other worlds than this one. I always assumed it was where the birds and guides hung out. Even though I'd never seen them before our stint on Mount Rixford, I knew about them." He set his jaw in a hard line. "I have no idea if it's last night's dragons heading our way, but it doesn't really matter."

The blue-white of the guides surrounded them and a high-pitched buzzing filled her ears.

John muttered several sentences in Sioux.

"Can I talk with them?" Cara asked.

"Not the way you normally do. Hold on. They're giving me instructions."

Buzzing alternated with his halting words. Cara assumed he sometimes had to hunt for how to answer them since he'd said his Sioux was rusty.

She shifted from foot to foot, waiting. It was hard. Adrenaline flooded her system, and she wanted to *do* something, not just stand around. The air grew warmer quickly and filled with the rotten carcass stench she remembered all too well from last night. She wanted to bat the birds out of the way so she could see where the dragons were, but they were all that stood between her and dragons' fire, so she clasped her hands together.

John turned to her. "Are you willing to share blood with me? It will make you stronger and increase our odds of success."

Cara stared at him. "Huh? I'm scarcely a vampire."

"You don't need much. I'll cut the balls of our thumbs and hold our hands together."

She hesitated, not understanding how something that small could possibly have any impact.

"Cara!" John grasped her hand. "We don't have much time. The guides outlined two strategies. I have to know which one we'll use."

She held out the hand he wasn't holding. "Here."

John released her hand and nodded once, sharply. He turned for the helicopter, but the buzzing intensified until it hurt her ears. "Fine," he snapped and extended an arm in front of him. Light blasted across his palm and a cut formed.

Cara understood she was supposed to follow suit. Hoping it wouldn't hurt as much as it looked like it did, she held her hand next to John's. Light flashed. Blood welled, and he held their hands together to let the deep red fluids mingle.

"I suppose what the guides did is close to sterile," he muttered. "I was on my way to get a scalpel from my kit when they called me back. That should be enough. Hold your hand out again, and they'll heal the cut."

Protests that it was impossible died when her hand emerged unscathed from the light. Neither the cut nor the healing had felt like anything beyond a mild, tingling warmth. Cara did a quick inventory, but she didn't feel any different.

The birds began squawking and cawing and rose higher in the air, forming a black banner. She could see the fire dragons through it, and her stomach twisted in outrage. The creatures were almost upon them. She counted twelve and grappled with the specter of certain defeat. Three had almost been too much for them.

What the fuck would they do against so many?

Fire spewed from the nearest dragons, and bushes flamed into pyres. A sulfur smell joined the rotting flesh reek that emanated from them. She'd always associated reptiles with a clean, antiseptic scent.

Not reptiles. They only look like they are.

Bright, clear light surrounded her. Guides. She repeated what she'd done the previous night and opened herself to their presence, their energy. It was easier than it had been. She didn't feel like a puppet anymore, but more like mistress of her own destiny.

"We will direct you." The buzzy murmur formed words inside her mind.

"So much for running things myself," she muttered. Part of her felt annoyed, but a bigger part wanted all the help she could get. She'd truly ventured into *terra incognito,* and it would be worse than stupid to insist on doing things her way.

Next to her, John whooped crazily. Power crackled around him, crashing and flashing until all she could see was an afterimage of lightning strikes. Two dragons exploded, leaving the bloody contrails she remembered.

"Pay attention!" The voice in her head sounded furious. Her first instinct was to cringe, but anger rushed in on its heels.

"Don't use that tone with me." Cara spoke out loud. Whatever those things were, either they'd understand—or not. She wasn't some dumb kid anymore, and she'd speak up for herself, goddammit.

Tingling heat began in her feet and spread through her body. She extended her hands because she had no choice, and their backs speckled with bird shit.

"Let the power flow through you. Don't fight it. Once it reaches its zenith, fling it at a dragon. Pick the large, black one on the far right."

"How will I know when the zenith is?" she cried, feeling her body inflate with unfamiliar sensations. When she glanced down, she was surprised everything looked the same, not swollen to grotesque proportions.

The guide didn't answer.

Last night, they'd commandeered her energy. Today, she was partway on her own. She liked that aspect, but she wanted to be sure to get it right. Cara had never liked making mistakes.

She focused inward, letting the heat sensation grip her, and imagined absorbing lethal power from the earth. When she was so full, she was about to shatter into a million pieces, she stretched her arms skyward toward the huge, black dragon and let go. Booming blasted her and she staggered backward, but the dragon burst into fragments. Its scales may have been ebony, but it left the same red smears across the sky as the others.

"Yes!" she screeched, shaking a fist at what was left of it.

"More." The telepathic sending was implacable.

She took stock of how she felt. Not too bad, considering. Next, she scanned the sky. Seven dragons remained. John must've gotten rid of two more while she worked on hers.

Maybe they could do this after all.

Cara invited the prickly heat into her body a second time. It was more uncomfortable, and sweat ran down her face and sides as she grappled with it. Stinging and burning accompanied the power, intensifying by the minute. She bit back a scream, and then got hold of herself.

How much more can I stand?

If I let go now, will it be enough to destroy the damned thing?

Cara was panting in harsh, little gasps when she sighted another dragon and let the power burn a fiery track through her guts on its way out her fingertips. For long moments, nothing happened.

"Believe in yourself."

The fucking voice again.

Nothing to lose, so Cara willed the dragon to explode and was thunderstruck when it did, alongside two others. The sky above her ran blood red, yet nothing dripped from the brilliant streams crisscrossing above her. The birds cackled and squawked, flying in formations of twos, threes, and fours as they turned their barrier into an ever-shifting collage of feathers.

Four dragons to go.

Fire burned on all sides of them, thickening the air with soot and smoke. A low moan from beside her caught her attention.

John was on his knees, gasping for breath, his face ashen. Both hands were splayed flat on the rocky dirt as if he exhorted the earth to give him more.

She fell to the ground next to him and grabbed his upper arm, shaking him. "Talk to me."

"I'm all right," he gritted out. "The magic. It burns a hole right through you. Not used to it."

"No kidding." She tugged on his arm. "We have to get up."

"I know. I know. I'm down here because I fell down, not because I want to be. We're not done yet."

He struggled to his feet; she stood next to him. Cara blinked hard, staring through grit-filled eyes, grateful to still see only four dragons. At least they weren't replenishing themselves by some arcane mechanism.

Jesus! That's one more than we faced last night.

A gray dragon dive-bombed them, leaving a fiery trail scant inches away. The guides converged on it, putting out the fire. Now that she wasn't consumed by focusing and honing whatever mechanism her body used to obliterate the dragons, the birds' angry vocalizations filled her ears with caws, squawks, and the occasional squeal when one burst into flames and fell to the earth.

"Can we do this?" Cara clapped a hand over her mouth. "Never mind. We have to."

He gripped her hand. She felt a heave of power roll through both of them. It was enormous, enough to flatten her if she hadn't been hanging onto John. Her vision blurred, and her hearing faded before the magic left them, auguring skyward.

One more dragon detonated.

Both of them were panting hard.

Before they could regroup, the remaining dragons flew straight toward them, fire streaming from their mouths. Two reds and a black.

"Get down!" Mark screeched from behind them. "Now."

John dragged her to the earth seconds before the report of a high-powered rifle deafened her. Mark fired again and again.

"What's he doing?" she screamed at John, who lay in the dirt next to her. "Can bullets kill those things?"

"I have no idea," John shouted back over the rifle's roar. "Wouldn't think they'd even penetrate the scales."

Cara twisted so she could see Mark. He stood next the chopper, an assault rifle slung around his neck. Instead of firing more shells, his hands were raised in front of him, and he chanted in Sioux. Lightning flashed from his fingertips, and his eyes blazed with dark fire.

Once. Twice. A third time.

Each dragon took a direct hit from Mark's magic. They flew in tired circles and didn't look nearly as substantial as they had before Mark shot them with bullets and magic.

The sky split in a black-tinged line; rain poured from it. A drenching deluge from a cloud-free sky. Cara stared, not understanding where the water was coming from. She blinked hard. And then did it again, not believing any of this. Not only was a sky that was clear of clouds producing torrential rain, the dragons were gone.

For now.

So were the birds and the guides.

John dragged her into an embrace and slashed his mouth over hers while they lay in muddy puddles. Cara kissed him back, not quite believing they'd gotten a reprieve. She wrapped her arms around the man beside her, reassured by the heat of him and the muscles beneath her fingertips. He kissed her harder, alternating kisses with words she couldn't understand.

"Cara. Darling," he tore his mouth from hers. "I want to find a tower somewhere and lock you into it. A dragon-free tower where nothing can hurt you. Not now. Not ever."

"Thanks." She licked his lower lip. "I'm scarcely Rapunzel. We'll do this together. Just like we did today."

"I'll figure out the magic. So I can do better protecting us."

"Slow down, tiger." She smiled. "First, we've got to get clear of these mountains. One project at a time."

Instead of answering, John kissed her again.

"I'm delighted you two care about each other, but we need to get moving." Mark's dry, understated words spurred her into action.

Cara let go of John and scrambled to her feet. Water sluiced down her body and plastered her hair against her skull.

John stumbled upright. "How'd you do that?" he asked his father.

Mark shrugged. "Made my own bullets with silver and iron. The combination weakens most anything magical. The rain that finished them off was a piece of cake."

"John said you were a weather-worker." Cara felt heat rise to her face. To be talking with anyone about magical skills felt so far in left field, she may as well sign up for the *Twilight Zone*.

"Comes in handy." Mark pointed to the bird. "Let's go. We bought ourselves a window here. I don't want to waste it."

Cara piled into the chopper and buckled her seatbelt. Water dripped from her sodden clothes until she sat in a puddle. She stared out the Plexiglas window, still expecting something to reach out and snap them back to the stinky, sooty plateau where they'd done battle.

Nothing did. The bird rose into the air, cleared the pass, and reached Highway 14 before anyone said much of anything.

"I'm going to put her down and fuel up," Mark said. "Anyone want anything while we're on the ground?"

Cara swallowed disbelief. "How can you sound so...cavalier?

So normal? Do you march out and fight evil every day, so it's become commonplace?"

John twisted to meet her gaze. "No. But my dad is one of the bravest men I've ever known. Have him tell you about his life someday."

"Enough." Mark moved the cyclic and adjusted the fuel mix as they headed for a small, private airport. "I did what was needed. Both of you were at the end of your reserves."

Reserves.

Cara sucked in a breath, still smelling dragon stench. "That blood ritual thing," she started, but her voice trailed off. She had questions, but wasn't certain how to couch any of them.

"It's permanent," John said. "Wait till we're in the air again, and I'll tell you all the things I didn't have time for earlier."

The chopper settled to the earth, skids lightly touching down. Mark jumped out, presumably to locate a fuel truck.

"Did you want anything?" John asked.

Cara glanced outside at what appeared to be a small fixed-base operation, but they'd probably have vending machines. Then she looked at herself. Soaking wet, stinky, sooty.

John read her thoughts easily. "It'll be all right," he said. "We came from the fire. We have every right to look like shit."

He smiled easily at her, as if they hadn't just escaped disaster for the umpteenth time. "Coffee and a pastry or sandwich, maybe?"

"You're on, bud. Food's my weak spot, and you've got my number."

He waited until she crawled down the aluminum steps to follow her. Though she tried for nimble, Cara's body ached in places she didn't even know she had muscles. She was in prime condition, for chrissakes. Why did she feel so bad?

John took her arm, and together they walked into the deserted building. The vending machines she'd predicted lined one wall, along with a refrigerator that turned out to hold several six-packs of beer and a selection of premade sandwiches. Instructions about where to leave money were plastered on the outside of the fridge.

Cara selected two cans of Starbucks, a tuna sandwich, and a chocolate bar. "Do you think your dad will want something?" she asked.

"I do. Thanks for thinking about me," Mark's voice drifted from the doorway. "I'm not picky. Whatever you're having will be fine."

He swooped into the room and grabbed a beer out of the fridge, chugging it down before tossing the bottle into a recycling bin. "See you two out at the bird. Truck's almost done refueling us." Mark loped out of the room.

Cara stared after him. "Booze and flying?" She kept her voice low.

John shrugged. "FAA hasn't caught him yet. He doesn't drink much of anything, so it's not really a problem. You're not the pilot. Would you like a beer?"

"Uh-uh. I don't drink. Not after growing up with an addict."

Contrition crinkled his face into a sheepish look. "I'm sorry. I wasn't thinking."

"Nah. It's okay. It's not that I've never had anything to drink, but it didn't add much to my life, so I'm good without it." She narrowed her eyes, wondering if John drank. If he did, would it make a difference? Leif had been a terrible drunk. It hadn't impacted his performance in the mountains because he was young enough for his body to absorb the punishment of daily infusions of booze...

"Cara. You're a million miles away. Did I hurt your feelings?"

She shook her head. "No. I got stuck in yesterday. What about you? Do you drink?"

"Very little. The thing about med school and residency is the hours are long, and you never know when you'll need to be running on all cylinders at a hundred ten percent alert. My recreational time, when I got any, was devoted to hiding in the mountains where my cell phone didn't have reception. Booze doesn't go well with solo climbing either."

Relief made her knees weak. She hadn't realized how important his answer would be to her. Or that he was starting to look like a permanent part of her life.

John gathered their selections, placing them in a paper lunch sack that he plucked from a stack on the counter next to the fridge. "Ready?"

"Yeah. Thanks for being you."

He rolled his eyes. "Really? You tangled yourself with a man with no job. I'm not the two kids and a house in the suburbs type."

Cara laughed and looped a hand beneath his elbow. "Know something?" She grinned broadly. "Neither am I."

CHAPTER 13

John wanted to say a whole lot more, but waited until they were heading skyward again. He unwrapped his father's tuna sandwich, so he could eat it more easily and began on the ham and cheese he'd selected. The bread was dried out, but he was hungry and the food disappeared fast.

"Not exactly haute cuisine—" Cara crumpled plastic wrap into a ball and dropped it into their lunch sack "—but it was wonderful." She popped the tab on a can of coffee and drank deep.

"Here." Mark handed headphones back to her. "You forgot to put these back on. Easier to talk that way."

"Thanks." She settled them around her head, noticing she'd been the only one without them.

"Magic burns through a whole lot of calories," Mark said. "It takes time to replenish, and that's why you were so hungry."

"Oh, I'm almost always hungry," Cara replied with a grin, "but it's good to have an alternative justification."

"Let me explain things," John cut in. "It'll make more sense if she gets at least some of this in order."

"I was telling it in my own order," his father protested.

"Maybe for a Native American," John said, "but we're not particularly linear, and she's not one of us."

"Not yet," his father countered. "I have a feeling she's well on her way. Especially after she got a dose of your blood."

"Let's start there," Cara spoke up. "What exactly was that? Why'd we do it? Will it have long-term effects? If so, what will they be?"

"Hold up." John said. "If you ask too many more questions, I'll never be able to remember them all. He undid his seat harness and moved to the rear seat across from hers. "This will make it easier to talk because I can look at you without a permanent kink in my neck." He buckled back in.

Cara gazed at him, an expectant look on her face, but apprehension rode beneath her expression too.

He resisted an overpowering impulse to gather her close, stroke her hair, and shield her from every bad thing in the world. Even though he wanted to do all those things, they'd do her a grave disservice. She needed knowledge, not protection. "Remember when I told you all people have some level of magic?"

"Yeah. Not sure I believed you, though." Cara drew her dark brows together and steepled clasped fingers beneath her chin.

"We tend to drum it out of children when they're very young, so it fades out of memory and possibility by the time they grow up. Because of your affinity for the mountains, I was banking on your strong suit being earth, just like mine. The guides confirmed that, so it made sense to strengthen your potential ability with an infusion from me."

"You're a doctor. How does that work?"

He reached for her hand, and she wove her fingers with his. "This isn't Western medicine, so I can't explain exactly how it works other than as a subtle alteration in how you manipulate the world around you."

She frowned. "Subtle, huh? Not quite the word I would've

picked. So your blood was why I could hear the guides clearly this time?"

He nodded. "And why you could channel earth magics to destroy the dragons—or at least move them away from our world. Last night, the guides commandeered your energy. Today, while they focused it, you did far more on your own."

"Is that what I was doing? Channeling earth power?" A corner of her mouth twisted even farther downward. "First time was easy. Next time, it felt as if I was wrestling with greased lightning, and it wasn't interested in cooperating."

"That would be because the first dragon ran your energy supplies low." Mark spoke up. "Over time you'll learn to modulate how much you pay out."

"Magical energy is a whole lot like physical energy," John added. "You have to titrate it, or you feel like you ran up against a brick wall."

"Makes sense. I was wondering why I felt so crappy." Cara squeezed his hand. "Not so different from climbing."

"We haven't had a decent night's sleep for a week, piled on top of everything else," John reminded her. "You have every right to feel less than a hundred percent."

"Magic is one part belief, two parts ability, and ten parts practice," Mark said. "It's the practice part where my son falls short. He's got ability to burn. Always did."

The radio crackled, and Mark keyed his transmitter to talk with someone about his amended flight plan.

John listened, amazed as always by how smoothly his father spun fabrications. To hear him tell it, he'd run into smoke, become confused, and ended up in trouble. By the time the conversation was over, the other man was bending over backward to make certain Mark had whatever he needed for a safe journey back to Bakersfield.

Mark glanced over a shoulder, grinning. "There. That's handled."

John rolled his eyes. "You're shameless. You stretched the truth until it could've been a tabloid headline."

"For the best of reasons," Mark countered. "If I'd told him what we'd really been up to, I'd be on my way to one of the few remaining state mental hospitals."

"End justifies the means, huh?"

"Sometimes, yes." He waved a dismissive hand. "Go back to the magic tutorial."

Cara wiped a smile from her face. "I really like both of you. It's even fun listening to you spar with one another. How can I leverage what I did today, learn from it so I can do better, and make my ability last longer?"

"Same thing I want to know." John traced a finger down her grime-caked cheek. "First on the agenda is getting cleaned up, though. I still smell dragons—on everything. Once we're clean, if we're really lucky, maybe we can find a real bed and—"

"Don't distract me. If I practice extra hard, what can I expect?" she persisted.

"Dad?" John tapped his father's shoulder. "I don't know how to answer her."

"If you truly believe in the world beyond your five senses, you should be able to develop your skills," Mark replied, his words slow and thoughtful.

"What does that mean exactly?" Cara straightened, rotating her shoulders. "Will I ever be as strong as either of you?"

"Probably not," Mark replied. "But you're an unknown quantity right now. Do you have any idea about your bloodlines?"

Cara shook her head. "No idea who my father was. Mom, she had a bad drug problem. She never said much about where she came from, but I always thought she was kind of a Heinz 57."

"Grandparents?" John probed, intrigued by his father's line of thought.

"Nope. No aunts, uncles, or cousins, either. None that I knew about, anyway. The family had pretty much written Mom off.

Like as not, she scammed or stole from them enough times, they gave her a wide berth."

"I'm sorry." Mark's words brimmed with compassion. "It's a hell of a way for a little girl to grow up."

Because John was looking right at Cara, he saw her eyes glisten with sudden tears. He wanted to pull her close and tell her all that was behind her, but something in her face—a stubborn, well-honed pride—stopped him.

"Nothing for you to apologize for." Cara aimed her words at his father. "Not all kids are dealt a hand with five aces. I managed."

"You more than managed." John angled his body across the slender aisle and kissed her cheek.

Cara focused her unusual multicolored eyes on him. "That's only because you see the end product. I wasn't nearly this well put together ten years ago."

"Ten years ago doesn't matter," John murmured. "Neither does tomorrow. What does is right here and right now. If we take care of that, everything else will work out."

"Your mother used to say that," Mark broke in.

"I remember." John pictured his mother's unruly mop of red hair and shrewd blue eyes. "She ran interference between me and Nana. And made the best wild blueberry pie, ever."

"I bet you and your dad both miss her," Cara said.

"More than you can imagine," Mark replied. "Audrey was one of a kind. Fate truly smiled on me the day I met her when I was stationed in the U.K."

"You'll have to tell me about it sometime." Cara's eyes shone warmly.

Emotion buffeted John. Cara was genuine, the real deal. She wasn't faking her interest in his family. "Mom would've liked you," he said.

"At least that's one out of two." Cara shook her head. "Never mind, I hate how bitter I sound whenever I talk about my own mom. I also hate to drag the conversation back to dragons, but when will they come back?"

"I have no idea," John said.

"I don't, either," Mark added. "But they will be back. My magic confirms it. And Ma's been planning for this for years. It was one of the reasons she was so put out when her only grandson shirked his duty to his family and his tribe."

"Ouch." John bit back a snort. "Silver-tongued devil with the authorities, but plainspoken as hell with me."

"I care about you," Mark countered. "You're my blood. In a backhanded way, getting us out of hot water with the FAA helps all of us. It keeps your medical license clear of splotches and my pilot certifications good to go if we need to fly somewhere."

"My guide certificates too," Cara added. "I have to recertify periodically, and they look for things like mental stability, so I have to authorize access to my medical records. But this is just another sidetrack. Back to dragons and blood."

"You're on. Dragons and blood it is," John said.

"I asked this before, and maybe there isn't an answer—or not one I'd understand—but how did your blood change something in me?"

"It reminded your spirit of its essential power," John replied. "Like Dad said, believing is a big part of this. So even if you've never tried to tap into anything paranormal before, the seeds of your ability have always been there. My blood opened channels so the guides could talk with you, and—"

"Did you know it would do that?" she demanded. Spots of color warmed her cheeks.

"No." John shook his head. "I had no idea what effect if would have. I'd never have thought of it on my own, to be honest, but the guides were insistent. Something about you called to them, made them certain you held building blocks of magic they could utilize."

Cara knit her brows together and studied her hands. "Fascinating."

"Ma will know more once we get you home," Mark said. "She can touch you or toss bones or read tea leaves—or whatever she's up to these days. One of her gifts is sensing power in others."

John glanced outside at a smoky sky. The spine of the mountains was passing beneath them. Had it been clear, he'd have been able to see California's Central Valley.

"How long before we land, Dad?"

Mark tapped a few keys on the dash-mounted nav system. "Forty minutes, give or take. We had to detour pretty far south."

John still had Cara's hand. He stroked it, overcome with tenderness and a fierce protectiveness. "Feel like closing your eyes until we get there?"

"I'm still pretty keyed up. How about if you tell me about the history of your people?"

"The Sioux Nation? That's a rather tall order. Once upon a time, there were seven branches. The word, *Sioux*, refers to seven council fires."

"I thought your tribe mainly lived in the Midwest and the Dakotas and Canada. How does it happen you ended up in California?" Cara asked.

"You're sharp for a white woman." Mark chuckled. "I'm impressed. My grandmother, also a tribal shaman, wasn't particularly thrilled about the job, so she and my grandfather tried to outrun their destiny—"

John sat up so abruptly, the seat harness cut into him "Hold it right there. How come no one ever told me about that before?"

"Ma didn't want to encourage you in the same craziness." Mark's simple words pinged true off John's magic.

"Did my mother know?" John demanded.

"Of course. We didn't have any secrets between us," his father replied. "Now go on with your history lesson."

"Any more family secrets sitting in a back room, waiting to stick their tongues out at me?" John struggled to get his mind around not being the first Cassavettes to believe being named shaman was an overrated honor.

"If any occur to me, you'll be the first to know."

"Yeah, like I was dead last to hear about this one." John didn't know whether to slug his father or hug him. Mark could've kept his mouth shut in perpetuity, but for some reason he'd decided now was a good time to come clean.

"Hey!" Cara closed her other hand over his, sandwiching it between hers. "What happened to my history lesson?"

John shut his eyes for a moment and visualized sitting at his grandmother's knee as she told him stories about his people. The old woman was a compelling storyteller, and the legends had stuck with him. "Our history comes in the form of stories and legends. It's much more typical of how Native people view the world."

Cara's eyes sparkled with enthusiasm. "I've always loved stories."

He locked gazes with Cara. "You're on. If any of this gets boring, just speak up."

"How could it be boring? I want to know everything about you. Plus, you're lucky to have a history that defines you, whether it's in legends or history books."

"You have a personal and family history too, even if you don't know what it is—yet. And you and I will create our own history."

She glanced down; color suffused her tanned cheeks. "That feels a bit premature."

"Not to me." Wanting to hold her was irresistible, but scarcely possible given the helicopter's spartan seating.

"Thanks for the vote of confidence, but a mutual future needs a whole lot more discussion before it's a done deal."

"You can have all the discussion you want." He disentangled his hand and stroked her cheek.

"We can save that part for later. I've always loved legends. Pick one of your favorites, and tell it to me." She held out her hand toward him, and he grasped it again.

"How about a story about how the crow ended up black? It seems relevant since the kites are black too."

"Sure."

John collected his memories and began to talk, recognizing the same intonations his grandmother had used.

"In days long past, when the earth and the people on it were still young, all crows were white as snow. In those ancient times, the people had neither horses, nor firearms, nor weapons of iron. Yet they depended upon the buffalo hunt to give them enough food to survive.

"Hunting buffalo on foot with stone-tipped weapons was hard, uncertain, and dangerous. The crows made things even more difficult for the hunters, because they were friends with the buffalo. Soaring high above the prairie, they could see everything that was going on. Whenever they spied hunters approaching a buffalo herd, they flew to their friends and, perching between their horns, warned them.

"'Caw, caw, caw, cousins, hunters are coming. They are creeping up through that gully over there. They are coming up behind that hill. Watch out! Caw, caw, caw!'

"Hearing this, the buffalo would stampede, and the people starved. They held a council to decide what to do.

"Now, among the crows was a huge one, twice as big as all the others. This crow was their leader. One wise old chief got up and made this suggestion. 'We must capture the big white crow,' he said, 'and teach him a lesson. It's either that or go hungry.'

"He brought out a large buffalo skin, with the head and horns still attached and put it on the back of a young brave, saying, 'Nephew, sneak among the buffalo. They will think you are one of them, and you can capture the big white crow.'"

Cara's hand had relaxed in his, and John glanced at her. Eyes closed, she leaned against the seat back with her lips curved in a soft smile.

"Go on." She opened her eyes and caught his gaze. "I loved it when Momma would tell me stories. She did sometimes when I was really small, and she wasn't too drunk. Back then, it was mostly alcohol. It was only as I grew older she branched out into harder stuff."

"Sure I'm not boring you? That it's not too much a little boy's story?"

"Yes, I'm sure."

John nodded and picked up the threads of a tale he knew word for word. Even though he hadn't thought about it in years, he wasn't surprised he'd never forgotten.

"Disguised as a buffalo, the young man crept among the herd as if he were grazing. The big, shaggy beasts paid him no attention. Then the hunters marched out from their camp, their bows at the ready. As they approached the herd, the crows came flying as usual, warning the buffalo, 'Caw, caw, caw, cousins, the hunters are coming to kill you. Watch out for their arrows. Caw, caw, caw!'

"All the buffalo stampeded off and away—all, that is, except the young hunter in disguise under his shaggy skin, who pretended to go on grazing as before.

"The big white crow came gliding down, perched on the hunter's shoulders, and flapping his wings, said, 'Caw, caw, caw, brother, are you deaf? The hunters are close by, just over the hill. Save yourself!'

"The young brave reached out from under the buffalo skin and grabbed the crow by the legs. With a rawhide string he tied the big bird's feet and fastened the other end to a stone. No matter how the crow struggled, he could not escape.

"Again the people sat in council. 'What shall we do with this big, bad crow, who has made us go hungry again and again?' they asked.

"'I'll burn him up!' answered one angry hunter, and before anybody could stop him, he yanked the crow from the hands of his captor and thrust it into the council fire, string, stone, and all.

"Of course, the string that held the stone burned through almost at once, and the big crow managed to fly out of the fire. But he was badly singed, and some of his feathers were charred. Though he was still big, he was no longer white.

"'Caw, caw, caw,' he cried, flying away as quickly as he could. 'I'll never do it again. I'll stop warning the buffalo, and so will the rest of the Crow nation. I promise! Caw, caw, caw.'

"Thus the crow escaped. But ever since, all crows have been black."

John blew out a breath. Hearing the story again brought back memories of being young and carefree. It was a restorative place to visit, even if he couldn't remain in childhood's halls for long.

"Thank you." Cara's voice was soft. "That was a beautiful story."

"I always liked that one too," Mark said. "John's not the only one Rose told it to. Redemption is possible, but it marks us in different ways."

"Never thought about it when I was little, but I'm sure that's true." John chuckled. "Thanks for asking to hear a legend, Cara. We all needed a break from being immersed in second-guessing where the dragons might strike next."

"We're close to the airfield," Mark said. "How about if you give Ma a call and tell her we'll be there soon."

"Do you still not have a cell phone?" John asked him.

"Nah. Too new-fangled. Plus the electronics aren't a good mix with magic—at least for my generation."

John pulled his cell out of an inner pocket, grateful the battery still had a charge. He tapped the keys that would raise his grandmother and listened while the phone rang and rang. Answering machines weren't something Rose Cassavettes believed in. Neither were cell phones, and now he knew why. No one had ever mentioned that they interfered with using magic before.

Why would they have? I left home determined never to summon so much as enough power to light a candle.

The phone kept ringing. John finally disconnected. "That's odd. She's not there. Did she have something planned for today?"

"Not that I know about," Mark replied, and twisted to spear John with a worried expression. "Sure you called the right number?"

"Yeah, Dad. I wouldn't have gotten it wrong. Besides her name came up on my display."

"We'll be on the ground in five minutes. Be ready to grab your stuff and make a run for my SUV. Something about this doesn't feel right to me. I've had this naggy, wrongness jabbing me for the last half hour. It was one of the reasons I asked you to call her."

John pushed his magical senses outward, hunting for whatever his father felt, but he came up dry.

"What is it?" Cara moved her hand to his upper arm.

"I wish I knew. Things seem normal to me, but I've had so little practice looking at the world through a magical lens, likely I wouldn't notice anything wrong—even if something was there."

The bird touched down, the transition not as elegant or gentle as when they'd refueled. That as much as anything spoke to how worried his father was. Mark was a talented pilot, one who could fly any craft in his sleep.

He shut down the engine and set the controls for non-operation. "Ready?" Mark asked, his voice tight.

"We're right behind you," John said and waited while Cara followed his father down the ladder. He handed her pack down to her and his medical bag. His pack came last, with him right behind it.

By then, his father had pulled alongside the helicopter in his dark blue Ford SUV. John didn't see how he could've gotten there so fast, but he didn't ask questions. Cara had already tossed his pack and medical bag into the back of the car. He hefted hers in after everything else.

"Where should I sit?" she asked.

"Front seat between us," Mark said. "Hurry. Longer I'm on the ground, the worse things feel."

John got in behind Cara and slammed the door. His father took off with a squeal of tires. He hadn't tied the bird down, which spoke volumes since a strong wind could damage the craft.

"I'll get it later," Mark muttered, likely having helped himself to John's thoughts. His father's mind-reading magic had bothered the crap out of him growing up, but today he didn't give it a second thought.

"If you don't get back here to secure the chopper, I'll do it," John said.

"Thanks, son."

John deployed his magic one more time. Darkness enveloped him until he felt like he was suffocating. "Jesus," he muttered once he'd broken free. "What was that?"

"Damn! It's really not good if you feel it too," Mark said.

"Yeah, but do you have any idea what it is?" John asked again.

"I know both of you are worried, but can you explain what you're sensing?" Cara asked.

"Not long now, and we'll find out." Mark pulled into his mother's driveway and sprang from the car, running hard for the front door.

John followed with Cara close on his heels.

Cara raced into the house, ready for damn near anything. It was a modest stucco home in a neighborhood of similar structures. The grass was mowed and the house clearly lovingly cared for. Native American artifacts graced the walls. Comfortable, well-used furniture was scattered about, along with books and music atop an intricately carved grand piano tucked beneath dormer windows.

"Son!" Mark's voice rang from the rear of the house.

Boots pounded across what sounded like a tile floor. "Shit! Stand back, Dad."

Cara ran for the sound of their voices. She crowded into a small sewing and craft room, from the looks of its contents. A tall, thin woman sprawled on the floor, her long black and silver hair tangled about her. A tan skirt, rich with beadwork, was twisted around her legs, and a white, linen shirt covered her torso and arms.

John knelt beside her, his fingers around her wrist and his head angled atop her chest.

Cara scooted to his side. "Please tell me she's still alive."

John raised haunted-looking blue eyes to hers. "Yes, thank God. Dad. Call 9-1-1."

The sound of his footsteps dashing for the living room, where she'd seen a phone, filled her ears. "What do you think happened?" she asked John.

"Maybe cardiac. Not looking like a stroke. Too soon to say for sure." He continued his assessment, moving his hands over his grandmother, poking, prodding, listening. "Could you bring my bag?"

Cara bolted to her feet and sprinted for the car. Moments later, she dropped his medical bag next to him. John fished a stethoscope, a penlight, and a blood pressure cuff out of it and went back to working on his grandmother.

"If you need me, I can help," Cara said. "I'm an EMT."

"Thanks. I wasn't thinking. Check the capillary return in her feet and hands."

Cara scooted to where she could hold one of Rose's feet, gratified when it was warm. At least the woman's circulation wasn't shutting down. She checked Rose's pulse and pressed on toenails. "Not bad. Might be normal, except I have no idea what her baseline looked like."

"Hmmm. Try her hands."

Cara repeated her motions. "Same thing. Except her pulse is slightly stronger here."

Mark came back into the room. "Ambulance might be a while. All their emergency personnel are tied up with fire victims. What happened to Ma? Ach, scratch that. Will she make it?"

John rocked back on his heels. "I can't find anything much wrong with her, other than she's not conscious. I checked her head. No big contusions like would've happened if she fell and hit her head. Her pupils are equal, and they contract when I shine my light in her eyes. Her heartbeat's strong. Respiration's normal."

"Then why is she unconscious?" Mark demanded.

John turned his hands palms-up. "I have no idea, and it bothers the crap out of me. I even checked with my magic, and she should be conscious."

Mark narrowed his eyes. "Not liking the sound of that. Let me get close to her."

John moved aside, watching his father intently. "If you're thinking this is some kind of dark mojo, maybe you shouldn't have called for help. We won't want her in the hospital unless one of us is with her all the time to keep an eye out for whoever did this to her."

"Hang on." Mark knelt next to his mother. "I don't know anything yet. Not for sure." He began to chant, low and urgent, in Sioux.

Cara turned the implications over in her mind. "What the hell do you mean by *dark mojo*?" she demanded. "I don't understand."

"Ssht." John got to his feet and led her down the short hallway and into the front room. "If some kind of malevolent power got its claws into Nana, Dad will figure it out."

"You have to say more than that," Cara pressed. "I understand things like vessels exploding and blocked cardiac arteries. And broken bones. And sprains. And altitude sickness. But I don't understand this. There's no fire here, so presumably no dragons. No kites. No guides—"

John dropped his hands onto her shoulders. "More than one kind of dark power exists in the world. Nana always was outspoken, and there were those who took exception to her views." His face creased with worry—and contrition. "So long as she was shaman, the guides and birds stood between her and her enemies..."

Understanding rocked Cara. "She ceded—or whatever the word is—them to you."

"Yeah, which left her unprotected."

"What exactly happened to her? Did whoever's out to get her stick pins in an effigy or something?"

John sent a pained look her way. "Maybe. That method is quite effective, so long as you have some material from the victim. Skin or hair or fingernails…"

"Jesus! I'm getting this image of old women gathered around a cauldron, like in Macbeth."

He tightened his hold on her shoulders. "Sometimes it's men too. Like Dad right now and the incantations he's sending into the spirit world, asking them to drive the darkness out of Nana. This is a different reality, one I tried my damnedest to escape from." He narrowed his eyes. "I'm stuck here, but you could still leave. You're not in so deep, you couldn't back out. Dad could alter your memories. Hell, maybe I could, but you know so much now that he's a surer bet."

Her stomach twisted sourly. Had John just decided she was too high maintenance, required too much by way of explanations? "That would mean leaving you." She tilted her chin at a defiant angle. "Not happening—unless you changed your mind about getting to know me better." Cara waited, barely breathing. Normally, she wouldn't have been quite so blunt, but she needed to know which way the wind was blowing before she gave John any more of her heart.

Walking away now would hurt like hell. Later it might not be possible.

Maybe it's better this way. Safer to be alone where there's only me to worry about.

Now if I could just get myself to believe that.

He moved his hands to the sides of her face. "No. I haven't changed my mind. You're all I think about. But I can see where being dropped into a bad episode of *Supernatural* would rattle anyone. You're worried about Nana. So am I. Playing by Western rules, she'd be on her way to Bakersfield Memorial, but we have to make certain why she's unconscious. If it's some kind of spell—and I'm guessing that's it because of how long Dad's been working on her—leaving her alone in a hospital room is a bad idea. She'd be vulnerable to a worse attack. One that might truly kill her."

"These enemies, can anyone else see them?"

"Not usually, so you can see where the hospital would be a problem. It's not as if they could ask the Sheriff to post a guard, if we told them she was in danger. Well, they could, but it wouldn't help."

"Shit." Cara rubbed a hand down her face. "None of this is easy, is it?"

"No, it's not. Back to you and me." He stroked her cheekbones with his thumbs. "We weren't done with that part of the conversation. I haven't changed my mind, sweetheart. The more time we spend together, the more I care about you."

"So you're not trying to get rid of me with all that bad episode of *Supernatural* talk?" Cara hurried on before he could answer. "All you have to do is say the word. I can rent a car and drive home from here. Work things out with the insurance company about the Subaru if I can't get it back—"

He put a hand over her mouth. "Stop. Is that what you want to do?"

"No."

Relief streamed from him in long, bright waves, just before he drew her tight against him. How could she see emotion as something physical? "Must be the magic," she muttered against his shoulder and hugged him back.

"What's that about magic?" He drew back, and his mouth twisted into a lopsided smile.

"You're kind of shimmery and glowing."

"Yeah, that's *your* magic, not mine. It's developing. So—" he tilted her chin upward "—you'd better be damn sure about linking your star to mine. There'll come a time when no one can stuff your power back into a box, and you'll be stuck with it, even without me."

"I'll take my chances." Emotion spilled through her. Even with how prickly she was, he still wanted her.

"Thanks, Cara. You'll never be sorry you gambled on me. I'll make certain of it."

"Fingers crossed, you feel the same way about me after we get some time under our belts."

She raised on tiptoe and kissed him once, quick and hard. "I'm feeling selfish even thinking about you and me. How do you suppose your grandmother is doing?"

He inhaled raggedly. "Dad would've yelled if he needed me. He's still chanting, but it's not the same refrain, so my guess is she's improving. I'm calling 9-1-1 back." He let go of her and moved toward a black, wall-mounted landline.

Cara chewed on her lower lip. "Are you sure that's a good idea? Your grandmother's unconscious. Maybe she had a series of TIAs. Maybe there's something else you can't assess properly outside a hospital environment." She ran out of words.

Even after his dark mojo tutorial, she still couldn't break out of the traditional way she viewed bodies and how they worked —or broke down. It was his grandmother, for god sakes. His flesh and blood. Surely he'd see the value in making certain nothing horrible had happened. After all, Rose wasn't a young woman—

"This is Dr. Cassavettes." His voice cut into her thoughts. "I'm here with Rose Cassavettes. She's my grandmother. At the moment, her vitals are stable, and there's no need for emergency transport. If she requires further assessment, I'll drive her to the hospital myself."

"Thank you, Doctor," blasted out of the phone's speaker. "We're hard-pressed here moving personnel to and from the fire lines. Could grant you emergency privileges if you had the time to help out—so long as your license is current. We've called in all our EMTs and paramedics, and we're still short."

"Let me take care of my grandmother, first."

"Sure thing. Call back if you need us."

John turned to Cara. "It's been pretty quiet from Nana's craft room. Let's see how Dad's doing. He'd have called me if he needed me, but still…"

Cara bit back protests that they really needed to package up his grandmother and drive her to the nearest hospital. A large, sprawling agricultural community, Bakersfield had several to choose from, including the one John had mentioned earlier.

John beckoned to her and headed down the hallway.

Cara followed him back into the craft room. Mark sat on the floor with his mother's head cradled on his lap. He'd stopped chanting, but the frantic expression had left his face. He nodded at them and gave a thumbs-up sign.

Rose's color was better. The ashen quality beneath her copper skin had receded. John knelt next to them and checked his grandmother's pulse. Still holding onto her wrist, he locked gazes with his father. "What'd you find?"

"Dark spirits were working their way through her defenses, but you know your Nana. She wasn't going down without a hell of a fight. Whoever was behind this covered their tracks well. Didn't want to waste time following a thread backward to reconstruct who did this, so I called on her totem spirits, and they cleansed the taint. She'll be back with us soon enough."

"Totem spirit? What's that?" Cara asked.

"In Rose's case, it's an elk," John replied.

"And you know this how?" Cara drew her brows together, trying to understand.

"Because we sense the animal spirit within her," Mark answered.

"Of course. Why didn't I think of that?" Cara exhaled sharply, kicking herself for her sarcastic rejoinder. "Geez. The world's shifted off its axis, and all the rules changed. I need to learn everything I can as fast as I can. What are the two of you?"

"Are you asking what our totem animals are?" John said.

Cara nodded.

"Dad's is a bear. Mine is a wolf."

"Yes, but who determines that?" she pressed.

"Our animals come to us in dreams when we pass into manhood," John explained. "Or womanhood."

"Is any of this written down anywhere?" Cara looked from one to the other of them.

Mark glanced at her. "Our stories are written, but not in any White Man's language. The most important parts are in pictographs, not letters."

"Before the missionaries came and introduced Latin letters," John broke in, "Native societies wrote things down with images rather than words just like all primitive people."

"What happened to your totem animal when you walked away from your culture?" Cara skewered John with a sharp-eyed gaze.

A corner of his mouth twisted downward. "He kicked up a hell of a fuss at first, but finally stopped bothering me. I haven't heard boo out of him in years."

"Do you think he'll come back?" The concept was fascinating and alien and mesmerizing all at the same time.

"Depends what John does next," Mark replied. "He may need that animal energy before everything is over."

"If there's not a book I can read, will the two of you teach me?" Cara looked down, hoping she hadn't asked for something impossible, something that wasn't allowed. Maybe only the guides could impart secrets.

"Of course we'll help," Mark said. "Might be a good opportunity for John here to take a crash course himself. He always was too smart for his own good, but I bet he's forgotten a lot."

"No kidding," John mumbled.

Rose thrashed from side to side, moaning, and her dark eyes flashed open.

"Ma. It's okay. Don't struggle." Mark lapsed into Sioux after that. His mother answered in the same tongue, but she stopped fighting his hold on her.

"Good to see you've rejoined the living. Can you sit up?" John wrapped an arm around her shoulders, supporting her.

"Yes. Yes. I'm fine." With surprising agility, Rose got her feet under her before her gaze lit on Cara. She stalked toward her, hands extended, muttering in Sioux.

It was unnerving to have the older woman close on her. Between her gaunt build, her strongly boned face, and her long, tangled hair, she looked more apparition than human. Cara held her ground. "What's she saying?" she asked John.

"That I've seen you before." Rose switched to English. "You were in my vision, leading my grandson through fire."

Cara swallowed disbelief, but it didn't go down as hard as it had when she'd run up against sorcery on Mount Rixford.

I'd better get used to the paranormal. It'll be part of my world from now on.

"Yes." Cara held herself tall. "That was me."

"Of course it was," Rose sputtered. "My sendings are never wrong. Sit with me where there's space, which isn't in here." She swept through the door, imperious and regal. "One of you will get me a glass of water and something to eat." Rose hadn't turned around, but her voice was deep and clear.

Whatever had happened to her hadn't impaired her mental processes.

John shot a meaningful look at his father. "I'll make her up a plate," Mark said. "Hope to hell she has food in the house for once. She gets so wrapped up in her magic, she forgets to eat."

"Not the end of the world if one of us has to run to the corner market," John replied and placed a hand under Cara's elbow. "Come on. Nana doesn't like to be kept waiting."

Cara smothered a smile. Even though she'd only spent a handful of minutes with Rose in a conscious state, she'd come to the same conclusion. She walked ahead of John down the hall to the living room. Rose sat in a rocker that was covered with a colorful knitted quilt. Cara picked a chair cattycorner from her and started to sit.

"Come here, first," Rose said.

"Where?" Cara asked, not seeing any closer chairs.

"Kneel next to me. I want to touch you." When Cara hesitated, Rose added. "I'd never hurt you. You're special to my grandson. Physical contact is how I draw information. Your life path is joined with John's, and I want to know why."

"You can tell that by touching me?" The words, underscored by skepticism, made their way past her throat despite her efforts to stifle them.

"It's what I just said, isn't it?" Irritation accentuated Rose's question.

John moved to his grandmother's side. "Be nice, Nana."

"Nice is overrated," she growled as Mark placed a glass of water on the table next to her. She drained it and held it out to him for more.

"It's fine." Cara dropped to her knees next to where Rose sat. "I want to know what she finds out too, since I'm such a neophyte to all this."

"Move back." Rose made shooing motions at John. "Your energy is so overwhelming, it interrupts my concentration."

"When you're done mapping Cara, I want to know what happened to you," John said.

Rose turned her shrewd, deep-set eyes his way. "You mean why I was stupid enough not to watch my backside?"

"If you know who did this to you, tell us." Mark's voice boomed from the kitchen. "I'll make the son of a bitch sorry he was ever born."

"Retribution bites back," she retorted and bent forward, hands hovering over Cara's head.

Warmth enveloped Cara, and she closed her eyes, embracing the sensation.

"Good," Rose murmured. "Don't fight me, and this will go

faster." She arranged her hands so that one was atop Cara's head and the other on her right shoulder.

Something akin to an electric shock—except it wasn't unpleasant—tracked through her body. Imagery marched through her mind. Her mother, a young, carefree version of her mother, and bunches of people she'd never met. Next a collage of mountains, one after the other, bombarded her as if Rose was shuffling through a deck of her memories.

As quickly as they'd surfaced, the images receded leaving her mind a black, velvety pool.

"See this place?" Rose spoke into her mind much as the guides had.

Cara nodded.

"Feel it. Remember it. You need to be able to find it on your own."

"What is it?" Cara asked.

Rose moved her hands away and directed a string of Sioux to John. He knelt next to her. "It's the center of your essence, your psyche. The home of dreaming and power."

Cara absorbed the information and looked up at Rose. "How can I find it on my own?"

"If you clear the clutter of your thoughts, it will find you."

Cara arranged her face into what she hoped was a receptive expression, rather than a grimace. "I was hoping for more of an instruction manual."

"That, young woman, is because you're still thinking with your White Man's mindset."

"It's the only one I have." Cara batted back defensiveness.

John settled on his haunches next to Cara and took her hand. "What'd you find, Nana? When you mapped Cara."

Her stomach tightened. She wanted to know, but she was afraid of what the old woman with the clairvoyant eyes would say. She gripped John's hand harder, and he squeezed back. "It'll be all right," he murmured.

"And why wouldn't it be?" Rose asked dryly.

"She's not like us," John cautioned. "Not attuned to information from the spirit world."

Rose snorted something that sounded like laughter. "I was accessing her memories—and reading her blood. The spirits had nothing to do with it. Beyond that, until rather recently, you weren't exactly part of *us*, either, as I recall."

He inclined his head. "Fine. I deserved that. Now can we move past it?"

"Maybe." She took another glass of water from Mark. He held a plate with a sandwich balanced on it. "Put that down." She pointed at a table. "I'll get to it."

"Ma. You don't eat enough," he protested.

"I said I'd get to it. Either go back to the kitchen or sit down."

Mark rolled his eyes and clumped to a recliner in the corner. He looked at it, and then sank to the floor in front of it in a cross-legged sit.

Cara sat stock still, waiting. Could unlocking memories of her family, of who she was, be as simple as Rose laying hands on her?

"You look like a canary waiting for a snake to strike," Rose observed. "Take a few deep breaths. I'm not going to tell you your mother was an axe murderer. You must not know much about your family, or you wouldn't be so nervous."

"That's true. I don't know anything—except about mother. And not all that much about her."

"Both sides of your blood are from the Old Country. Same part of Ireland, Johnny's mother came from. It's likely why the two of you get on well."

"What part was that?" Cara asked.

"Northern tip," John answered, "County Donegal. Is that why she holds the ability to work with earth power?" he asked his grandmother.

"Like as not."

"Do you know where my father is? Or if my mother is still

alive?" Cara's eyelids prickled, and she blinked back unexpected tears. She had to do a better job riding herd on her emotions.

"No, child. To both questions." Rose leaned close enough to lay a hand across Cara's cheek. "The mapping doesn't work that way. You must've spent time with your father when you were very young. The memories are there; I merely drew them to the surface. I didn't find out anything you couldn't have on your own."

"But I had no idea my family came from Ireland."

"I gleaned that from your blood." Rose hesitated. "Knowing is complex. The things we hold here—" she tapped her forehead "—are but a fraction of everything in our minds and our collective memories. You hold tribal memories as well as individual ones."

Cara nodded slowly. "That place you tapped into—mapping you called it—I asked you before, but how can I find it on my own?"

"I can teach you," John said. "It's a lot like meditation."

He directed his next words at his grandmother. "What did you discover about her magical ability?"

"She has the seeds of mild power that she can cultivate. She'll never come close to your level of proficiency because her gifts are so much less."

"Whew!" Breath whooshed from Cara. "I'm relieved. With everything that's happened, I wasn't sure I wanted the responsibility of saving the world heaped on my shoulders."

Rose skewered her with her discerning gaze until Cara couldn't look away. "That particular task belongs to my grandson. Your job is to help him."

"And yours is to eat the fucking food I made you." Mark flowed to his feet and dropped the plate into his mother's lap. He stood over her, glowering.

Cara waited for Rose to rebuke him. Instead, she broke into gales of laughter, picked up half the sandwich and began to eat.

Once it had disappeared, followed by the second glass of

water, Mark snatched up the glass. "I'm off to get more, but when I get back, I want to know who was stupid enough to raise dark power against you."

"How about if you brew us up some tea?" Rose suggested. "And there's a tin of butter biscuits in the cupboard."

Mark had started for the kitchen, when Rose said. "It was the Cree's shaman, Two Horses. Bastard's been after my guides for years. Guess he sensed they weren't linked to me anymore, and he thought he'd swoop down and convince them to join him."

Mark punched the wall so hard plaster rained down, muttered, "He's history," and stomped into the kitchen.

Cara expected Rose to tell her son to cool off, but she did no such thing. An almost feral smile spread across her face. "Nothing less than he deserves," she said. "He's been a thorn in my side for a very long time. If I hadn't been so focused on scrying where all of you were, I'd have sensed his trap and not fallen into it."

Questions jostled Cara, but one rose to the surface. "Are the guides so fickle, they'd switch allegiance?"

"Sometimes." Rose spoke slowly. "Depends what he had to offer them. They weren't all that sure they wanted Johnny here. I had to do a lot of tall talking to get them to seek him out and test him."

"You might've let me know," he muttered.

"Not the way it works," she said primly and picked up the second half of her sandwich.

Mark carried a kettle and a trivet into the living room and set them on a table before returning the way he'd come.

Cara got to her feet and trotted into the kitchen. "Can I help?"

"Sure." Mark grinned at her. "Cups are in that cupboard. Sugar's in the blue canister over there, and cream's in the fridge."

"How about those cookies?"

"Oh, the butter biscuits? They're not sweet, but Ma's always loved them. I'll bring them along." He bent close, his voice low.

"Don't take anything she says amiss. She's forthright like that because power runs so strong in her."

"Don't worry," Cara whispered back. "I like her. I've always appreciated a no-bullshit approach."

"She likes you too."

"How can you tell?" Pleasure warmed her. If she was going to be part of John's family, she wanted them to respect and care about her. Not like her family had been. Cold and distant and harsh.

"Because you're still here and not on your way to wherever you live."

"There is that, huh?" Cara tried not to laugh, but it was impossible.

Mark joined her, and they both hooted and cackled until tears rolled down her cheeks.

John trooped in from the front room. "What's so funny in here? Nana wants her butter biscuits."

Mark thrust the tin into his hands. "Here."

"Sorry." Cara wiped her eyes with the backs of her hands.

John hugged her with the biscuit tin between them. "Don't ever apologize for having fun."

"I'll try to remember that."

"Do I have to get my own teacup and biscuits?" Rose called.

"Oops." Mark snorted back another peal of laughter. "Johnny has the biscuits. On my way with those cups, Ma."

CHAPTER 15

John set his cup aside and wiped his fingers on a napkin. Afternoon was drawing to a close, and he was tired.

"Hey, Dad."

"Yeah?" Mark looked up from a book he'd been buried in for the last hour. Leather-bound and dog-eared, John assumed it was some sort of spell book.

"Mind if I borrow your car? Or maybe you could drive me to one of the rental lots."

"Take mine," Rose said. "Where are you going?"

He bit back a protest that he wasn't sixteen anymore and said, "Depends on Cara. I could drive her home, or we could figure something else out for tonight—after we've scared up something for dinner. Butter biscuits only go so far."

"You can leave for a short time, but you're not done yet," Rose said.

"Huh?" John looked blearily at her. "Don't worry, Nana, we'll clean up after tea before we go."

"Not what I meant. You and Cara are headed back into the mountains as soon as you get a few hours' rest."

For a minute he didn't understand, and his groggy brain pedaled in circles. "They told me they need medical personnel on the fire line, but how could you have known—?"

Rose stood and stalked over to him. "Do you think the dragons went away? Those fires are raging worse than ever. The dragons are in hog heaven. They thrive on big, uncontrolled fires. No one will be able to put them out until you convince those abominations to leave for good."

John got to his feet so he faced his grandmother, looking right into her unnerving eyes. When he'd been a child, he was certain her gaze followed him everywhere. Who knew? Maybe it had.

"Do you have some ideas how we can accomplish that? I'm not trying to shirk my duty, but last time dad bailed us out with his weather working."

"Don't forget my silver and iron ammo," Mark said with a grin.

"I didn't." John glanced at Cara. Dark circles rode beneath her eyes, and she looked as trashed as he felt. "Maybe after we've eaten and slept a little, Cara could stay here with you," he ventured.

"The hell I will." She sprang upright.

"Who said anything about me staying here?" Rose looked down her nose at him. "Mark and I will be there too, but we won't get there the same way you do." She rubbed her palms together. "I do love a good fight. It's been a long while since I've been in one."

John peered at his grandmother through slitted eyes. He recognized the stubborn set to her shoulders all too well. He didn't have the energy to argue with her, and he spread his hands in front of him in a gesture of no contest.

"You obviously have some kind of game plan mapped out, Nana. Feel like sharing it?"

"Watch your tone, young man."

John closed his jaws with a *clack,* so he wouldn't blurt out something he regretted. He didn't see Cara stand, but she made her way to his side and wove a supportive arm around his waist.

"If you have something in mind, I want to hear it too." Mark shut the book and glanced up expectantly.

Rose walked to a window and looked outside. Magic simmered around her, surrounding her in layers of color. She was obviously searching for something. Minutes ticked past before she turned and gathered her long hair into a bunch, draping it over her shoulders. After flexing her fingers in front of her, she clasped her hands together.

"It's not quite five-thirty," she said to John and Cara. "Keys are in my car. Get a quick meal and find yourselves a bed. You're welcome to the back room here, but I suspect you're interested in more privacy than it allows."

"Nana, please." The last thing John wanted was a lecture on sex from Rose.

She sent an annoyed look zinging his way. "Please, right back. Part of your task is to complete your linkage to Cara. It will allow her better access to your power, and you to hers." She took a breath and blew it out. "Return here at midnight. Sometime between now and then, see if Emergency Services, or whatever agency is dealing with the fire, would be willing to transport both of you to the front lines. I'm betting they're using helicopters, and it's faster than driving."

"It might work. They did say they needed docs and EMTs," Cara murmured.

"I'm sure they still do." Rose's deep, melodic voice held a dry note.

"What will we be doing, Ma?" Mark asked.

"We'll focus our astral selves."

"Not a good idea." Mark tapped the tome in his lap with an index finger. "We're not nearly as strong in that form."

"Better that way than not at all," she retorted. "I'm sure they have all the roads blocked off."

Her son shrugged. "We'll take my bird. The air's so thick with smoke and debris, likely no one will bother us. Whoever's monitoring ATC will just think we're one more emergency chopper delivering water or personnel."

Rose scrunched her forehead into a frown. "That might work."

"It's going to have to," Mark said. "I'm going to get myself some dinner from that drive-in two blocks over. You want anything, Ma?"

She made a face. "I don't see how you can eat that trash."

"I didn't ask for a commentary on my food consumption. You should eat too. Want me to make you another sandwich? Or is there something I missed in the freezer?"

She strode to where he sat and plucked the book out of his lap, examining the spine. "Good choice. I need to read up on some things in it too."

Mark got to his feet. "Last chance for junk food."

"Find me a salad and maybe something with chicken in it."

"On my way." He focused his next words at John and Cara. "I'll transfer your stuff into Ma's car before I leave." Mark went out the front door, whistling a discordant melody.

"That tune used to bring all the crows in the neighborhood," John remarked.

"They're likely not listening today," his grandmother said. "Get moving." She dropped the book on a table and clapped her hands together.

John scanned the rows and rows of books lining shelves on two sides of the room. "Anything here I should read?"

"Of course, but not tonight. If we survive this, you can embark on the course of study you should've mastered ten years ago."

John detached himself from Cara. "How about if you get Nana's car out of the garage? I'll meet you out front."

Rose grabbed a set of keys from a hook near the front door and tossed them Cara's way. She caught them handily and faded into the kitchen. He heard the door into the garage open and close.

John walked to his grandmother. "I understand you're angry

with me—and you have every right to be. I can't change what happened ten years ago. Hell, I can't change what happened yesterday. I made choices—they may have been bad ones—but you can't force anyone to do anything. That never works out well."

He stopped to take a breath. At least she wasn't arguing with him. "The important thing is I'm here now, and I'll do everything I can to address this problem. I hope to hell it's good enough. I'm counting on you and Dad to help until I get up to speed."

A stubborn expression crossed Rose's face, and she opened her mouth, but he held up a hand. "I know full well if I'd done my part, you wouldn't have to bail me out at all—or maybe not as much. Nothing I can do but play the ball from where I tossed it. I'm grateful for your help."

"And I'm grateful you came to your senses."

Love for the old woman filled him and he hugged her tight. When he let go, he said, "Do something for me."

"If I can."

"Keep an eye on Cara. Make sure nothing happens to her."

An unreadable expression flitted across his grandmother's face, but it made his stomach twist into a hard knot of fear. "Tell me." He gripped her shoulder. "What have you seen?"

Asked a direct question, seers had to answer with the truth.

"Tonight will be hard. I'm not sure any of us will still be alive at the end of it. In my vision, we walk into darkness, but I didn't see any of us come out the other side."

"Did you spin the timeline out far enough?"

Her mouth turned downward. "It doesn't work like that. I see what the spirits allot me, nothing more, nothing less. Let go. You're hurting me."

He uncurled his hand from her shoulder. "Do we at least rid Earth of the fire dragons?"

Rose shook her head. "I'm afraid I don't know that, either."

John balled his hands into fists. "If this is such a fool's errand, why are we even going?"

Straightening her spine, she said, "Because it's our task. And it's the right thing to do. I love you, grandson. Now get moving."

He started to say more, but she glided across the room and pulled the front door open.

"Thanks, Nana. I can take a hint. We'll be back at midnight. Or we'll at least check in by phone if we figure out transport into the mountains."

She closed the door behind him and he strode to the car, a late model silver Volkswagen, idling in front of the house.

Cara sat behind the wheel. "Did you get things squared away?" she asked once he was belted in.

"As much as I could. What do you feel like for dinner?"

She smiled crookedly. "For once, I'm not all that hungry. Maybe Chinese takeout?"

"You're on." John hesitated, searching for words that didn't appear presumptuous. They'd been through a lot. Maybe she'd rather curl up for a few hours by herself after they ate. He needed to let her know that whatever she wanted was all right with him.

"You're going to have to help me," she said as she guided the car through a residential neighborhood. "I have no idea where I'm going. While I was waiting for you, I pulled out my phone, but it's dead so I can't use the GPS. I dug through my pack and I have the charger with me, but it needs an AC plug."

"Turn right here. In half a mile, you'll come to one of the main drags. Go left. There are several Chinese places and some chain motels."

"Great." She fed more gas to the car and it sped up. "Are you good with getting food and taking it to our room?"

"Yes, but we can get two rooms if you'd like some time by yourself." John kept his gaze trained on her and saw her wince.

Cara braked hard and pulled the car to the curb. She turned so she faced him. "Stop being so fucking polite. And stop trying to second-guess what I want. If you want two rooms, speak up. If not, don't chuck the ball my way. Christ!" She let go of the wheel and tossed her hands skyward. "There's a whole lot that's new here. I need to believe you and I are working together—that maybe we have a future as a couple—not that you're unsure what you want to do with me."

He captured her hands with his. "You want plain speech? You've got it. I say we find a room, order dinner delivered, and take things from there."

Something in her face relaxed, and she ran her tongue over lips so split and chapped they had to hurt. "Then why offer to waste money on two rooms? Holy shit! A woman needs to feel wanted."

"I do want you, Cara." He paused a beat. "I also feel guilty as sin for dragging you into this mess, so I don't want to presume anything. I've already taken plenty of advantage of you."

"No, you haven't."

He fielded the full force of her eyes that were shading to gold in the afternoon's fading light. "How can you say that?"

Her voice softened. "Because everything I've done was offered freely. Where's the nearest motel that's not a dive?"

"Go left at the light. There's a Red Lion about half a block down on the right."

Cara ferried the car back into nonexistent traffic. "What exactly did your grandmother mean when she ordered you to *complete your linkage* with me? Was she telling us to have sex?"

"Yes and no."

"You have to say more because I don't understand." She pulled into the check-in area of the motel and put the car in park.

"I will right after I book a room for us. Would you like to come in with me?"

Cara glanced at herself. "Nah. One dirty, smelly guest is probably enough cluttering up their lobby. First thing both of us are going to do is clean up."

"Before we order dinner?"

She nodded. "I've spent weeks without a bath in the mountains, but I like to be clean when I can be."

He angled his head and kissed her, loving the taste of her lips on his. Before things got out of hand, and judging from the hot tension between his legs, that could happen damned fast, he pushed the car door open.

"Twin beds, right?" He grinned at her.

She swatted his arm. "We'll just end up shoving them together."

He exited the car and trotted inside, wondering if they'd make it as far as any bed. They might stay in the shower until they'd run the hotel's hot water down to nothing. Chuckling, he dragged his wallet from a back pocket and asked for their nicest accommodations.

A short while later, he got back into the car brandishing keycards and hotel propaganda. "Turns out we won't need to find a restaurant. There's one here and they have room service."

"Even better. Which way is our room?"

He directed her toward the back of the building. Once she parked, she got out and went around to the back, popping the trunk. "Take your pack," she said.

He peered at both their packs and his medical bag arranged in the tight trunk space and shouldered his pack. "You're wonderfully organized."

Cara shrugged and handed him his medical kit. She hucked her pack over her shoulders before shutting the trunk. "One of the first rules you learn in the backcountry. Never get too far afield from your gear. It's your lifeline. But I can't take credit this time. Your dad transferred our stuff. Remember?"

He opened one of the hotel's many side doors with a keycard and held it for her. "Third floor. Do you want to take the elevator?"

She shot him an incredulous look. "You're kidding, right?"

John laughed. "Yeah, second backcountry rule. Never turn down an opportunity for conditioning."

"How'd you guess?" Laughing right along with him, she led the way up three flights to the top floor.

"We're in 323," he said and followed her to the end of the hall. Since the card was already in his hand, he slotted it into the latch and turned it.

Cara walked inside and whistled. "Jesus! What is this? The John F. Kennedy suite?"

"You're close, but if it has a name, the desk clerk didn't tell me. All he said was he was certain we'd be comfortable."

Cara shucked her pack, and John placed his doctoring supplies on a table. That done, he removed his pack as well. The two-room suite had a living area and double doors that opened into a bedroom where a king-sized bed butted against one wall. Flat screen televisions graced several walls. Patios sat off both the living and bedrooms with comfy looking chairs.

"What I can see of that bed looks awesome, but I'm too dirty to touch sheets I plan to sleep on." She cast a longing look at the bed before sinking onto a chair and bending to unlace her boots.

He knelt in front of her and batted her hands away. "Let me." He tugged the laces out of their eyelets and levered her boots off her feet, stripping her socks off after them. Once her feet were bare, he held one between his hands and massaged her instep and the ball of her foot.

She arched into his touch. "Damn that feels good."

"Yeah, my feet always take it up the ass when I backpack. We haven't had much of a break since we came off Kearsarge."

"Want to tell me more about what your grandmother meant by her linkage comment?"

John switched to her other foot to buy himself a moment.

"Whatever it is, just tell me," she said. "You're working out a palatable explanation of something you think I won't like."

It was precisely what he'd been doing, but her astuteness stunned him. "How'd you know?"

"I read people really well. Have to in my business. Worst mistake I've ever made was Ruth and Christopher. If I'd been more on top of how frayed their emotional state was, I could've—"

"Maybe not. The fire dragons make people crazy."

"You and I didn't run pell-mell into the heart of the flames."

"They weren't as strong as us. Everything we did on that trip was a struggle for them. Between you and me, we had to help them over and over."

Cara nodded. "Yes, and that's something else I feel responsible for. I didn't vet them as thoroughly as I should've, and by the time I realized they weren't all that competent, retreat wasn't possible because of the fire."

"Don't blame yourself. The trip got a whole lot harder really fast when the fire blazed out of control."

She wriggled her foot in his hand. "Back to your grandmother."

John nodded, and ran a hand up her calf, continuing to knead her tight muscles. "Nana has an old-fashioned side. In the world she inhabits, sex goes with marriage. So she was urging us to have sex, but also to pledge ourselves to one another."

He reluctantly let go of her leg—in case she wanted to collect her things and storm out of the room. When she pushed her foot back into his hand, relief hammered him.

"Is it some kind of Native ceremony?" she asked, her eyes sparkling with what could only be enthusiasm.

"You could say that." She'd already shared his blood, so they had that part nailed. His old antipathy for everything linked to his roots caught him by surprise, and he couldn't figure out what to say next. How to describe the archaic ritual that bound a man and a woman through this life and all lives to come.

Cara jerked her foot back. "You're hedging again. Do you not want to tell me because you don't want us to do that?"

A frustrated groan bubbled past his lips. His scant experience with women was coming back to bite him in the ass. Because words weren't working, he dragged her off the chair and into his arms, slanting his mouth over hers, and putting his heart and soul into a kiss.

CHAPTER 16

Cara tumbled to the floor with John's arms firmly around her. Before she could protest, he'd covered her mouth with his own and pushed his tongue inside. Heat flashed from her toes, sweeping all the way to the top of her head, shocking her with its intensity.

She wrapped her arms around him and buried her hands in his hair, holding his mouth against hers. Her tongue tangled with his and she bit his lower lip, almost as if she was hanging onto him. Willing him to brand her, make her his in every way that counted.

John ran his hands down her back. When he reached the bottom of her stretchy top, he jammed his fingers under it exploring bare skin. Everywhere he touched her, lust bloomed. Her nipples pebbled, and her breasts grew heavy with wanting him.

Moaning, she writhed against him, against the cock that had turned into a tantalizing thickness, pressing into her belly. There had to be a way to get him inside her body, but her brain wouldn't cooperate. At least her boots were off. She let go of him and reached between them, undoing, unzipping, unbuckling.

Not sure how she accomplished the impossible, Cara could've

crowed with triumph when she found his cock beneath its layers of fabric and drew it out.

He made a decidedly male sound against her open mouth and pushed her pants south, but the angle was awkward. John ripped his mouth from hers. "Clothes have to go." His voice was harsh with wanting her, and he was breathing hard.

"Does that mean I have to let go of you?" Cara stroked his wonderfully erect cock, rubbing her thumb around the velvety head.

"Not for long, darling." He pried her fingers off him and tugged her top over her head, followed by her sports bra.

"Two can play that game," she announced and unbuttoned his shirt, slipping it down his shoulders, along with his vest. "You have the most beautiful body," she murmured, tracing the hard planes of muscles that cut across his shoulders with her fingertips.

"Not as beautiful as yours." He filled his hands with her breasts, rubbing her already hard nipples into achingly stiff peaks.

Cara started to tug his pants down his slender hips, and then realized he still had his boots on. "Damn it!" She slithered down his body and made short work of undoing his bootlaces and tugging the heavy fabric and leather climbing boots out of the way. She'd begun on his socks when he rasped, "Leave them for later."

She dragged his pants the rest of the way down his legs, followed by his underwear. His cock drew her, standing hard and proud from a mat of curls just as red as his hair.

She licked her way up his legs, tasting salt and soot. When she reached his cock, she couldn't resist swiping her tongue across it. The sharp tang of him made her crazy with wanting more, and she took him into her mouth, licking, sucking, teasing as she worked him with a hand.

He made a sound like a big male cat purring and threaded his hands into her hair as he thrust into her mouth. Her crotch throbbed relentlessly, beating between her legs with a rhythm all its own. She threw a leg over one of his, pressing her core against him, not caring about anything but the ridged flesh swelling even harder inside her mouth and the climax that bubbled low in her belly, so close it was almost upon her.

It wasn't how she'd envisioned making love with him for the first time, and she had thought about it. After their few kisses, she'd begun plotting seduction schemes, desperate to lose herself in his clean mountain scent and feel his limbs wrapped around her.

"Cara." Her name was part entreaty, part prayer. He tugged gently on her head, but she didn't want to let go of him. He pulled harder, and his cock slid from her mouth. He turned her onto her back and drew her pants down her legs, followed by her panties. The heat of his gaze raked her body as he ran his hands from her breasts down her hips, settling one between her legs over the distended place that had grown so sensitive a breath would tumble her into ecstasy.

He knelt between her legs and she wound them around his waist, opening herself for him. Her heart thudded against her ribcage; breath clotted in her throat. She wanted the man kneeling above her more than she'd ever wanted anyone. He wrapped a hand around his cock, but didn't press it inside her.

"I could look at you forever," he panted. "You're the most beautiful, the most perfect woman imaginable. You look like one of the ancient goddesses with all that dark silky hair, and I've never seen the like of your eyes."

"Could be the work of the wee folk." She winked lazily. "Now that we know I hail from the Emerald Isle."

"You never know, darling."

"Stop talking and make love with me." She thrust her hips upward and seated him at her entrance. She had to have him now, or she'd dissolve into a million motes of nothingness. "I need you." The words held such raw heat, she almost didn't recognize her own voice.

"Not as much as I need you. I'll do the best I can, sweetheart, but I won't last long."

"Neither will I. Hell, if you keep looking at me like that, I'll come just from the lust in your eyes."

He pushed into her, slowly, so slowly she almost couldn't stand the tension building in her belly. She reached for her clit, intent on feeding the orgasm that tormented her, just out of reach.

He batted her hand away. "We'll do this together. Trust me. I'm walking that same fine edge. The longer we can hold out, the sweeter the fall." He sank full length into her, stretching her with his length and girth. Instead of withdrawing, he stayed quiet, teasing her with small muscle contractions.

Cara squeezed back.

Supporting himself on one arm, he cradled a breast, tweaking her nipple, and then he withdrew just as slowly as he'd inserted himself. She grabbed his hips, trying to pull him back inside, but he was strong and he kept to the same, glacial pace.

Cara giggled.

He bent and brushed his lips across hers. "What's so funny?"

"You're like a glacier."

He kissed her again. Longer this time, while he sank back inside her. When he moved his mouth away, he said, "Only you would come up with that analogy."

"Probably so."

The tide moving through her body heated, scorched her with need so fierce everything else in the world paled. His strokes grew faster, until their bodies pounded together.

She dissolved into a climax that shook her to her toes, and she kept on coming as a second peak rocked her, followed by a third.

John growled, a savage, untamed howl that augured into her soul. He slashed his mouth down on hers, and she felt him shudder deep inside her as he kissed her.

He rolled her into his arms and they ended up lying on the

carpeted floor on their sides, breaths still coming hard like an out of control bellows.

"I guess we have our priorities straight," she said when she could talk.

"How so?" He nuzzled her neck.

"I figured we'd clean up, then maybe order dinner, and then once we were fed and clean, we'd—"

"—make love like two refined adults rather than rutting beasts?" He grinned and her heart melted.

"Yeah. Something like that. How about that shower?"

"I don't want to let go of you." His cock twitched, not having deflated much.

"I feel the same way, but we need to be cleaner. God knows when we'll get another opportunity."

He let his tongue drift up the side of her neck until it tickled her ear. "Another one of those mountain lessons?"

"Indeed. Never let an opportunity for anything pass you by. Come on." She wriggled free, dislodging him from her body. "We can continue this under hot water."

She got to her feet and made her way into a bathroom that was as big as her bedroom at home. A Jacuzzi tub sat in the middle of the floor, and a shower with multiple spray heads and glass doors was positioned in a corner across from it. She opened the shower door and turned on the water, figuring out which adjustment went to what spray head by a process of elimination.

John joined her. "Wow! Looks like something for an Iranian prince. Or a wizard with tech skills."

She hip butted him. "Well today it's for us. Water's hot. Soaps and shampoos and conditioners are all in that basket." She pointed and ducked beneath the many jets shooting water in all directions.

He followed her in, grabbed a small bar of lemon-scented soap, and proceeded to wash her with it. Once she was lathered to her chin, she turned to him with a twin bar and worked the dirt and grime off his skin, paying particular attention to his perpetually erect cock.

"That part's not dirty," he teased. "At least not as dirty."

"I like to be thorough," she shot back.

"Lean your head under the spray so we can experiment with all these little shampoo bottles."

"You too," she countered and detached one of the sprayers to sluice water over his head.

She ended up facing away from him, head tilted beneath a nozzle and wet hair streaming down her back, when he wrapped her in an embrace from behind. "You have the finest ass," he murmured in her ear. "Gets me excited as hell."

She butted herself against him, splayed her hands on the wet marble, and spread her legs. "You're on."

Unlike their first lovemaking, there was nothing slow about how he entered her this time. He pounded into her and reached around to rub her clit. He bit and nipped her shoulder, and she shuddered as another climax ripped through her.

"That's it, darling." His throaty voice caressed her ear. "Now me."

She felt the spasms of his release and tightened around him, willing him the most pleasure he could contain. He pulled out of her and turned her in his arms. Water pounded down on them as he closed his mouth over hers, kissing her thoroughly before he let her go.

"Ready to get out?" He smiled at her, his expression tender and protective and other, deeper things she couldn't interpret.

"No, but we should. We also should probably stock up on condoms. I quit using birth control years ago. Didn't need it." She flipped off the taps and opened the steamy glass door to grab thick towels off a nearby rack. Wrapping one around herself, she handed him another.

Taking it, he began toweling himself off. "You being pregnant wouldn't be the worst thing in the world."

"Right now it would. I wouldn't be able to work for a few months, and after that, the baby wouldn't see much of me. I'm gone, sometimes for months at a time."

"Darling, you're not alone. Not anymore. We'll figure things out as they happen." He picked up a comb off the ledge and worked tangles out of her hair, leaving it wet and streaming down her back. Then he went to work on his snarled locks.

A warm tide rolled through her. When it reached her heart, it cracked open and spilled over. He'd just said they'd face the future together, that he wasn't going anywhere. Even if things didn't work out, it was still nice to be wanted in the moment.

When did I get to be such a cynic?

Somewhere between Mom and Leif.

Cara answered her own question and winced inwardly. Truth always caught up to her, no matter how much she wanted to paint the world in rosy tones.

"You never did finish telling me about that ritual your Nana expects us to complete." Cara quirked a brow his way. "You leapt on me like a caveman in the middle of that, and here we are."

He furled a brow right back. "Do I hear a complaint?"

Cara shook her head, smiling. "No. But I do want to know what she expects of us. If there's some magic bullet out there that will confer protection once we face the dragons again, I want to know what it is."

John walked to where two white terrycloth robes hung on hooks near the bathroom door. He pulled them down and handed one to her. "If you still feel like dinner, we can order something from room service. While we're waiting for it, I'll fill in the details I can. Then we need to grab a couple hours' sleep."

She let him bundle the robe around her. "Sounds like a plan." Cara threaded her arms around him. "I really, really like you. So much it scares me."

"Good to hear, Cara, because I'm falling in love with you."

She jumped back as if he'd shot her. "It's too soon," she mumbled. "Way too soon to talk about love."

"Why? Define too soon?" He draped an arm around her shoulders and led her into the living area and a well-padded, beige, leather sofa. Sitting, he drew her into his lap.

"Too soon is… Well, too soon. You have to get to know someone really well, first. And then you live together. And then if they don't have too many horrible habits, you—"

He placed a hand over her mouth. "It's only the past seventy or eighty years people have done things like that. Lots of places in the world they still don't. We're scarcely kids anymore. I know the qualities I've looked for in a woman, and you must know what you'd like in a man. What you need."

Fear made an end run around her heart as all the miserable years with Leif popped up to taunt her. She'd been alone for the best of reasons. So she wouldn't make another mistake. "You make it sound so…clinical and analytic."

He cradled her head against his chest with a hand. "What I feel for you isn't clinical or analytic. It's warm and tender and sexual and protective. I want to stand by your side and take care of you. I want us to have a life together. Children if you want them."

Her eyelids prickled dangerously. Tears weren't far behind. "What if we're wrong for each other?"

John stroked her hair. "We're not."

"Yes, but how do you know? Sex was great, but it takes a whole lot more than that to build a life on."

"We'll figure it out, sweetheart. I know we will. That's the other part of what Nana was talking about. It's an archaic concept, but we plight our troth to each other. It goes along with making love. We don't have to do it right now," he hurried on. "The ritual is brief and we can share the vows whenever it feels right to you."

Conflict raged within her. A deep, elemental part of her wanted to be with John forever, but she was frightened of anything that smacked of long-term commitments. Nothing human-spawned lasted forever that she could see. Only the mountains did that. They were solid. You could count on them to be the same every single time.

"Penny for your thoughts?" He angled his head to look at her.

Cara ducked her chin. "I was thinking about the mountains and how they're always the same."

"Yup. They are. And they're rough on the unprepared. People get lucky and skate by, but look at how many big name climbers are dead. You throw the dice enough times, take enough chances, and one of those chances sends you to the hall of the mountain gods."

"What are you saying?" She looked up into his striking blue eyes, noticing flecks of silver around the irises.

"That I'll care for you for the rest of your days—and beyond—if you'll have me. I'm willing to take a chance on us."

Cara wanted to say the words, wanted it so bad she could taste it, but they refused to leave her throat. "I— I need a little more time." Tears welled, and she brushed them away.

"Take all the time you need, Cara. My offer doesn't have an expiration date." He tapped her upper chest gently with two fingers. "The answers you need are here, not here." He touched her forehead. "On a much more prosaic note, I'm going to order a salad and chocolate cake. What do you want?"

"Ooooh, both of them. And soup too. Any kind. I'm not picky. And French fries if they have the real kind, not the frozen ones."

"Let's see if I can remember all that." He set her on the sofa, walked to the other side of the room where a house phone sat on a small, wooden table, and dialed room service.

Her mind raced in unproductive circles. Maybe what she needed to do was not think for a while. Watching John on the phone, Cara remembered her cell and got up, intent on plugging it into shore power. She might need it later. Since she was already next to her pack, she pulled everything out of it, sorting, deciding what to take to face the dragons later that night.

John joined her. "Good idea," he said. "We'll be better fighters if we're not burdened by fifty pound packs."

"Yes, but we need all three ropes and an assortment of hardware…"

They were still debating what to take—agreeing about almost everything—when room service knocked on their door. Cara hurriedly stuffed things into their packs and got a valet sack from the closet to hold everything they weren't bringing with them.

John flowed to his feet, and she watched his graceful movements as he loped to the door. Maybe things between them would work out after all.

She hoped so. He was an amazing man. Before she could stop herself, a catalogue of the traits she admired—integrity, intelligence, competence, honor—marched across her mind. He had them all, plus the self-discipline to do the right thing, even if it inconvenienced him.

The door swooshed shut, and he rolled the cart to a nearby table, set for two. Cara pushed to her feet and joined him.

"You're smiling." He pulled out her chair and settled her into it.

"So are you."

He sat across from her and placed the salad bowl between them, handing her a fork. "It's because being with you makes me happy. Dig in, sweetheart."

Maybe because he wasn't trolling for her to say something nice back, it was easy to let go of the chokehold she usually had on her emotions.

Cara murmured, "You make me happy too," before she began to eat.

CHAPTER 17

John wakened to the subtle vibration of his watch. He'd set it to get them moving at eleven-thirty. Red-tinged moonlight spilled across the bed, and the air that wafted through the open window smelled like smoke. Cara lay on her side, an arm tossed across her face. She'd fallen asleep almost before she was done eating, and he'd carried her to their bed.

Watching the deep rise and fall of her chest, he hated to wake her, but there wasn't any choice. He'd called Emergency Services once he was done eating. As he'd suspected, they were delighted to have him. He'd emailed his credentials, but they still had to send Cara's. He figured she kept a copy of her EMT cert somewhere in her phone, but he didn't know the passcode to get into it.

He'd expected an argument regarding his request to help out tonight, but the 9-1-1 operator hadn't given him one whit of trouble. Maybe she understood the crazy schedules many M.D.s kept. When he'd said he was free around midnight, she'd jumped on it and given him instructions where to show up for helicopter transport into the mountains.

"Cara." He touched her shoulder, and she came awake instantly.

"Yeah." She twisted toward him. "Show time?"

Savage protectiveness raked through him, and he pulled her close. He wanted to insist she remain behind, somewhere safe, but he wouldn't insult her by suggesting it. She'd refuse, anyway. In truth, she was as strong as he was. Not magically, but every other way.

He muffled a snort and reminded himself that his magic was almost an impediment since he'd used it so infrequently.

Cara wriggled against him. "I love it when you hold me, but we need to get moving. I just caught a glimpse of the clock."

He kissed her hard and let her go. Cara rolled off the bed and padded toward the bathroom. He got up and began pulling on the stack of clothing he'd sorted and left by the bed.

"What happened to the things in the valet bag?" she called from the other room.

"I picked the cleanest clothes I could find for both of us. They're in here."

She walked into the bedroom to a pile of her things and dressed fast. "Not only do I get a valet bag—" she grinned at him "—I also get a valet."

"A true valet would have laundered everything for you," he informed her archly.

"Clean clothes are nice, but scarcely critical. Why these ones barely stink at all." Cara flashed him a mischievous grin before bending to shinny into her socks and boots. "We need to get moving if we're going to be at Rose's by midnight."

"After you fell asleep, I got things squared away with Emergency Services. You need to email them your EMT certificate, but we're meeting them at the airport around midnight."

"Does your grandmother know?"

John nodded. "Yeah. Called her too. Among other things, she extended her blessings."

"Huh? For what?"

"She's clairvoyant, remember? Far as she's concerned, we're something like married."

The set of Cara's shoulders stiffened, and she walked briskly to her phone. Unplugging it, she pocketed both it and the cord. Then she shouldered her pack and picked up the valet bag. "Ready."

"Not going to comment on Nana's approval?" He slid into his own pack, buckling the waist belt, and snapped up his medical bag.

Cara had the door open, but she stopped on the far side of it. Keeping her voice low, she said, "Not right now. We have a job to do. Single-minded concentration is why I'm still alive. I can't think about you right now. Or about us."

John tugged the door shut and took her free hand. "Smart woman. I'd do well to borrow a page from your book."

Except he couldn't. Cara was at the forefront of his thoughts. He liked having her there, and didn't try to move her away from center stage.

They walked through the silent hotel and down three floors to where they'd left the car. Once they were en route, Cara pulled out her phone and tapped its display. "Where do I send my EMT cert?"

He rattled off an address, and she tapped a few more keys. "There. All done. This might be a stupid question, but how do we know the dragons will show up?"

"Because they see us as a serious threat. They won't overlook an opportunity to squash us."

"How will they know we're there, though?" she persisted. "There's a bunch of this magical stuff I don't get. Probably most of it."

"They'll know. I listened to the news for a little while after I got our itinerary squared away. Everyone is saying how this fire isn't responding to normal efforts at eradication. They're frantic because of how fast it's spreading."

"Did you sleep at all?" She laid a hand on his thigh.

"Yeah. Probably not enough, but it took a while for me to wind down."

"I've been thinking—" Cara began.

"Always dangerous," he teased to lighten the mood and make it feel less like they were running headlong into Armageddon.

"Be serious. The last two times, we've fought right next to each other. Maybe our ability to destroy these things would improve if we attacked from different angles."

"Say more."

"High places are comfortable for me. I have ropes and hardware. Depending on the terrain, I could climb to a stable ledge or platform or something and fight them from there."

"By yourself? I don't think so."

"Why not? You're not going to turn into one of those overbearing, overprotective men, are you?"

Good point.

He picked his words carefully. "I still see this as my fight. You got roped into it, and I appreciate the help, but if something happened to you, I'd never forgive myself."

"It's not only your fight. It's everyone's. We've covered that ground. You spin the wheel. You take your chances." Her voice rose with emotion. "I've lost clients before. Ruth and Christopher weren't the first, even though how they died was a stupid waste. If I beat myself up for every climber who overreached himself, or who didn't listen and ended up at the bottom of a rock pile, I'd have quit guiding years ago. My track record is better than most guides, but far from perfect. Find me a guide who's never lost a client, and I guarantee you it's one who doesn't go to anyplace dangerous."

Her intensity caught him off guard. "Cara. Back down. It's all right."

"I will not *back down*. Besides, I'm not done yet. You say you want a life with me. If you do, you have to trust my judgment about what I can do. You can't coddle me or protect me or shut me in a tower."

John swallowed hard. She was absolutely correct. "Touché. Apologies. We're a team. You're a more-than-equal member."

"Good." She settled back against her seat. "You won't bring one hundred percent concentration to whatever we face if you're diverting your attention worrying about me."

"Another good point." He followed flashing signs into the airport and drove to the helicopter area. "Once we get to ground zero, we'll assess what we have to work with and plan from there."

He turned off the car and got out, using the clicker to pop the trunk. She had her pack buckled into place by the time he got to the open trunk. John hefted his pack over one shoulder and shut the car, locking it.

"No medical bag?" she asked.

"They'll have supplies in spades there. Besides, I have some things in my pack. So do you. We should be fine. This way." He took off at a lope for the flight line with her right beside him.

A chopper sat on the tarmac, its rotor whirling lazily. When John drew close, a man got up from where he sat on a lawn chair. Tall and rawboned, he had long, black hair and a colorful bandana tied around his forehead. Oil stained blue jeans, motorcycle boots, and a T-shirt that had once been white hugged his body like a second skin. "Dr. Cassavettes?"

"Yup. That's me. We're not late, are we?"

Brown eyes sparkled merrily, and the man, who looked around fifty, shrugged into a battered leather jacket. "Nah. I like to be early. Lets me preflight the bird and warm her up." He turned to Cara. "Ms. Carlisle?" He broke into a grin. "Of course it would be you. I remember you from the Hindu Kush—and a few other places too. Used to fly climbers in and out of there."

"Terry? Oh my God, I never thought I'd see you again." Cara

hugged the pilot before stepping away. "When you took off to rescue those two men who were still stranded on that glacier in Pakistan, weather was closing in fast. I wanted to stay to make sure everyone was safe, but the authorities forced all of us to leave. They were afraid the storm would trap us. Did the guys make it?"

"They made it into my chopper, but one of them was dead by the time I got him back to base camp."

"Damn." She turned toward John. "It was a group of Koreans. They got into big trouble climbing Tirich Mir. My group came across them on our way down and did what we could to help."

"Well, thanks to you only one of the nine didn't make it," Terry said. He focused his next words at John. "I don't know how well you know this woman, Doctor, but she's one hell of a mountain climber. Keeps a cool head when the world's turning to shit around her. Come on. We're out of here."

John followed Cara and Terry, bending low to avoid the spinning rotors. He handed his pack up before climbing the ladder and settling into one of the rear seats. Cara sat in the right seat across from the pilot.

Terry passed him a set of headphones. "Sit back and enjoy the flight. ETA is about thirty-five minutes. It's really smoky up there, but I'll do the best I can to find a spot to set the bird down."

"Not sounding good," Cara said.

"It's not. If I can't land, we'll send you down in the basket. There are injured I need to transport out of there."

"We can rappel out of the chopper," Cara said. "It'll save time, and then you can drop the basket for us to package up the injured."

John thought about the logistics of what lay ahead. Getting away to fight the dragons might take time. Triage for severely injured would have to be his first priority. If this chopper couldn't land, he wondered what the hell his father and grandmother would do. Mark was a fine pilot, likely as skilled as Terry. Would he shove safety aside in the interest of getting on the ground no matter what?

Nothing I can do about that.

Next he thought about the binding ritual. The one he and Cara hadn't done. Would that added margin of safety protect her? Especially if she followed through with her idea about fighting separately from him?

Not much I can do about that, either.

John ground his teeth together. He'd be the first to admit he was a control freak. He liked his I's dotted and his T's crossed. It was one of the reasons medicine had been so appealing. He appreciated the ability to assess problems and fix them—with science firmly on his side.

He'd have to get over that. Cara had chastised him soundly earlier. Not that he hadn't deserved it. Tonight was a fly by the seat of his pants endeavor. He'd need to be able to switch gears at a moment's notice. Kind of like working in an ER when it was on fire.

The analogy made him smile grimly.

Smoke filtered into the helicopter. When he looked outside, not only was it black as pitch, he couldn't see either the moon or the stars. "Instruments?" he asked.

"You betcha," Terry replied. "Wouldn't want us to chuck into the side of one of these mountains, would you?"

John didn't answer. He thought about his dad again. Mark had instruments, but they weren't nearly as sophisticated as the ones in this craft.

The radio crackled to life spouting a conditions report and Terry responded, asking a question or two.

"I saw ropes lashed to your packs." Terry was obviously talking to them now. "How long are they?"

"If you're asking how far we can rap," Cara replied, "maybe seventy-five feet."

"You don't need double rope," Terry said. "I'll be up here, and I can untie this end."

"Good point. Then you can increase my estimate."

"We'll split the difference at around a hundred feet. Hey, Doc. You ever rapped out of a bird before?"

"No, but I've rapped off plenty of rock faces."

"This is a little different," Cara cut in. "You won't have the rock to stabilize yourself."

"I'll be fine."

"Yeah, you will be because you're going first, and I'll check your knots and your harness." Cara sounded so fierce, the evidence of her caring touched him.

"Harnesses, huh? Guess we should get them on now." He stretched an arm toward the packs, but couldn't reach them, so he undid his shoulder harness. A warning blast filled the cockpit.

Terry laughed. "Been trying to figure out a way to squelch that fucker for months. Never did figure it out."

"I'll hurry," John said. The craft bucked and shuddered in the unstable air. Luckily—or maybe luck had nothing to do with it— Cara had lashed the harnesses right on top of the ropes. He tugged them out and handed hers up to her.

Back in his seat, he slid his sit harness up his legs and buckled it into place. He'd just reached for his shoulder belt, so the infernal warning buzzer would shut the fuck up, when it quit on its own. The silence was wonderful, except he didn't understand it.

"Why'd it stop blaring?"

"We're hovering. Here's where you get out." Terry gestured to Cara. "Remember how to do this?"

"Of course I do. You stay put. I'll keep my headphones on so we can communicate from the ground, and I'll send them up with last basket. How many wounded are you transporting?"

"Three, plus a paramedic to watch over them."

Cara worked her way past him and undid the latches on a door in the belly of the chopper.

"Can I help?" John hunkered next to her.

"Yeah. Get the longest rope. It's on the left hand side on my pack. I've been thinking how to do this. We're going to tie our packs into the basket and lower it. Once it's down, we'll go."

John detached the rope and watched her work. She was fast and skilled. It didn't take more than ten minutes before he was on the ground next to the basket, and only a couple more before she joined him. He'd gotten their packs out of the basket while he waited, but the air was so smoky his eyes watered, and his lungs began to burn immediately.

"Jesus! This is horrible," she muttered, glancing up. "Can't even see the chopper."

John keyed his mike to communicate with Terry. "Tell them we're ready to receive whomever they want to send with you."

"I already did," Terry replied.

Boots pounded toward them. Two medics came into view, a stretcher between them. John bent over the moaning man. Burns covered one leg. The fabric of his firefighter's suit had scorched until it bonded with his flesh.

"Did anyone give this man something for pain?" John demanded.

"Nope. Chopper with more supplies crashed," one of the medics said, tightlipped. Cara directed them as they transferred the injured man into the basket and strapped him in.

John bent to his pack and extracted his medical supply kit. He drew out a prefilled syringe of morphine and injected it into the man's good leg. "That'll hold him until he gets to a hospital."

Cara keyed her mike. "One coming up. Untie my rope while you're at it."

The basket began its trajectory upward, and the two paramedics grabbed the stretcher and ran back into the smoky gloom, presumably to snatch the next patient.

The rope slithered into a heap at their feet. John returned his medical kit to his pack. Cara coiled the rope and reattached it to her backpack. Minutes dragged past. The basket had long since *thunked* to the ground next to them. Fire flashed and flared, accompanied by loud booms. The ground began rocking beneath their feet, almost as if an earthquake was rolling through.

"What's going on?" Terry demanded. "I need to get this man to a hospital."

"Don't know," Cara said. "Did you radio the command center?"

"Yeah. No one answered."

John exchanged a look with Cara, and she made a chopping motion with one hand.

John keyed his mike. "We're putting our headsets in the basket. Take her up."

"What about the other two injured?" Terry asked.

"I have a feeling something bad happened," Cara said. "Get out of here before you can't." She dropped her headset into the basket. John did the same. Silently, she detached her helmet from her pack and buckled it into place. John already had his on. He'd donned it before he rapped out of the bird.

"I hope your father had the sense to turn around," Cara said, settling her pack on her back.

John hoped the same thing. His dad was in his fifties. Rose in her seventies. The smoke and debris clogging the air would be extremely hard on them. He dragged his pack into position on his back and secured it. "Stay close," he told Cara. "With this much smoke, either one of us might lose consciousness."

"Like glue," she agreed and clicked on her headlamp. The light didn't help much, so John left his off.

They followed a well-beaten four-wheel drive road for half a mile. At least the smoke didn't grow any worse. His lungs ached, and his eyes felt like they were lined with shards of glass. Cara trudged beside him, silent, uncomplaining. She had a quiet strength that he valued. No wonder she'd been successful as a guide. Her simple presence instilled courage and helped others believe in themselves.

The path through spindly mountain mahogany opened into a clearing. Cara moved to his side and raised her head, swinging it from side to side so they could see in the beam from her light.

"Jesus! If I didn't know better, I'd say an avalanche flattened this place." Adrenaline poured through him, leaving a sharp, metallic taste in his mouth. The remains of a field hospital spread across the clearing. Ripped tents, crushed furniture, twisted metal equipment cases. Nothing whole remained.

He cupped his hands around his mouth. "Hello. Anyone here?"

Cara whistled. The strident notes sharp enough to reach a long way.

A figure detached itself from deep in the shadows at the far side of the clearing and ran for them, screaming and sobbing. John and Cara bolted toward the woman. John reached her first and wrapped his arms around her, holding on tight.

"Hush. You're okay. Pull yourself together and tell us what happened."

The woman, a short, thin blonde, who was soaked to her skin, gradually stopped screeching until all that was left were snuffly sobs. "N-nurse," she stammered. "I'm a nurse. One minute I was working on someone. Next minute, the fire got us. It came out of the sky and rampaged through the whole camp. M-my patient incinerated in front of me. Just went up like a torch until there was nothing left. I tried to stay with him, help him, but the heat was too much. And the ground was bucking and heaving. I crawled because I couldn't stand up. When I got to the vehicles, I kept crawling until they were between me and the worst of the explosions."

"What did you do then?" Cara asked. "How'd you get so wet?"

"Creek. There's a creek back there. Figured it was the safest place, so I crept into it. It's where I was when I heard you."

"You did great." Cara patted her arm.

The nurse panted, wrapping a hand around her throat. "Hurts. Too much smoke. And no, I didn't do great. I abandoned my patient to save myself." More tears welled, creating tracks down her sooty face.

"Your patient was already beyond saving. You did the right thing, even though it feels bad right now." Cara's voice was gentle. "I know it hurts, but we need you to keep talking for a little bit more. Are you the only one left?"

"I don't know. I called and called after the explosions, but no one answered. Then I tried my two-way." She tapped a radio attached to her belt. "I was just so terrified. Couldn't figure out what to do."

"What's your name?" John asked.

"Robin Nelson."

"Do any of the vehicles have fuel, Robin?" At her nod, he said. "I want you to take one and drive out of here. When the road branches, take the one that leads lower."

"I know the way," she said. "I grew up in these mountains."

"Good. Get moving."

"What about you two?" Robin swept her wide-eyed gaze from one of them to the other.

"We'll be okay. Helicopter just dropped us off. He'll be back soon as he drops his passenger at the hospital," John lied smoothly.

"If you're sure." Robin squared her shoulders. "I'm better now. I just kind of lost it there. Been a nurse for thirty years. I had no idea a body could burn so fast and not even hardly leave any ash." She shuddered. "Still gives me the creeps."

"We're sure." Cara smiled. "Now get moving." She mirrored John's words, and they seemed to do the trick. Robin trotted back in the direction she'd come. An engine sputtered to life, and an ATV rolled past them with Robin hunched over its controls.

John waited until she was gone. "What was that you called this earlier? Show time?"

"Yup. Looks like the dragons beat us here."

John didn't hesitate, and he didn't ask first. He took one of Cara's hands. "Repeat after me. Heart of my heart. Bone of my bone. Blood of my blood. We shall be joined forever more."

Cara stood tall and gripped his other hand too, as she repeated the words of the ancient ritual back to him.

"You won't be sorry." He cradled her face in his hands.

"Let's make sure we both live long enough to find out." Cracking a grim smile, she dropped her pack to the ground and rooted through its top compartment.

CHAPTER 18

Cara pulled her GPS out of her pack along with a topo map. She needed to know where they were to mount any kind of defense that made sense. She'd just linked her life to John's, and it felt right in a way little else had. She wanted to revel in having not thought an emotional commitment to death, but she couldn't afford to shift her concentration away from survival.

"Do you think it's odd there's no, erm, human remains?" she asked. It felt macabre to her, but maybe she was overreacting.

"Not really." His voice held a somber note. "Dragon fire burns extremely hot. Hot enough to incinerate anything it touches until nothing's left but ash. Robin was smart to make a run for it. Last two times we had the guides and birds to modulate things."

"Awk! I'd forgotten about them. Where are they?"

He shrugged. "I have no idea. And I don't know how to summon them. Nana would, but she's not here, either."

Got to work with what we have, not waste time wishing for what isn't here, Cara lectured herself, narrowing her focus to the map in front of her.

The smoke was better near the ground, but the flare of fires roared around them. They were still below timberline, which was around eleven thousand feet at this latitude.

Timberline.

"John." She looked up at him from where she crouched over the map. "I just had an idea, and it's a damned good one."

"Are you going to say more about that, or make me guess?"

She folded the map so their current location was in front of her and hit the on button for her GPS device. It had built in maps as well, but they weren't nearly as detailed as the one spread across her knees. "Remember climbing out of Rae Lakes?"

"It's unlikely I'll ever forget it." He hunkered next to her and focused his red-rimmed eyes on the map.

"The fire was beneath us, not showering us with burning debris. We can replicate that, and it will make our lives easier."

"Go higher. Excellent idea. I'm ashamed I didn't come up with it myself."

Cara clicked through screens on the GPS and zeroed in on their precise position on the map. "We're here." She stabbed the paper with a finger. "Let's see if another of those ATVs has fuel. I say we follow this welter of roads as high as we can. Once we get above timberline, we'll be out of the way of falling trees or anything big catching fire—except us—but that feels manageable."

"We might not be able to drive quite that high," he cautioned.

"However much altitude we can gain before we have to walk will help," she countered.

"Couldn't agree more. I'll locate the stash of vehicles. There have to be more ATVs." He pushed upright and loped into the smoke, disappearing from sight shockingly fast.

The ground rocked beneath her, and she stuffed things hastily back into her pack and stood. Tremors bit deep into the earth. She took off running for John and the vehicles. If they got really lucky, the four-wheel drive roads wouldn't fall victim to earthquakes and slough off the mountainside or become so choked with rock fall, they became impossible to navigate except on foot.

"If that happens, please let it be after we get high enough for my plan to work," she muttered.

The sputter of an engine coming to life was welcome. She had no idea how many vehicles were parked here, but most of the personnel and equipment had likely come by road, not air.

She made her way toward the sound. The smell of oil and gasoline grew stronger. Her gut twisted with anxiety. If a dragon got frisky and decided to target either fuel tanks or fuel cans, they'd be in deep shit.

Don't think about it. Maybe those bastards have no idea gasoline burns.

A sea of vehicles came into view from Jeeps to quads to dirt bikes. A couple of large, military transport vehicles sat off to one side, their flat decks covered with tarps. John was bent over a quad, pouring gas into its tank out of a five-gallon jerry can. She ran to his side. "Where's the one that's running?"

"Over there." He jerked his chin to the right. "Already topped off its tank. I figured we should take two. That way if something happens to one of them, we won't be dead in the water. Besides, both of us would be a tight fit on a single one of these with our packs."

"I like the way you think."

"There." He set the can aside and flicked the ignition switch. The engine purred to life. "You take this one." He stood aside. "It's newer and will be easier to drive."

Cara thought about the map she'd folded and stowed. "Do you need my map?"

"Nah. I grew up four-wheeling these roads. They'll come back to me."

A muted growl reverberated beneath their feet, and the ground undulated, making balance a task. She straddled the quad, checking for where the controls were. They had to get moving before escape wasn't an option. They had yet to see a dragon, but she felt certain they were flying above the smoke laughing their heads off.

"Follow me to my quad, and then I'll be headed hard right up the mountainside." John strode toward the clearing and jumped astride the idling vehicle.

Cara nosed hers after him, gratified when they left the remains of the field hospital behind. How many people had died here? Fifty? A hundred?

Don't think about it, she cautioned herself again.

A hell of a lot more people would die before this was over if she and John couldn't stem the tide somehow. Even though she tried not to think about the guides or birds, her mind returned to them if she wasn't vigilant. She willed them to show up because she and John had no chance at all without supernatural assistance.

"There's always a chance," she murmured. "It's when hope dies that all your chances go with it."

She unclenched her fingers from the controls, realizing she held them in a death grip. She'd kept her eye on the altimeter watch strapped to her wrist as they climbed. At least so far, John had chosen roads wide enough for any vehicle to navigate. The clearing had been just over nine thousand feet. They climbed through ten, and were approaching ten five, kindling her optimism. This might go better than she thought, so long as she remained absolutely present.

An enormous boom rocked her, and the quad canted alarmingly. She fed it gas, urging it to keep its aggressive tires attached to the earth and ride through whatever the disturbance was.

A flaming tree pitched off the mountainside above her, whooshing past with inches to spare. Another followed. The heat seared her, and she dragged her hood over her helmet to shield her hair. Sweat beaded her forehead and dripped down her sides.

Ahead of her, John slowed to about five miles per hour. The

snail's pace made her want to scream, but he could see the road. She couldn't. Damn, but she wished they had radios.

More burning brush fell past them, dotted by the occasional tree engulfed in flames. Trees had to be getting scarce above them. Had to be. She guided the quad as close to the bulk of the mountain as she could, wishing for an overhang to protect them.

The road was a series of zigzag switchbacks. John turned hard right up the next one and stopped, pulling his quad to the side. She parked next to him, squinting through thick smoke. A jagged fissure split the road, growing wider by the minute.

"We can make it," she screamed, "but we have to go now." Without waiting for him to answer, she gunned her quad, aiming for the narrowest spot, and prayed. It wouldn't be pretty if her quad T-boned into the widening hole.

The front wheels scrambled for purchase. Cara stood, throwing her weight forward as she flung the throttle full open. After a gut-wrenching moment when she was certain she'd have to abandon her quad, it shot forward, tires hugging the solid dirt on the other side.

"Yes!" She would've fist-pumped the air, but she needed both hands to control the ATV.

John roared up behind her. "Christ, woman! You have nerves of steel."

Cara laughed. "If we get out of this, you'll have years to decide if wanting me in your life forever was a hasty choice. Come on. The trees are definitely thinning out."

She drove faster than he had, hoping to hell some major obstacle wouldn't rise up through the gloom and throw her and her quad off the increasingly narrow road.

Three more switchbacks dumped them onto a narrow plateau. A few scrubby trees grew in clumps, but for all intents and purposes, they'd made it. She skidded to a halt at the place a rock pile signified the formal end of the road—at least for vehicles, and jumped off, pocketing the keys. Driving out of here was unlikely, but keeping her options open appealed to her.

John joined her. "Do you want to keep climbing?" He eyed the track on the far side of the rocks.

Cara visualized the map. She had an almost eidetic memory when it came to topography. Another five hundred feet would buy them a lot, plus it would place them on a football field-sized mesa. Maybe visibility would improve. Regardless, the earth wasn't heaving and rolling—at least not at the moment.

"Yeah. Nothing to lose. All we need is another five hundred feet. We can knock that off in twenty minutes."

"Lead out. I'm right behind you."

Cara sprinted up the road. Her lungs burned. Her eyes watered. Her throat had passed beyond sore an hour ago. She focused on the rocky earth beneath her feet. Every step was one step closer to—

To what?

Not to a summit. She wasn't climbing a mountain. Not to safety, either. She shook her head hard to clear it. Where they were going was safer, a strategic move to up the odds in their favor.

But it was a hell of a long way from safety.

Feet clicked off on her altimeter. Three hundred. Four hundred. She was grateful the earthquakes had slacked off—and that the road was as good as it was. The smoke was worse. Her eyes felt swollen and hot. She rounded what she hoped would be a final switchback when the unmistakable *whump-whump* of chopper blades buffeted her.

She didn't want to stop until they hit the mesa. Not even for long enough to ask if John thought it might be his dad. Who the fuck else would pilot a bird into this hellish maelstrom?

Cara dug deep and moved faster. Behind her, John's panting filled her ears. Thank God he was as strong as he was and could keep up. She had a hideous feeling something unspeakable was almost upon them.

"Think it's Dad," he rasped.

Cara was running. She didn't turn around to answer. The next bend deposited them onto the mesa she knew had to be here. It was just as broad and flat as she'd seen on the map, which was a relief. Sometimes places that looked flat on a map weren't nearly as level as she hoped they'd be.

Mark's silver bird with its red markings sat at the far end of the plateau, its rotors turning. Mark pelted toward them with Rose close behind him. Cara tried to keep moving, but her muscles were out of oxygen. She planted her feet and bent forward, hands on her thighs, sucking the smoke-filled air. It helped some, but it also made her light-headed.

John threaded an arm around her. "Get closer to the ground," he said.

She let herself sink to the earth and pulled her shirt in front of her nose and mouth to filter out some of the crud in the air. At least her head quit whirling.

Mark and Rose reached them. "Told you they'd be here," Rose said, sounding vindicated. "When there comes a day I can't find my own blood with magic, that'll be the day I'm dead."

"Yes, Ma." Mark bent over Cara. "You all right?"

"Yeah." Cara muttered. "Fine. How the hell did you ever fly through this?"

"Very carefully." A satisfied grin split Mark's weather-beaten face. "Not much worse than flying through hellholes in the Middle East."

Cara scrambled to her feet and scanned the smoke-filled skies. "How can we fight what we can't see?" she demanded.

The air developed the blue-white quality she associated with the guides. Sure enough, a flock of kites descended on them, squawking and cawing. Relief cascaded through her. "Never thought I'd be glad to see those fuckers. Not after the way I first met them, but I could kiss every single black, feathered head."

As if to test her words, a kite swooped right in front of her, hovering. Cara bent and pressed her lips to the top of its head. It did an aerial summersault and rubbed its beak across her cheek.

"Did you have something to do with them showing up?" John asked, directing his words at his grandmother.

"Now how could I have done something like that?" she asked with a sly inflection. "They're bonded to you now."

John rolled his eyes. "Yeah, except I haven't got the first notion of how to communicate with them when they're not right in front of me."

"We'll have to fix that," Rose said with conviction. "But first we have a few other items that require our attention."

Cara scanned the skies. They'd cleared to some extent, maybe because of the guides. Her sore throat thickened with apprehension and she pointed skyward. "I liked it better when I couldn't see. Not really, but holy shit, look at all of them."

She tried counting, but there were too many dragons. They flew in lazy circles, as if they had all the time in the world—and they knew it.

Rose narrowed her eyes. "They're stronger. Fire feeds them. Misery feeds them. Chaos feeds them."

"Means we need to find a way to derail their train," John muttered.

Cara chewed her lower lip. They needed a strategy, and a surefire one at that since it didn't look like they'd get a second chance. Right now the dragons were teasing them like a big cat whose prey was cornered. They wanted to have a little fun with their adversaries before well-aimed blasts of fire ended them forever.

"Uh-uh." Rose shook a finger her way. "No negativity."

Cara drew back. "What? You can read my mind?"

"Of course. You're linked to my blood. It opens you to me."

"Nana, there's scarcely time for that," John broke in. "We need a plan."

"You think?" Mark's tone was acidic.

"No time for snappy rejoinders, either." John trained serious blue eyes on his father.

Light surrounded them, along with the buzzing Cara associated with the guides communicating. Mark, Rose, and John responded in Sioux. Fire rained down, punctuated by angry screeching from the kites. Impatience ate at Cara until she'd almost bitten through her tongue. It grated that plans were clearly being made, and she had no voice in them because she didn't know the language.

First order of business. I'll teach myself Sioux just as soon as we get out of this.

Determination burned through her. They'd find a way to the other side of this. They had to.

John gripped her hand. *"Can you hear me like this?"* His voice resonated in her head.

She nodded. "Can I talk to you the same way?"

"Doesn't matter. All you need to do right now is listen."

The old Cara bristled, racing to the fore. "What if I don't agree?"

The corners of his mouth twitched as if he wanted to smile. *"Listen first. After that feel free to add to the plan. Watch what you say, though. Nana is convinced the dragons can hear us. Dad's not so sure."*

Cara made come along motions with one hand.

"They draw strength from each other. There's also a link, like an umbilical cord, from them to their home world. It's how they find their way back and forth." He paused to take a breath, but Cara suspected he was girding himself to deliver a difficult strategy. One with significant risk.

"We have to get them to split up. The only way to do that is for us to split up." He set his mouth in a thin, hard line. *"I argued, but I was outvoted."*

She gestured for him to go on since she wasn't supposed to ask anything out loud. Like what her role was.

Even though he was using telepathy, he bent close to her, and the guides formed a circle of light around them. *"Dad will do what he did last time. He'll start by blasting as many as he can with ammo. Once he's exhausted that approach, he'll call rain and summon thunder and lightning. Enough of it should annihilate their connection with their home world. Meantime, I'll head north with a group of guides and birds. You'll head south with another group. Nana will go west, back the way we came with her own group of guides and engage the dragons that way."*

"But there's nothing to the west but a big drop to the Central Valley," Cara protested. She clapped a hand over her mouth, and her eyes grew large. "Rose is taking the chopper, right?"

John's gaze burrowed into hers and he shook his head. *"Wrong. Nana can barely drive a car. It's an astral thing. Don't ask questions. No time to answer them. The last part of the plan is for Dad to lend his weather working power to assist each of us once he's done here. A hard rain should finish them off, if they have no way to return home."*

Cara blinked back astonishment. There were holes in the plan big enough to pilot a 737 through. "What if—"

He shook his head. *"Run hard for the edge of the mesa and beyond. Whether you go up or down is your call. The guides and birds will follow. Once you've drawn off a group of dragons, do exactly what you did last time. Draw earth power, let it use you as a conduit, and destroy them one by one."*

A pained look crossed his face, and he clasped her hard against him. "I love you, Cara. I'll find you when it's over."

"But this could take days," she mumbled.

"No. It'll go much faster than you think."

"Son!" Mark yelled just before dragon fire rained down in earnest.

John sprinted north surrounded by blue-white light and a flock of birds. Sure enough, a group of about ten dragons wheeled away from the main group, following him.

The strident report from Mark's rifle got her moving. If she stayed put, one of his bullets might ricochet and nail her. Cara hoped to hell John was right about the guides and the birds offering her—a non-Native American—protection. They had before, but that was then and this was now.

She put her head down and bolted for the southern end of the plateau. At first she was alone, but then light, blessed light, surrounded her and the kites' cawing pounded against her ears. She didn't waste time looking up. If the dragons had sent a cadre after John, they'd do the same for her.

The edge of the plateau loomed before her. Down was a non-starter. Too much tinder. Cara felt her way across a barely-there ledge system to the next peak over and started up it.

First opportunity, she'd make a stand, but if she remembered the map right, a patch of dicey climbing stood between her and where she could launch an offensive against the dragons.

Cara picked a likely chimney and shinnied upward. Her pack caught on sharp rocks, its fabric ripping when she tore it loose. As she worked her way upward, she asked the mountain gods to watch out for John. What was the point of that binding ceremony if they didn't tackle their foe together?

"Stop thinking," she hissed in frustration. "Climb. One foot. One hand. Next foot. I know how to do this."

Buzzing morphed into voices in her head urging her to hurry.

Cara hurled caution to the winds and leapt from one precarious stance to the next. It worked, and the place she'd envisioned rose to greet her. A horseshoe-shaped patch of rocks with a large lake at its center.

Shucking her pack, she hurried to the lakeshore and spun to face the sky, which was filled with dragons. She started counting and then gave it up for wasted effort. What difference did it make if there were hundreds of the bastards flying above her? The best she could do was to pick them off one by one. Fire rained down on her, deflected by the guides and squawking birds. When the guide's voice in her head fed her instructions, she followed them.

Power flowed from the earth through her, but she wasn't nearly as strong as she'd been last time she'd battled the dragons. By the time the first one exploded, she sank to her knees, gasping for air. Stars spun across her vision, and her aching lungs rebelled.

What the fuck is wrong with me?

Nothing much. A different inner voice shot back acidly. *Not enough sleep. Smoke inhalation. Dehydration. Crashing blood sugar.*

"Get up!" the voice exhorted, not bothering with telepathy. "We've barely begun."

Cara tried. She planted one foot in front of her, knee bent, but before she could force herself upright, blackness descended, and she pitched headlong onto the rocky ground.

The voices escalated, turning to a screech that scoured the inside of her head. What she wanted didn't matter. Her comfort didn't matter. She was the conduit the guides needed, or the dragons would win. Cara gathered her long years of living with extreme hardship in the mountains, and focused every shred of her self-discipline into a desperate lurch that got her standing.

The minute she had her feet under her, power surged, filling her with a pins and needles electricity that fried her from the inside out. A guide grabbed one of her hands. Another did the same on her other side. They raised her arms until her fingers pointed at one of the wheeling monstrosities overhead.

"Release!" a guide shrieked.

Cara felt a dam burst inside her, and the power that had boiled through her boot soles exploded out her fingers. Two dragons shattered into streaks of red gore. The victory heartened her, but not by much. She was amazed her hands were intact. It had felt as if protoplasm shunted out her fingertips along with the magic.

"Again," a guide urged from behind her.

"No resting," another voice intoned.

Cara worked with the guides, aware of birds cawing and

chittering in a black-feathered canopy above her head. For some reason, her power didn't impact them at all. She started to ask why, but the guides must've been mind readers in addition to everything else because one said, "They are of the earth, like us. Anything earthbound is impervious to its destructive nature."

"Good to know," Cara mumbled, not understanding any better than she had before.

She channeled magic until it prickled, cut, and burned. Liquid ran from her nose. When she curled her tongue to taste it, the rich copper tang of her own blood made her shudder. Her cheeks grew wet with drippings from her eyes. Was she crying blood as well?

The thought was so grotesque, she shied away from it. Cara swayed alarmingly. The only thing holding her up were the guides, one on either side. Her vision grayed from the edges in toward the center and a bone-deep weariness pushed from her center outward.

Was this what dying felt like?

She'd exerted herself past the point of collapse many times before. Forced herself to keep going in the face of cold and hunger and sheer misery because there weren't any good choices.

That's it.

Her muzzy brain latched onto the problem. The guides were using her, draining her. Choice had packed up and left long ago.

"Let go of me." She wrenched at both arms, trying to rip them loose from the guides' iron grips. She may as well have been chained to a wall with manacles for all the good her efforts did.

"You can't quit now. There's only one left." The guide's voice was liquid silk in her feverish mind.

"I have to. You're killing me. One more will be the end of me." The minute the words were out, Cara recognized truth in them. The guides would drive her until her body had no more resources. They didn't give a shit. No one would save her. She had to save herself.

"Let me rest for a minute," she pleaded. "Then we'll get the last dragon."

"No! No rest. Keep the channel open for us, human woman," the guide growled low, right next to her ear.

It was a hell of a time for experiments with unknown ability, but Cara took a breath and a chance. With what was precipitously close to the end of her strength, she pulled the power back into her and refocused it right at the guides. It wouldn't kill them. They'd be impervious to its destructive nature just like the birds were. Would it at least make them let go of her?

Cara bit her lower lip so fiercely, pain ratcheted through her and gave it everything she had. With a surprised yelp, the guides let go as a unit, and she hit the ground hard. Even if she died, escaping her role as a human lightning rod was an enormous relief.

Sprawled in the dirt, her last conscious thought was about John and his father and grandmother. Had she done enough? Had she done her part? Would the others die because she'd failed to annihilate the last dragon?

Aw Jesus. God. Please, please let it be enough.

Darkness hit her like a runaway semi. If the guides launched a gargantuan effort to get her up again, she never knew about it.

CHAPTER 19

*D*ashing away from Cara at Mach ten was one of the hardest things John had ever done. She was a climber, not a warrior. Not that he was much of a warrior, either, but he still felt responsible for her being on the front lines and not back home in Visalia operating her guide service.

He sucked back his frustration. What he'd told her was true. If anything happened to her, he'd never forgive himself, but he had to concentrate on what was unfolding around him right now. He'd given Cara what protection he could through the binding ritual, and it was actually the lynchpin that had decided things. Without it, his grandmother might have rethought her insistence about them going four different directions.

Blasts from his father's assault rifle bombarded his hearing. He reached the edge of the mesa. Was he far enough from his father to take on the dragons from here? Going down the mountain seemed unwise. Too many things the dragons could set on fire. He glanced up. Another mountain rose not far from the one he stood on top of. Getting to it would be easy enough, but climbing it would require ropes and hardware. He had a rope, but Cara had most of their hardware.

He hacked out black phlegm, courtesy of all the smoke he'd inhaled and turned to face the dragons. If the guides wanted him to move higher, they'd let him know.

John scanned the skies. Light flared from his father's ordnance. His grandmother's energy pulsed in the middle of a blazing white nimbus suspended over nothingness. Light from the guides surrounded her, but it paled in comparison to the illumination streaming from her.

He'd always known Rose's magic was potent, but that knowledge had remained in the conceptual realm until today. His grandmother was a freaking powerhouse with magic to burn.

Why the hell had she shunted him into being the Sioux's shaman? No matter how long or how hard he studied, he'd never be as strong as she was.

"Pay attention!" A guide's voice—in English this time—cracked like a bullwhip.

"Yes," another chimed in. "Do your part or all will be lost."

Sucking in a tight breath, John opened a channel for earth power to pour through him. He understood teamwork from medicine. He had a role to play here, and it didn't include gawking at his grandmother or watching the pretty lightshow his father's bullets made against the night-dark sky he could finally see.

A red moon—a fire moon—crested the horizon, casting an eerie glow over the mesa. John ignored it too and loosed power at one of nine dragons pouring fire down on him. The birds and guides deflected the worst of it, but their protection wouldn't extend forever if he couldn't make a dent in the numbers ranged against them.

He fought against weariness and inertia. No sleep. Not enough food or water. Breathing smoke for the past few hours didn't help. The constant punishment had damaged the small vessels in his lungs, and they'd take time to recover. On top of all that, he was frantic about Cara. Was she all right? Were the guides protecting her like they said they would?

"Focus. Stop making excuses." He spoke out loud to steady himself and sent destruction winging toward another dragon. He hadn't been kidding when he'd told Cara this would play out fast. According to everything he'd ever read and heard, magical battles never lasted long.

Thunder rolled through the sky, followed by jagged forks of yellow lightning. His father must be deploying magic to destroy the dragons' link with their world. Would the ones left here give up once it was gone?

John didn't think so. They'd have nothing left to lose, and they'd be furious. More peals of thunder shook the earth under his feet. Dragons' frantic bugling followed. The group targeting him flew in a tight circle just before they turned as a unit and headed right toward him.

At least they were closer. It made his job easier. Power flashed through him and two more dragons exploded, leaving shiny red trails across the sky. Four down. Five to go. How maneuverable were they? Wings tight against their scaled bodies, they looked like a squad of suicide bombers.

John ran back toward the middle of the mesa. It beat the hell out of staying put and having them plow into him.

The guides buzzed directions, and John spun to face the dragons. More thunder boomed, followed by a deluge from the sky. Rain came down so hard, the droplets felt like shrapnel jabbing into him.

Mark raced toward him, whooping like a mad man. Raising his rifle, he skidded to a halt long enough to fire into the five remaining dragons. "Add your magic," he shouted. "Double whammy."

John skinned his lips back from his teeth and reached deep. He'd never asked much of his power before, so he had no idea how deep the well ran.

Guess I'll find out.

He focused bright, shining earth power on each of the

dragons in turn. Between that and the weather working and his father's silver and iron ammunition, the creatures exploded one after the other until the sky ran red with their remains. The moon took on an even eerier glow, as if someone had painted it with blood.

Mark clapped him on the back. "Nice work, son. I'm off to see if Ma needs me. I'm guessing she doesn't, but I'd rather have her tell me that herself."

"I'll find Cara. Meet you back at the bird."

"It's as good a plan as any."

John prodded his tired brain into action. "Dad. Before you go. Did you break the gateway?"

A feral, satisfied smile spread across Mark's face, and John wondered if he'd ever known his father at all. "Yeah. It's gone. They can build another one, but it'll take them years."

"How can you know that?"

Mark shrugged. "I just do. You'll learn to listen to your magical side. To trust it." Mark chanted a few words. His astral self detached from his physical body and leapt off the edge of the mesa, moving toward where John had last seen his grandmother.

Dragons. Astral projection. Magic. Gateways.

Shit! What happened to the world I signed up for?

It's gone, but for the best of reasons. That destiny Nana nattered on about caught up with me, and I need to find a way to square it with living my life—

Something jabbed him in the back. He twirled, expecting a renegade dragon they'd missed. Instead it was a bird. The kite had pecked him hard enough to hurt.

"Yes?" He looked askance at the bird.

"Cara needs you," a guide said.

John didn't see how he could have even an iota of adrenaline left, but his heart slapped into triple time rhythm, and his stomach twisted into a sour knot.

"Do you know where she is?" he asked.

"Of course," another guide said. "Follow us. The way is steep and precarious. You will need our help."

The guide's words turned out to be more than prophetic. Long before he reached Cara, John's respect for her climbing skill edged up many notches. In places, the guides lifted him. In others, the birds helped. There were moves he could've made—maybe—but not without ropes and hardware.

He asked the guides how much farther. They didn't answer. Next he asked if Cara was alive.

"You hold the answer to that, shaman. Use your power," a guide said in Sioux probably because the Indian words held a snotty, patronizing note that wouldn't have come through in English.

John tried extending his power to sense Cara, but he needed all his concentration to climb the vertical rock walls. Had the guides lost their collective mind? He didn't see how anyone shy of a mountain goat could've managed this route. If he wasn't careful, he ran out of air and ended up gasping, panting, and immobile in a place where moving so much as a toenail would've sent him catapulting into the void.

His resources were fraying, dangerously thin. He'd been in this place before and needed both water and a quick source of carbs to replenish himself. And to sleep for a week, but that wasn't likely to happen in anything like real time.

"Soon," a guide said.

It was the first encouragement any of them had offered, and John latched onto it. He could do *soon*. Hell, he could do whatever he had to. Cara needed him.

He staggered onto a flat area with a good-sized lake. Was this the right place? Now that he didn't have to concentrate every drop of his existence on climbing, he scanned the area. A dragon came into view, its scaly hind legs planted on the lake's rocky shore. Its gray color had blended in with the boulders at the end of the lake. The thing held Cara in its forelegs.

She wasn't moving.

Red haze covered his visual field, and John bolted for the far end of the lake, drawing magic as he closed the distance between him and the dragon. The guides and birds created a semicircle with him in the middle, and he felt them thrust magic into him. At first the sensation was alarming. He couldn't hold that much magic and not implode into atoms scattered through the magical universe.

"Treat our aid as if it came from you," a guide suggested smoothly as if absorbing enough power to light a small village was an everyday occurrence.

Since he didn't have any better ideas, John focused the borrowed power to determine how he could wrest Cara from the dragon. Its talons pressed into her, leaving red streaks where they'd broken through her flesh. Blood splashed her cheeks and chin.

Fury boiled hot. How dare the dragon hurt his love? He'd make him pay if it was the last thing he ever did. John made a grab for the collected calm that had always carried him through in emergencies. Could he destroy the dragon without hurting Cara? He sent his magic outward, searching for the answer to his question. When it zinged back, he screeched, "Fuck!" The thing had married its essence with Cara's. If he blew it up, Cara would crash right along with it.

"What do you want?" he screamed at the dragon not expecting an answer. Not expecting it to understand English.

"Reestablish the gateway."

John stopped a few feet from the dragon—and Cara. The words in his head hadn't been English, but he understood them just the same. Maybe the guides' magic had something to do with that. Maybe his own was zipping into ascendency. It really didn't matter which.

He shrugged and turned his hands palms upward. "I can't do that. It's gone for good."

"Then your mate is gone for good as well."

The dragon bugled and blew fire skyward.

John lunged at it. He hit it squarely in the side, but he may as well have pitched up against a boulder. The dragon didn't so much as shudder.

What's made with magic can be unmade.

The dragon sent fire at John. He rolled out of its path and pulled power like a maniac, sending it auguring into Cara. His bond with her had to trump whatever the dragon had done. He located the shining threads of their troth, feeding them, strengthening them until he was certain she was his and his alone.

Shifting gears fast, he sent earth magic right into the dragon's heart. It exploded, showering him with the red gore he'd seen splattered across the sky. John leapt forward and gathered Cara into his arms. She had fallen to the rock-littered earth when the dragon blew up.

Had the surfeit of magic injured her further? Had he hurt her when he fed power into their troth bond?

The dragon's remains stung like viscous, liquid fire where they touched his skin. Cara was covered with the stuff, and her skin bubbled and blistered before his eyes. She moaned softly, still deeply unconscious. He walked into the lake with her, not bothering to remove their clothes.

The guides followed them in, and the water developed a soothing, healing aspect, feeling like a balm. He cupped water in a hand and rinsed dragon bits and blood off Cara's face and hair, crooning to her in Sioux. Once she was clean, he sent magic into her, healing magic. Were the guides still feeding power into him? Or was this his own? John had no idea, but he found the broken places inside Cara.

The scorched lungs.

The cuts and bruises.

The blistered skin.

The fear that had seared her soul.

The place the dragon had dug its essence in deep.

Western medicine might have helped with her physical hurts, but the place the dragon had claimed bit deep; so did her fear. Instead of feeling he was failing her by not getting her to an emergency room immediately, he trusted his magic. Believed it was the best thing—the only thing—to bring her back to him.

Chanting rose around him in Sioux, and he joined the guides' musical voices with his own. The pool turned into something sacred, holy. It would save his love. Strong in that knowledge, he kissed her wet forehead, willing her back to consciousness.

Long moments passed with her limp in his arms. He upped the ante on his magic, feeding a steady, healing stream into her very psyche.

"Please," he pleaded. *"Return to me. I love you."*

Cara's eyes opened and she smiled wanly.

John clasped her more firmly against his chest. Relief boiled through him. "Thank God. I was getting worried."

Her smile grew brighter. "You and me both. I was trying to come back, but it wasn't easy. Like I was watching events unfold through a thick window, too thick to break the glass." She paused long enough to take an unsteady breath. "I'm not sure, but I think you just saved me from a dragon."

He brushed his lips over hers. "I did. And I'd do it a thousand times over."

"We can talk about all that mushy stuff later." She sounded so much like the Cara he'd fallen in love with, he laughed.

"What's so funny?"

"You. I'm just so goddamned glad you're alive and in my arms."

"I'm happy about those things too. I have no idea how you managed any of this, but I'm good, we can dry off now."

"My practical darling."

"Always. I need something to eat and drink, and then I'll be good to go."

He snorted. "I followed your route up here. My god, woman! You free climbed that with a full pack."

She raised a brow. "It would appear you did too."

"The guides were motivated to get me up here. They helped. So did the birds."

John carried her to the lakeshore, and she wriggled free and stumbled to her pack. He hadn't noticed it before. She must've shucked it earlier. Cara dug out nuts and dried fruit and a water bottle. He removed his own sodden pack, surprised when everything inside was still reasonably dry.

"Want something?" she asked and sat next to him, shaking her wet hair over her shoulders.

He took a handful of cashews. "Mostly I want you. What happened before I got here?"

Cara shook her head. "What didn't? The climb up here about did me in. I killed one dragon and kind of passed out. The guides weren't pleased. They fell on me like a pack of wolves."

One of the guides hovered nearby and said, "We woke you."

"Yes, if we hadn't," another guide cut in, "the dragons might have left with you as their hostage."

"After the guides roused you. Then what?" John dug into the dried apricots. Once he'd begun eating, he realized how much he needed fuel.

"I killed more dragons. They killed some. I killed some." She made a helpless gesture with one hand. "It's not very clear after that. The guides forced so much power through me, I knew if I couldn't get away from them, they'd be the death of me. I tried to tell them, but they didn't care." She closed her teeth over her lower lip, looking embarrassed. "I, well, the thing is, it was experimental because I really don't know all that much…"

"What'd you do?" John pressed.

"Redirected the earth magic to make the guides let go of me. After that, I passed out for good."

Anger buffeted him. The guides were far from sensitive to

human physiology. "She's right. You could've killed her," he sputtered at the guides.

"Possibly, but only one dragon remained," a guide said. "And we needed to destroy it."

"Unfortunately, we need human energy to focus our own," another guide broke in.

"When the last dragon took it upon itself to capture your mate, we were not able to intervene," a third guide said.

"We are sorry, shaman," they said in unison. "We failed you."

John's anger frittered away. The spirit guides had their own rules, and their own system of seeing the world. He wouldn't change them. In their own way, they'd done their best to keep Cara safe from harm. "You didn't fail me," John replied after a pause long enough to get his roiling emotions under better control. "My beloved is unharmed."

"Only because we herded you here in time," one of his guides noted smugly.

John shook his head. "No. The dragon wanted to return to its world. It was using Cara as a bargaining chip. It wouldn't have killed her until it lost all hope of returning home."

"You may be correct," the guides intoned in unison. "You no longer have need of us, so we shall depart."

"Thank you for your assistance against our foe." John matched the guides' formal intonation.

"No thanks needed. Look for us again soon. We must learn to work together when the stakes aren't quite so desperate."

A crooked smile turned one corner of his mouth upward, and John really meant it when he said, "I'd like that."

Two kites flew close, clacking their beaks within inches of his head as if they were saying, *we told you so*, just before they soared high into the air, and the entire flock vanished, along with the guides.

John blinked hard, staring at the empty space where they'd stood. Magic may have chased him down—forced him to accept his calling—but it would take time to get used to it. He took her hand. "And here I thought medicine was my future—my passion."

"Maybe it still is. You have the best of both worlds now. Your traditional training, and now ever so much more."

"What do you mean?"

"You used our bond, not Western medicine, to bring me back." Cara smiled softly. "I felt it kindle and burn within me. Just before the—"

"The what?" John asked, wanting to know.

She scrunched her forehead in thought. "The dragon. It did something kind of like planting an anchor inside me. It hurt when it happened—our bond fought hard against it—but the dragon's branding hurt even worse when it ripped out of me. You did something to make our bond strong enough to break the dragon's hold."

John pulled her into his arms. "I'm so sorry. I had to act quickly. I sensed the dragon had linked itself to you. If I'd destroyed it, you'd have died too." He took a ragged breath. Nothing would do right now but the unvarnished truth. "I took a chance. A big one. I was banking our bond would be stronger than whatever the dragon had jerry-rigged."

"You guessed right, but maybe it was a few steps better than a guess." Cara turned in his arms and wound hers around him. "Thanks for insisting on our vows. At the time I was skeptical. Not that I wasn't feeling more and more certain you were the only man for me, but I didn't see how the ritual could do us any good when we were so far away from one another."

She leaned her head against his shoulder. "I'm babbling. Don't mind me."

"Babble all you want, darling."

She drew back so she could look at him. "If the dragon needed to bargain to go back to its world, then your dad must've destroyed the gateway. Are they okay? Your nana and your dad?"

"Dad is fine. I suspect Nana is too. And yes, the gateway is gone." He hugged her again. "Damn, you feel good in my arms."

"Well, I can't feel too good. We need to get back to your dad's bird or the ATVs or something before hypothermia sets in. I might have dry clothes in my pack. They should be since they were in a dry bag. I'm going to change into them. You might want to at least consider dry socks. We'll have to rap down those cliffs we scaled to get up here."

"Dangerous territory." He cupped one of her breasts.

"The cliffs are challenging." Her green-gold eyes twinkled. "If you're anywhere near as trashed as I am, watching me change clothes isn't dangerous at all. I could sleep for a week, and I bet you could too."

He cradled her head against his chest. When he thought how close he'd come to losing her forever, it chilled him to his bones. "I am never, never leaving your side again," he murmured.

She leaned into him. "What we did today—the way we did it— worked. The dragons are gone for now. Sometimes doing what's hard is the only way through."

"Another mountain lesson," he murmured.

"Yes. That one might be number thirty-four or thirty-five."

"Someday, you'll have to write them all down for me."

"Someday I will. I love you holding me, but I want out of these wet clothes."

His were clammy and sodden as well, and he dug things out of his pack to change into. It did feel better to trade out the wet garments for dry ones. They might've moved faster, but a few kisses snuck in, distracting them.

Finally ready, they were unfurling ropes and preparing for the journey back when he heard a chopper heading their way. "Looks like we won't have to down climb those cliffs after all."

Cara shielded her eyes with one hand. "I wouldn't be so sure about that. Nowhere here for him to land."

John looked at the rocky ground with a critical eye. "We could clear some rocks, but let's see what Dad and Nana have in mind."

A small box dropped from the bird, landing a few feet away. He walked to it, and picked it up, prying it open. A brief note in his grandmother's handwriting fluttered out.

"What's it say?" Cara bent over his shoulder, reading.

John smoothed the paper and read it too.

See the two of you at home.

You made me proud today.

"Woman of few words," Cara noted.

"Sometimes very few. But these mean a lot. She's never been lavish with praise, and she hasn't said she was proud of me—or anything close—since I left the tribe behind twelve years ago."

"I'm proud of you too." She wound an arm around his waist and kissed his cheek.

The unexpected praise warmed him, but it also made him uncomfortable. He'd done what needed doing not for acclaim, but because it was important. "Let's get moving. I hope we can find a way through the fire when we get lower. The firefighters will be able to put it out now, but it'll take time. Days if not weeks."

Cara chewed her lower lip thoughtfully. "If I remember the map right, and we stay headed north once we get back to the ATVs, we'll miss that big fissure and we should come around on Bakersfield from the northeast."

John played it through his mind. "Yeah. I know that road. And you're brilliant. It just might work."

"It will work." She made her way to where the cliffs began and set up a rappel off one of the boulders.

"How can you be so sure?"

"Because we deserve to have something go right after what we've gone through."

He folded her against him. "We've had the most important thing of all go right. Us."

She swatted his back. "Let go, silly, and clip into this rope.

Now's not the time to get sidetracked. Save that for after we're down."

"You are not a *sidetrack*." He threaded the rope through his breaker bar, double-checked his knots, and stepped backward into space, controlling his descent with one hand.

"Keep those compliments coming," she called after him. "You might win me over yet."

"I already have," he told her when she landed next to him on a narrow ledge and recovered the rope to set up their next rappel.

"That may be true—" she smiled coquettishly "—but I'm told men like women who play hard to get."

"I love you, Cara. Be whomever you want."

"You too. Always." She made a sweeping gesture with one hand. "Your rope, buddy."

CHAPTER 20

Cara guided her ATV over a rocky Jeep track. Despite the bold red line on her map, it was obvious no one had done any maintenance on the road for years. They'd run into the odd boulder, but nothing so large they couldn't push it out of the way working as a team. The problem was more deep ruts and rocks that jolted her—or taxed her tired brain as she maneuvered around them.

She felt battered, and fatigue clawed at her to the point she had to remind herself to focus on the patch of dirt in front of her headlight. Dawn was breaking, but the staunch mountainside to her right would block the sun's direct rays for at least another hour. By then, they might be back at the airport where they'd left Rose's car. At least, they'd be close.

Cara rolled her shoulder blades. First one, then the other. The motion shifted the weight of her pack, and also made her feel a shred more alert. After she returned from an arduous time in the mountains, she usually replayed the dicey parts, running them through her head until she came to terms with decisions she'd made. It was how she'd grown as a climber. Being honest about her mistakes and learning how to do things better next time.

What she'd just lived through didn't fit nicely into any of her pre-constructed methods for dealing with cheating death one more time, though.

That's because I wasn't running my own operation. I was at the mercy of the guides and the birds. And then John saved my bacon from the dragon...

The dragon.

A grim laugh bubbled past her lips, drowned out by the engine noise from her ATV. Not that she hadn't imagined any number of supernatural creatures nipping at her heels in the mountains, but she'd never believed they were anything other than a product of her overactive imagination.

Until now.

The dragons aren't gone permanently, she reminded herself. *They're just gone until they can build another gateway, or bridge, or whatever the fuck it was.*

Maybe by the next time the bastards showed up, she and John would be better prepared.

They came to a fork in the road, and John turned left. Soon the bumpy, uneven surface gave way to graded gravel, and he pulled his vehicle off to one side. She guided hers to a stop right behind him and swung a leg over the seat, not surprised to find herself stiff and sore. Her cell phone trilled from inside her jacket, and she fished it out, thinking the waterproof case was worth its weight in gold.

"Hello?"

"Cara? That you? I got this number off your guide service page from the Net."

She glanced at the caller ID, but didn't recognize the string of numbers. "Yes. Who is this?"

John dragged himself off his ATV and stumbled toward her, his eyebrows furled into question marks. Cara tapped the display to activate the phone's speaker and repeated, "Who is this?"

"Sorry. It's Terry. After I dropped the one dude off at

Bakersfield Memorial, I refueled, grabbed a quick bite, and headed back to the site to pick up more injured. When I couldn't raise anyone on my radio, I found a spot lower down to land the bird and climbed up to where I'd left you off." Harsh breath whistled though the cellular lines. "Jesus fucking Christ. No one is alive up there. And I looked. In fact, I've been looking these past two hours. If it weren't for the vehicles, I'd have thought I wasn't in the right place. And it might have been an artifact of the fire, but the sky came alive with light right after I got there. I don't scare easy, but this whole gig is too bizarre for words. Nothing worked up there, so I'm back where I left the chopper. Least I have cell and radio service here."

The tumble of words slowed but didn't quite stop. "Dr. Cassavettes. Is he with you? Did at least two of you make it out of that hell-spawned hole?"

"Yes. John is with me, and we're all right. We actually found another person at the site, a nurse, and sent her down the mountain on an ATV hours ago. Her name is Robin Nelson."

An uncomfortable laugh escaped him. "I mean, you're a wonder woman and all that rot, but how the fuck did anyone escape whatever happened up there?"

Cara thought fast. Whatever she said would be a story she and John would have to stick with. She sent a frantic look his way, and he nodded encouragement.

She leaned against her ATV and said, "I've been asking myself the same thing. You must've felt the shock waves from an explosion. They would've hit about the time you were five minutes or so out from where we rapped out of your bird."

"Yeah. I felt something, but figured it was just abnormal air currents from the fire being so close."

"And we thought it was an earthquake." John leaned close to the phone. "Dr. Cassavettes here, Terry."

"Damn! It's good to know the two of you are alive. And that nurse too. Wonder how she managed to survive."

"According to her, she was working on a patient when a series of explosions hit. Once she ascertained her patient was beyond anything she could do to save him, she made a run for the creek behind the parking area," Cara said carefully. "After we got her calmed down and sent her on her way, we combed the area for survivors."

"By the time we determined there wasn't anyone we could help," John cut in, "the fire was closing from below, but only from the southeast. We grabbed two of the ATVs and went the only direction we could. First we tried down, but the road was riddled with huge fissures. So we went up instead."

"I remembered a good-sized lake from the map," Cara inserted, weaving a smattering of truth with John's fiction. "So we headed for it. Could only take the ATVs partway. We climbed the rest and waited next to the lake until we thought we could get out of there. Even after we got back to the ATVs, we had to plot a different route because the way in had a hell of a deep fracture. We barely got across it when we were going up. By the time we headed down a fifteen-foot section of the road had caved in."

"Where are you now?" Terry asked.

"Out of the mountains. Maybe eighteen miles from Bakersfield on the northeast side," John replied.

"Want me to come pick you up?" Terry's voice held such anguish, it made Cara's heart hurt. He'd flown dangerous missions for over twenty years, and it was as close as he could come to saying he didn't want to be alone right now.

"Sure," Cara said. "Hang on and I can get you coordinates."

"No need. We're at the corner of…" John rattled off local road numbers.

"Be there very soon." Terry disconnected.

Cara dropped the phone back in her pocket, but not before she noticed over two dozen texts and messages, no doubt from clients wondering what the fuck had happened to her.

John wrapped an arm around her shoulders. "That was a kind thing to do."

She turned her head and smiled softly. "Things come full circle. That rescue Terry alluded to when he picked us up?"

John nodded. "I remember."

"Terry put his life on the line that day. And he's always come through—for me and lots of other climbers. It would've been hard for him to come right out and say he needed to lay eyes on anyone who survived the maelstrom up there, but I knew what he meant. And I also recognize what he needs right now because I've been there."

"Yes. Reassurance life goes on, even after cataclysmic events." John moved so he could thread his arms around her from the front, tangling his hands in her pack straps. "That story we concocted on the fly, it's a good one."

"Yeah. There's enough truth in it, it'll be easy to stick to. Robin was long gone before the rest of it played itself out, so we should be safe enough." She leaned her head into the crook between his neck and shoulder. Even through soot, smoke, and sweat, the forest smells that were unique to John clung to him, and she breathed them in hungrily.

"What do you want to do once Terry drops us at the airport?" John asked.

Cara thought about it. "At some point, I need to see if I even have a business anymore, but before I do that, I want to find a bed and sleep until I'm ready to wake up." She grinned at him. "If you're in that bed, it might take quite a while."

A stray thought intruded, and she frowned. "Crap. Rose said we should go to her house. Did she mean right away?"

"Hey." He brushed his lips across hers. "I'm sure she'll forgive us if we don't report for duty at six a.m."

"I hope so." Cara giggled. "Because we'd already be late." The *whump-whump* of a chopper drew her eyes skyward. "Looks like our limousine has arrived."

"You mean our air charter service." After one more kiss, John let go of her. "I'm actually happy to see him. Leaving the driving to someone else sounds like a winner right now." He flexed his fingers. "I used to drive miles on these back roads when I was a kid, but I don't remember my hands getting quite this sore."

"Better watch it, Cassavettes!" She elbowed him. "It's all downhill once you hit thirty."

"You'd know about that."

Cara snorted. "Never remind a woman of her age. How'd you know, anyway? I never told you."

"I read all about you on your website before I booked that trip. Didn't have to do too much math to come close. Besides, you're the one who brought it up." He retrieved the ATV's keys. "Better get yours too. I figure these vehicles belong to Emergency Services, and they'll want to pick them up at some point. We can leave the keys at their office or one of the hospitals."

She pocketed her keys and grinned. "Hey there, Prince Charming."

"Hey, yourself."

"In case I missed thanking you for saving my life, I'm grateful I'm still here."

John gripped her hand in his, and his blue eyes augured into hers. "I love you, Cara. I want to spend my life with you. I'd have gone to the mat to keep that dragon from hurting you."

Emotion thickened her throat. "I know that. The words don't come easy, but I'm falling in love with you too."

A complex panoply of emotion crossed his face just before he swept her into a hug and slashed his mouth down on hers. She threaded her arms around him, reveling in his solid warmth pressed against her. They were still lost in their kiss when Terry tapped her shoulder and cleared his throat.

Cara jumped and disentangled herself from John. Her face heated, and she grinned sheepishly. "Gosh. I didn't even hear the chopper touch down."

Terry grinned back. "I can see that. Do you guys have everything you need?" He gestured at the ATVs.

"Yeah," John replied. "We're good here."

"Come on, then," Terry said. "I'll get you back to the airport. It's the least I can do." He trotted toward his bird.

Cara read between those lines easily. Terry needed to feel useful. Like his efforts these past few hours had yielded something other than unsolved puzzles and missing, presumed dead, emergency services personnel.

"We appreciate it," she said. "It's been a long night for all of us."

She tried for a jaunty lope toward the chopper, but all she could manage was a tired plod in a more-or-less straight line. Bending low to avoid the prop wash, she stopped at the steps, removed her pack, and handed it up to Terry.

"You go on and get seated, Cara," Terry said. "I'll get the doctor's pack too."

"Thanks." She made her way to the left rear seat and fell into it, buckling in. Cara tried to keep her eyes open, but exhaustion claimed her before the chopper's rotors drew them skyward.

JOHN HATED TO WAKE CARA, but they were on the ground. She hadn't stirred during the short flight back to the airport. For the first time since their frantic race out of Rae Lakes Basin, her face looked relaxed, peaceful.

Terry leaned close, speaking low. "She can sleep for a while. Chopper isn't going anywhere the rest of today—unless they call me in for something."

"Thanks, but it's okay. She'll sleep better when she's not sitting up."

Terry's forehead creased with concern. "Probably so. Wasn't thinking. I'll get your gear out of here."

John moved into the seat across from Cara, leaving the narrow aisle clear for Terry to transfer their packs from behind the seats to the open doorway. He placed a hand on Cara's arm, and her eyes fluttered open.

"Hey, darling," he said. "We're here."

Cara shook her head. "Shit. I must've pretty much passed out." She squeezed her eyes shut and rubbed them with the backs of her hands before opening them again.

"Bodies are like that. They like to have the last word. Come on. We'll go back to the Red Lion. I actually rented that room for the next three days."

"You did, huh?" Her full, chapped lips curved into a rowdy grin. "I like men who plan ahead."

"Dr. Cassavettes?" an unfamiliar voice called from the chopper's open doorway.

John snapped his head around. "Yes?" He helped Cara to her feet and followed her toward the stairs leading out of the bird.

"I'm Dr. Johanssen. Eric Johanssen. Terry radioed he was bringing you in. I head up Emergency Services here in the Central Valley. I know you and Ms. Carlisle must be exhausted, but if I could have just a few minutes of your time to fill out a report, I'd appreciate it."

"Certainly. Of course." John joined Dr. Johanssen and Cara outside the reach of the wash from the slowing rotors and shouldered his pack. Cara already had hers buckled into place. The other doctor was slightly built, and his shaggy black hair was shot with silver. A deeply lined face held tired blue eyes and a square jawline. Dark slacks, a beige button-down shirt, and a tweed sports coat looked like he'd slept in them. Who knew, maybe he had. John pegged him at somewhere north of forty.

Eric offered his hand, along with a weary smile. John shook it, and Cara did too.

"I'm out of here for a few." Terry waved and loped toward the building.

"Don't get too comfy," Eric called after him.

"Eight hours," Terry retorted without even turning around. "The rules say I get eight hours of downtime."

Eric muffled a snort. "As if I need a reminder about FAA regulations."

"We don't have an august body like that standing between us and rest," John said, "so if it's all the same to you, let's get this over with. Or we could come in later on today and take care of your paperwork."

Eric leveled his gaze at John, his expression unreadable. "No. Let's do this now. Ms. Nelson's story was…strange, but she might've been confused. Stress and shock can addle the mind."

Cara angled her head to one side. "We were grateful to find any survivors up there, and we saw Ms. Nelson well on her way to safety. I'm sure she told you that."

"She did." Eric inhaled sharply, but didn't add to his words.

"What happened up on that mountainside was worse than *strange*." John wove what he hoped would be a believability spell into his words. Before he'd walked away from the tribe, he'd employed that particular casting more than once—mostly when he wanted to fool his grandmother, except it never worked. Hopefully, the good Dr. Johanssen wasn't as astute as Rose Cassavettes.

"How so?" Eric shot a meaningful glance John's way.

"Strange enough, I'm not sure anything we have to say will add to your understanding," John murmured still sowing magical seeds, "but lead out."

Eric herded them inside the terminal and then upstairs to a small, cluttered office on the second floor. John dropped his pack near the door and helped Cara off with hers, managing to lean close enough to whisper in her ear to let him handle this.

She sent an annoyed look skittering his way, but settled into one of two chairs. "Say." She smiled at Eric. "Could I have a cup of coffee or a coke?"

"Sure. I wasn't thinking, or I'd have offered," Eric replied. "Which would you prefer?"

"Coffee," Cara said. "One sugar. One cream."

"Since I'm getting something for her…" Eric eyed John.

"Let's make it easy. I'll have the same. Do you need help?"

"You're kidding, right? It's two Styrofoam cups. I think I can handle that."

"Appreciated." John waited until the other man left the room and scooted his chair right next to Cara's. "Brilliant move," he whispered. "But he won't be gone long. Trust me to get us out of here."

She met his gaze and mouthed, "Magic?"

The corners of his mouth twitched. "Yup. Let's see if it works."

"If not, I'll ply my feminine wiles to bail us out."

A laugh bubbled up from his belly, forcing its way out. "Just don't ply too many of them," he retorted right before Eric trotted back into the room, coffee sloshing over the sides of two cups.

"What's so funny?" Eric demanded, handing their cups over. "I could use a joke. Things have been downright grim around here."

"Nothing really. More delayed relief reaction to these past few hours than anything else." John took a slug of coffee. It was hot and bitter and had clearly been sitting in a pot for far too long, but the jolt of caffeine was welcome when it hit.

"Mmph." Eric grabbed two clipboards and a couple pens, offering one to Cara and the other to John. "Fill these out, please."

John worked his way through what turned out to be ten pages of repetitive questions, occasionally casting sidelong glances Cara's way. Her eyebrows were drawn into a thoughtful line as she scribbled answers to the endless series of questions.

"Here." She thrust her clipboard at Eric and downed the rest of her coffee. "Mind if I find the ladies' room and maybe more java?"

"Go right ahead." Eric bent over the clipboard she'd handed him, and Cara left the room.

"Here's mine." John passed his clipboard across Eric's desk.

"Who designed this form? And why don't you have computer terminals for people to sit at? It would go a whole lot faster than writing things out longhand. So much of this was me writing the same thing in a new box. Easier to copy and paste."

Eric rolled his eyes, the first halfway human gesture he'd made since showing up on the helipad, and John took it as a positive sign. "I've been arguing with the powers that be to revamp these forms for years. Give me a few to slog through your responses."

It worked for John. He focused *believe us* spells as fast as he could craft them and shunted them right at Eric, gratified when the other man flipped through the pages of Cara's account and then moved on to what he'd written. Eric was right to be suspicious, but even if John had written a blow-by-blow account of last night, the other man would never believe any of it.

Damned if you do and damned if you don't.

Cara slid back through the door and into her seat, handing him a fresh cup of coffee, twin to her own.

Eric laid the second clipboard aside and looked from one to the other of them. "How was it you discovered the lake where you ended up?"

"That's easy." Cara offered a pleasant smile, and John could've hugged her.

"Indeed it is," John seconded. "She—" he nodded toward Cara "—has an eidetic memory when it comes to maps. She recalled seeing it, and we agreed it was the safest place. In case the fires continued to head our way."

"But Robin was able to ride out of there," Eric protested. "You had access to the same type of all-terrain vehicle. Why didn't you simply follow her—once you determined there were no other survivors?"

"We tried." John layered lies with spells. "But by then the track Robin took had developed deep fissures from a series of earthquakes. They forced us upward."

"That was when I suggested we head for the lake. It was really hard to see with all that smoke," Cara added. "Disorienting as hell."

"You couldn't have driven all the way to that particular lake."

"Nope. We had to abandon the vehicles and climb," John agreed.

Eric narrowed his eyes. "That's really, really rough terrain. Near vertical granite cliffs."

Cara set down her coffee and offered her hands palms upward. "What can I say? I was a mountain goat in a previous life, and I guide for a living. We had ropes and hardware."

Never mind we didn't use them, John added silently.

Cara's upbeat response earned her a smile from Eric, and he set the clipboard down and folded his hands in front of him. "I'll probably never fully be able to picture what happened up there, but the fire crews are finally making excellent progress. Wind's died down, which helps. Do either of you want to stop by an emergency room?"

"We're not injured," John said, recognizing that Eric was within an angstrom of releasing them. "Just bone-tired."

"All right. I can take a hint. Thanks for your cooperation."

"You're quite welcome." Cara stood and extended a hand. Eric shook it. When he let go, she walked to her pack and hefted it over her shoulders. "See you out at the car," she told John and walked out the door.

John got to his feet as well and reached for Eric's hand. The other man's grip was crisp and firm. "You know where to find me if you have any other questions."

"Indeed I do." Eric released his hand, and John gathered his pack. He'd just turned to follow Cara when Eric said, "You recently finished your residency in family medicine, correct?"

John turned. "You nailed me dead to rights. Why?"

"What are your plans?"

John's face grew warm. "I was going to Africa with Doctors Without Borders, but that was before Cara came into my life."

"Ah. I see." The corners of Eric's eyes crinkled as he smiled. "We can always use doctors with climbing skills in Emergency Services. Think about it. If it sounds good, our main office in this region is in Fresno. You could get an application packet online and file it either that way or in person. We take both fulltime and per diem applications."

John didn't bother trying to hide his surprise. He'd spent the last hour doing his best to hornswoggle Eric Johanssen, and here the man had practically offered him a job. In fact, the expectant look on his face required an answer.

When he recovered a shred of equanimity, John said, "Thanks for the offer. I appreciate it. Always good to be wanted. Plus, I'll have a wife to support soon."

"From the looks of things—" Eric chuckled softly "—the last thing she'll need any man for is to support her. Congratulations, and best of luck regardless of what you decide about the job."

John retraced his steps down the hall and the stairs and out of the terminal. He caught up with Cara when she was nearly to his grandmother's car. "What kept you?" she asked and tossed her pack into the trunk once he opened it.

"He offered me a job." John placed his pack next to Cara's.

"Wow! That's a surprise." She pulled the passenger door open and dropped into the front seat.

"Sure was," he agreed and fed the key into the ignition. "Is back to the Red Lion okay with you?"

"Yup. More than okay." She didn't say anything for the next few minutes. "Funny about that job offer."

John glanced sidelong at her. "Why's that?"

"Because I was thinking maybe you could hook up with my guide service and be the team doc on my expeditions."

"When I'm not doctoring for the local clinic or Emergency Services or maybe Indian Health?" John laughed.

"Something like that. Told you that you guys were in demand." Cara laughed right along with him. "Aw hell," she managed through snorts and giggles, "let's not get too far ahead of the curve here."

"Right. How about sleep and sex and food, not necessarily in any particular order."

"I like how you think. The world will wait until we resurface."

"Maybe not Nana, but the rest of the world will definitely leave us be."

"I'll take my chances with Rose. She likes me."

"Indeed she does." John nosed the car into the Red Lion's half-empty parking lot. He couldn't wait to go upstairs and close the door behind himself and Cara. Maybe they'd sleep for a bit. Or maybe they'd shower first. Memory of her perfect ass blasted across his visual field, and his cock jumped to attention, achingly hard.

He turned off the ignition, twisted to face the woman who meant everything to him, and drew her into his arms.

CHAPTER 21

The kiss that began in the car had grown so heated, they'd grappled with one another through their clothes, reluctant to let go for long enough to head for their room. Her breasts ached, the nipples peaked with wanting the man by her side, and it took all her self-discipline not to reach for the tented out front of his trousers as they walked into the hotel. Considering the hour, they passed quite a few people in both the lobby and the stairwell. It was enough that they were smeared with dirt, soot, and God only knew what else. Plus, they probably didn't smell very swift. No point in compounding their sins with a display of public sex.

Cara stumbled through the door of their suite. It had taken an ungodly amount of time, lugging her heavy pack, to get there, but the door was finally barred against intrusion. Her crotch throbbed with need, and her underwear was slick with her fluids.

She unbuckled her pack and dropped it behind the door. John did the same and closed his arms around her from behind, filling his hands with her breasts. She leaned against him, loving the hard length of his erection butting into the curves of her ass.

He nuzzled her neck and murmured, "You taste like smoke."

"And sweat and probably dragon bits," she countered, turning in his arms and wrapping hers around him. "Want to hit the shower, first?"

He winked and then ran his tongue over the curve of her ear. "So long as we get a replay of our last shower, I'm good with that." He pushed his hard on into her stomach, and a flash of sexual heat blasted her.

She rubbed herself against him, gratified by the low, tortured moan that escaped at the increased contact. "We have to get these clothes off. How about this? Race you to the shower."

He held on tighter. "What does the winner get?"

"Position of their choice."

"You're on, wench!"

She jerked away and bent to unlace her boots. They'd take longest. Once they were off, the rest of her clothing would disappear fast. Next to her, John knelt to work on his own bootlaces. Cara toed one boot off, following it with the other and her socks. She slid out of her jacket and yanked her top over her head. Her sports bra came next.

"Not fair." John reached for her naked breasts. "You have the body of a goddess."

She rolled out of the way and got to her feet. "It's all fair, sweetie. I'm winning." Cara fumbled with the button and zipper that held her pants in place and pushed them down her legs, along with her underwear. Stepping out of everything, she sprinted for the bathroom and flipped on the jets. The water was cold, but she got into the oversized, multi-jet shower anyway.

John joined her moments later. He spun her to face him and covered her mouth with his own as gradually warmer water pounded down on them from every direction. Cara opened her mouth to his questing tongue, sparring with it, and she tangled her hands in his hair. He nipped her lower lip. She bit back, sucking his tongue and wishing it was his cock inside her mouth.

The cock she lusted after pressed against her belly,

tantalizingly long and thick and hard. She wanted to do everything. Touch him, kiss him, take him into her body. John shifted his hands from their slow, enticing journey down her back to her thighs. In a single, fluid motion, he lifted her, seating himself at the opening to her body.

Cara wriggled until he slid inside, groaning with pleasure as he stretched her, exploring her depths. She wrapped her legs around his slender hips and tightened herself around him.

She stopped kissing him long enough to say, "Thought I got to pick." Her words came out garbled because she was so hot, she could barely think.

He ran his tongue up the side of her neck. "Just say the word, darling. We can arrange ourselves any way you want to."

A host of lascivious poses raced through her mind in an XX-rated slideshow. All they did was stoke her lust. He lifted her and drove himself home. "We can get fancier later, darling," he whispered into her ear and upped his tempo.

Cara splayed her hands across his back, digging in hard. The only thing in the world was him inside her, and her body close to release as he thrust into her, growing thicker and harder by the moment.

"Now, Cara. Come with me now." His words washed over her, silky and smooth.

Maybe it was the power of suggestion, maybe it was his magic at work, but an orgasm boiled from the depths of her belly, followed almost immediately by another as the spasms of his release drove her over the crest once more. Panting and gasping, she clung to him, and he murmured musical words in Sioux.

"I want to learn that," she said when she could talk.

"Learn what?" He lifted her off his still-hard cock and let her down until her feet contacted the wet marble.

"Sioux."

He traced the lines of her cheekbones with his thumbs. "I'm sure that could be arranged."

She reached for the collection of soaps and shampoos in the small basket suspended off to one side and quirked a brow. "Sooner we get clean, the sooner we can get down to more of the same."

"What?" He grabbed a round of soap and lathered her breasts, belly, and legs. "No room service first?"

"Only unless you can't get it up without it." She cast a meaningful glance at his penis before covering it with foamy lather. "Not looking as if that's going to be a problem."

"I like a woman who knows what she wants. Turn around. I'll wash your hair. Then we'll get mine and we'll be clean enough."

A snort bubbled past her lips. "Another lesson from life in the backcountry. Since anything is an improvement over the stinky messes we were when we came into the room, we don't have to be too particular."

He massaged soap into her hair, and then rinsed it with one of the handheld jets. "Oh, I'm very particular. Never found a woman I wanted to spend forever with before."

Emotion sluiced through her until her heart cracked wide open and spilled over. Her throat was thick and speech impossible, so she worked on his hair until she got herself under control.

"You sound sure," she said and placed the shower nozzle back in its holder.

John turned her in his arms so she faced him and shut off the water. "I am sure." He kissed the tip of her nose. "Besides, we're already joined, one to the other. The words we shared before we separated to battle the dragons bound our souls together."

Confusion speared her. She hadn't thought the ritual was permanent.

Would I have agreed to it if I knew?

When the answer came, joy thrummed through her and she felt the quick, hot bite of tears. "You don't know me very well," she stammered, determined to be honest no matter what. No matter how badly she wanted to spend the rest of her life with John Cassavettes.

"I know the important parts. We'll figure out the rest as we go." He pushed the glass door open and stepped onto the bathroom's floor, grabbing two towels. He wrapped one around her and tucked the other around his waist. Once his was secure, he got another towel and placed it around her head to catch the drips from her hair.

"You're quiet," he observed. "Is anything wrong?"

Cara shook her head and toweled her hair drier before she locked gazes with him. "Can it really be this easy?"

"It can be anything we want it to be," he replied, his tone solemn. "We get to write our own script." He took a measured breath. "For example, I used to see my obligation to the Sioux as a millstone. It's not that at all. My grandmother bestowed an honor on me when she passed the shaman baton. She wouldn't have done it if she didn't trust me to rise to the challenge."

Cara closed her teeth over her lower lip. "Say more. I'm not quite getting the connection. I understand the part about the tribal stuff, but how does it apply to us?"

"Simple. The way we view what comes our way creates our future. If we look at something as an unwanted obligation, it becomes one. You got a rotten break growing up, and you picked a man who mirrored the emotional negativity."

Cara opened her mouth to protest she hadn't viewed Leif that way—not in the beginning, but John held up his hand. "I'm not quite done. That wasn't a criticism. You've kept to yourself these last ten years because you didn't trust yourself not to make another mistake."

Cara nodded. "That's true enough."

"For whatever reason, we found each other. I admire you. You're strong, gutsy, principled, and you love the same things I do. The mountains drew us together, and they'll be one of the things that defines us as a couple."

Cara winced. "Leif and I had the mountains. It wasn't enough."

John leaned close and kissed her cheek. "I'm not him. I'll never cheat on you, for one thing." He tipped her chin up with one finger. "Can you let go of the past long enough to take a chance on us?"

Well, can I?

The joy that had filled her earlier resurfaced. Her eyes flooded and she said, "Yes. I can do that. In truth, I already have in lots of ways that matter."

A smile began in his blue eyes and traveled to his mouth, and he gathered her against him. "You'll never be sorry."

"I hope the same is true on your end." Her words were muffled against his neck.

"Don't doubt yourself. You're everything I've ever wanted." He picked her up and carried her through the sitting room and into the bedroom, laying her across the bed.

WARMTH AND CARING—AND most of all hope—blazed from her, warming his soul. John gazed at her body, splayed out before him. "You're such an amazing gift," he said and settled on the floor with her pussy at mouth level. She let her legs fall open in clear invitation, and he fastened his mouth over her sensitive nub. He licked, sucked, and nipped while he plunged two fingers deep into her scorching core.

Her hips bucked and thrust as he teased her, backing off when she got close to release. His cock was so hard it was about to explode, and he wrapped his other hand around his shaft, building his arousal, but holding himself just shy of orgasm.

Her nub swelled in his mouth, and her muscles clamped down on his fingers. He lifted his face, and took in pebbled nipples and a lovely rose color splashed across her face and breasts. Her head was tossed back, her eyes closed, and her fingers grappled with the bedcovers.

"Incredible. Beautiful. Tell me what you want, sweetheart."

Instead of answering with words, she curled forward enough to latch her hands beneath his arms urging him upward. Once he lay atop her, she rolled them so she was on top, and she straddled him, taking the length of him inside her. The heat of her body almost undid him, and he drew strands of magic to hold himself back.

Cara sat astride him. He reached for her breasts, twirling the nipples between his thumbs and forefingers. A randy grin turned her into how he'd always imagined Aphrodite might look. She rose on his shaft and lowered herself, passion plain on her face. He traded her breasts for her hips and controlled their rhythm. Making love with Cara was perfect. Their bodies fit together as if they'd been made for one another.

The cadenced rise and fall of her hips quickened, followed by the rhythmic contractions that told him she was coming. When a climax shuddered from his balls, it caught him by surprise. He'd thought he was on top of his arousal, but his body had the last word.

Laughing softly because he was so happy, he pulled her into his arms and covered her mouth with his. She met his tongue and lips with ardent kisses, sometimes running her mouth and tongue to the side to tickle his neck and ear.

The sound of someone knocking intruded. John ignored it, thinking it must be one of the other doors. When it escalated, he broke their kiss and murmured. "Did you call for room service?"

"Nope. I was wondering when you'd had time to, but you're a magic man, so I figured maybe you sent a subliminal suggestion to the kitchen." A smile illuminated her face, making her even more beautiful. "Food would be great. I'm starving."

More knocking. Whoever was at the door wasn't going away.

"I didn't order anything," John said. "Honest, but I will see who's there."

He closed the bedroom door to make sure Cara had privacy and stopped by the bathroom to belt himself into one of the thick terrycloth robes the hotel left for their guests.

Either whoever had been at the door had given up, or they knew he was on his way to open it, because the insistent pounding had ceased somewhere between the bedroom and the bathroom. He rolled his eyes. Unless someone had mistaken his door for another, he'd bet his Sioux heritage that either his father or grandmother was on the far side of the door.

He considered sending his magic outward to assess just who'd bothered them, but gave it up. Magic was far from second nature to him, and he'd blown through a whole lot in the mountains. He tugged the door open.

Rose Cassavettes and her son stood there, knowing grins plastered across their faces.

John herded them inside. Asking how they'd found him was pointless. They'd tracked him with magic. "What?" he demanded, closing the door. "Were you just going to keep hammering until hotel security threw you out?"

"Whatever works," his father replied. "I tried your cell. You didn't answer."

Rose waltzed into the bathroom and came out with a robe tossed over her arm. "Pretty fancy digs," she said and strode to the bedroom door. After knocking once, she opened it and dropped the robe over a chair before shutting it again.

"Thanks," Cara called.

"I have ulterior motives," Rose called back through the door.

"What might they be?" John folded his arms across his chest. "Don't we get twenty-four hours off after last night?"

His grandmother shot him a condescending look. "How about if the two of you get dressed and meet us in the restaurant downstairs. We'll have breakfast—or more likely lunch at this point—and figure out what comes next."

Cara padded out of the bedroom, wrapped in the robe Rose had brought her. "I heard some of that," she said. "Neither of us has anything clean to wear. The hotel restaurant might not want us anywhere near the other dining patrons, but we could order something up here."

"Good idea," Mark said. "It's more private anyway."

"How about this?" John suggested. He glanced at a clock. "It's closing on two. There's nothing so pressing it won't wait until supper. Cara and I will buy some clothes that don't reek of smoke, and we'll stop by a laundromat and wash the dirty stuff—"

"That'll work," Rose broke in before he was done. "But give me your dirty clothes. I'll wash them up for you."

"You don't need to do that," Cara said.

"I know that," Rose snapped. "I want to. You're family now. Just like my Johnny. That's what families do. Help each other."

"I don't know much about the good side of families." Cara smiled shyly. "I'm looking forward to finding out."

Rose covered the short distance to Cara and gave her a quick, hard hug. "You'll be a good granddaughter-in-law. Have faith in yourself." Stepping away, she nodded to Mark, and the two of them walked to the door.

"Hand over those things you need washed. Shall we say six o'clock at my house?" Rose asked.

"We'll be there," John said.

Cara gathered their trashed clothing from off the floor, while John searched for the laundry bag he was certain he'd find in the closet. He pulled his pack open and dragged his clothing bag out, sorting to leave himself something to put on until they could go into a store and buy fresh duds. Cara did the same.

Soon, he handed a bulging sack to his grandmother. Rose snorted. "Climbing's dirty business, huh?"

"It is," Cara agreed. "Are you sure it's not an imposition?"

"We've covered that ground," Rose said, handing the bag to Mark.

"Would you at least like us to bring something to add to supper?" Cara persisted.

Rose smiled. "Surprise me."

Mark added, "Tomorrow or the next day, I can fly the two of you back to see if we can't retrieve your cars."

"Really? That would be great," Cara replied.

"Should work," Mark said. "They've reopened the road from where I picked you up through Lake Isabella." He pulled the door open, and he and Rose left.

John took Cara's hand and led her to one of the small, overstuffed couches. "I figured Nana would show up—just not quite so soon."

"It's okay." Cara leaned into him. "I like being cared about. It won't be a hard thing to get used to, and it was really kind of your father to offer his helicopter to rescue our cars."

"Dad's always been a gem. Nana is crusty and opinionated, but—"

"But nothing." Cara spoke over him. "I like her. Want to order something from the kitchen?" She reached for a menu on a side table.

"Sure. It's a long time till dinner, and we have every right to be hungry. How about the same as we got last time?"

Cara shook her head. "Hard to believe that was less than twenty-four hours ago. Sure. Salads, cake, French fries, soup. What else?"

"It's a great start." He waited while she dialed room service, noticing with pleasure that she added a couple of unsweetened iced teas to their order. "Thanks, I like my tea without sugar too."

"I have a feeling we like a whole lot of the same things." She put the phone down.

He pulled her into his lap. "I meant what I said earlier about us writing our own script. I'd like to doctor on some of your expeditions, and I think I'd like working for Emergency Services part time too."

"Would you want to live in Visalia?" She focused her forthright gaze on him.

"Sure. I cleared out my apartment in Las Vegas. Everything is in storage."

Cara nodded enthusiastically. "I have lots of room. Bought this five-bedroom house after the real estate market crashed and everything was dirt-cheap. I only live in a couple of the rooms."

Happiness swelled in him, and he cradled her protectively against his chest, with an arm around her shoulders. "We'll want to get married."

"I thought we already were." She quirked a brow. "Shouldn't you be down on one knee or something?"

"Western marriage, so the neighbors don't think we're living in sin," he clarified with a warm smile. "I'll get down on one knee if you'd like. And buy you whatever kind of rings you'd like."

"No rings. Too easy to snag on rock faces." A small line formed between her brows. "Will our plans fit with whatever Rose has in mind for you?"

He nodded. "Yeah. They will."

"How can you know?"

"I'll make sure of it. Like Nana said, have faith."

"Not exactly what she was referring to."

John thought about it. "Yes," he said. "I believe it was. No one will ask more of us than we have to give. It's important for me to believe that too. I'm not going to give up doctoring. You're going to keep guiding. We'll find a balance point that gives both of us what we need."

She nodded solemnly. "We'll make things work. I love you."

"Darling." He tightened his hold on her. "I love you too."

A stout knock announced room service, and John kissed her nose before he got up to answer the door. By the time he signed the chit and wheeled the tray inside, she'd moved to the table and helped him transfer their late lunch onto it. For a time they ate in a companionable silence. He liked that she didn't need to fill every second with chatter.

Cara set her fork down and glanced at the clock across the room. "Mind if I close my eyes for a few? I want to be awake for dinner at your Nana's house, and if I don't get at least a little rest, I'm afraid I'll pitch face down on her table."

"Of course I don't mind. I'll join you. I'm tired too. I'll just get my cell and set the alarm so we don't oversleep. I want to leave us an extra half hour to buy some clean clothes."

"Good idea." She got up and kissed the top of his head before making her way to the bedroom.

He located his phone and set it. Cara was already asleep when he walked across the thick carpet and into the bedroom. For a while, he watched her slumber. Dark hair still damp from their shower spilled down her shoulders and back. Protectiveness surged and he vowed to be worthy of the woman who'd dismantled long-standing barriers enough to trust in a future with him.

When his eyes refused to stay open a moment longer, he lowered himself to the bed, careful not to disturb her, and let sleep claim him.

This is the end of *Fire Moon*. There are three more books in the Alphas in the Wild Collection. *Hello Darkness, Alpine Attraction,* and *A Run For Her Money.* You might enjoy them as well. Available for individual sale as well as in a boxed set titled *Alphas in the Wild* that contains Books 1-3.

If you enjoyed this backcountry adventure romance series, you might like *Icy Passage.* It takes place in Antarctica, a place near and dear to my heart. Read on for a sample.

ABOUT THE AUTHOR

Ann Gimpel is a USA Today bestselling author. A lifelong aficionado of the unusual, she began writing speculative fiction a few years ago. Since then her short fiction has appeared in a number of webzines and anthologies. Her longer books run the gamut from urban fantasy to paranormal romance. Once upon a time, she nurtured clients. Now she nurtures dark, gritty fantasy stories that push hard against reality. When she's not writing, she's in the backcountry getting down and dirty with her camera. She's published over fifty books to date, with several more planned for 2018 and beyond. A husband, grown children, grandchildren, and wolf hybrids round out her family.

Keep up with her at www.anngimpel.com or http://anngimpel.blogspot.com

If you enjoyed what you read, get in line for special offers and pre-release special reads. Sign up for Ann's newsletter on her website or her blog.

ICY PASSAGE, CHAPTER ONE

Micah Greenwich sucked air as he pushed up from his squat, a weight bar balanced across his shoulders. He did one more squat before a wave of dizziness threatened to bring him to his knees. Gasping, he shucked the bar onto pins protruding from the back of the squat rack and grabbed one of the metal stanchions for support. A headache pounded behind one eye, and he felt nauseous.

"What the fuck is wrong with me?" he muttered, still clinging to the metal cage shoved in a back corner of the gym at McMurdo Station, Antarctica. No one was in the gym. Not at this hour. Granted, the perpetual night for part of the year, followed by perpetual day, yielded some odd circadian rhythms, but Micah rarely had competition for any of the gym machines or weight equipment late at night.

He glanced at the weight plates balanced on the ends of the forty-five pound bar, thinking perhaps he'd misjudged and put too much weight on it, but that wasn't the issue. He shrugged. Maybe he was getting sick. Something was going around. So far, he'd been lucky during his brief stint at the southern end of the

Earth and had avoided the colds and flus McMurdo residents passed among themselves like candy.

He wiped sweat from his face with a ratty towel and decided to call it a night—at least for working out. He still needed to stop by his lab. Because he was the newest and greenest microbiologist, he'd been assigned archaea, the most ancient single-celled life form on the planet. His cultures had taken a decidedly odd turn, though, a couple of weeks back—growing like mad and not looking like any prokaryote he'd ever seen. While he might have started with archaea, what was in his bins didn't look much like them anymore.

Another wave of nausea battered him, and he folded his arms around his midsection, wondering if he was going to vomit. Saliva flooded his mouth, but he choked it back. Even though he didn't feel like doing anything beyond finding his bed, he left the gym and made his way three buildings over to his lab. McMurdo was a series of prefab buildings with interconnecting doors and insulated tunnel-walkways, so you didn't have to go outside into the weather. Antarctica never got particularly warm, and nights were always bitter.

He glanced out a window at an inky sky shot with stars, and a reluctant smile split his face. It might be minus something outside, but it was beautiful too. He'd always loved wild, remote places, and Antarctica was about as wild and remote as it got—shy of signing up to be an astronaut, which was a long-standing dream of his.

Micah frowned, wondering if the astronaut gig was even possible. The United States had cut their funding for the space program rather dramatically. Besides, he needed more in the way of credentials to even be considered for something like that. With another swipe at his still sweaty face—the more he thought about it, the surer he was he was coming down with the flu—he pushed open the door to his lab and froze, not believing his eyes.

"Britta?" he called. "Marguerite!"

The women didn't answer. They sprawled face down on the floor in front of his main workbench, clearly passed out. Wondering if they'd gotten into the high-grade, ethyl alcohol he used to preserve things, he called their names again, louder this time. The longer he looked at them, the weirder he felt. They were too still. Sudden fear gripped him, making the nausea worse.

"Jesus fucking Christ. Why me?" he muttered, and raced to the women. He bent, grabbed Britta's shoulder, and shook her. When she didn't respond, he flipped her over and stared at her cherry-red face.

Fighting a deeply sinking feeling, he turned Marguerite over. She looked just like her friend and roommate. Micah squatted next to them and laid his fingers across their necks, searching for a pulse.

Nothing.

He placed his ear over their hearts, willing there to be something, anything, before he started CPR. Still nothing. He ground his teeth together, unnerved. How could there possibly be two dead women in his lab?

Even though he was pretty sure it wouldn't do any good, he tilted Marguerite's head back and breathed into her mouth before doing chest compressions. When he looked over at Britta, he understood he had to have help and lurched to his feet. Snapping up the wall phone, he punched in the after hours code for the clinic. As soon as one of the nurses answered, he screeched, "Send help now. Third micro lab."

His headache worsened. So did his twisting, roiling guts, but he went back to the women. He didn't need to be a doctor to recognize death. Despite the futility, he alternated CPR from one to the next. Five long minutes passed—but they felt like five years —before the door burst open.

"Christ!" One of the docs—Stewart maybe, Micah was too rattled to take a good look—pulled him off Marguerite. A tall, broad-shouldered woman Micah didn't recognize examined Britta.

"Looks like carbon monoxide poisoning to me," the female medic said flatly. "This one's well past CPR."

Dr. Stewart rocked back on his heels. "Yeah, her too." He trained his blue eyes on Micah. "What happened?"

Micah shook his head. "Damned if I know. I just got here. I had dinner in the mess hall, worked out in the gym, and then I swung by here to check on my cultures."

The woman narrowed her eyes and half-crawled to where Micah sat on the floor. She folded her fingers over his wrist and took him in with practiced hazel eyes. Her reddish hair was short, almost in a butch cut. She pressed her lips into a harsh line, frowning.

"I'm Ariana," she said, letting go of his wrist. "One of the nurse practitioners. How have you been feeling?"

"Bad," he admitted. "Think I finally succumbed to the community disease everyone else has."

Dr. Stewart joined them and squatted next to Micah. He ran a hand down the side of Micah's neck and listened to his chest with a stethoscope before exchanging a pointed glance with Ariana. "Where's the CO meter in here?" he asked.

Micah gestured behind him. "On that wall." He twisted to look at it, but the indicator light was green—safe. Maybe it was defective. His scientifically trained mind arranged informational bits into an unpleasant pattern. "The women," he said. "If I'd been firing on all cylinders, I'd have figured it out as soon as I looked at the color of their faces. They died from carbon monoxide poisoning, didn't they?"

"Probably," Dr. Stewart said cautiously. "But it's conjecture at this point."

"That cherry-red color is a dead giveaway," Ariana said with conviction. "Nothing else will do that."

"We'll wait for an autopsy before we make statements like that." The doctor eyed his colleague coolly.

"Yes, Doctor. Sir. King of all things medical." She set her lips in a thin line, clearly biting back further sarcasm. "Meantime," she ground out, "I'm pretty sure he—" she jabbed a finger at Micah "—has whatever killed these two." She stood and punched numbers into the wall phone. "I'm calling security."

Dr. Stewart sifted his hands through his untidy, blond hair. "Tell them to alert maintenance. Until we figure out what killed these two, we've got to get out of here. Now."

Micah straightened. "Wait a minute," he sputtered. "The meter says it's safe. For all we know, Britta and Marguerite got poisoned elsewhere and just happened to be in here cleaning when they collapsed."

Dr. Stewart got to his feet and hauled Micah upright. "For tonight, we'll put you in the infirmary and run tests to check if your hemoglobin's been compromised. I've got to alert the boss and talk with base security. We'll to get to the bottom of this."

"But my lab—"

Dr. Stewart made a chopping motion with one hand, and the rest of Micah's protest died unspoken.

Ariana hung up the phone and nodded at Dr. Stewart. "You take care of the boss. I'll deal with security and maintenance. Need to get the gas sniffer in here to make sure there's not a leak."

Micah tried to focus, but the room spun crazily. He really was wiped out. Much more tired than a thirty-year-old man had a right to feel.

"Can you walk?" Dr. Stewart nudged him.

Micah focused bleary eyes on the physician. "Yeah. I think so."

"How are you feeling?" Ariana asked the doctor.

He shrugged. "Normal. But it takes time for exposure to take a toll. Micah probably lives in this lab, except when he's asleep."

"Yeah, but," Micah pointed out, "those women didn't. They

clean all the science labs. Maybe one of the other ones is the problem."

The doctor folded an arm around Micah's waist supporting him, and led him out of the lab. "I'm on it. By the time you wake up, we'll know more."

Micah staggered through the door, flanked by Dr. Stewart and Ariana. "What are you going to do about the women?" he asked.

"You were there when I alerted base security. They'll take care of them," Ariana assured him. "For tonight, focus on getting well."

IT HADN'T BEEN JUST that night, though. Micah spent the next three days in the infirmary sucking bottled oxygen. When that didn't clear his red blood cells fast enough, the doctors ordered chelation treatments. In the meantime, he had a chance to think, and he didn't care for what he came up with. Besides, it was so fantastic, no one would believe him.

Maintenance had given his lab, and the other three microbiology studios, a clean bill of health, which meant he could go back to work tomorrow. Even more disturbing, the entirety of the science wing where the dead women cleaned showed zip in the way of evidence of a gas leak. In the interest of thoroughness, maintenance had checked the female dorms too, and found exactly nothing. Autopsy was conclusive regarding cause of death, but no one could figure out how the women had been exposed to a big enough dose of carbon monoxide to kill them.

The same was true for him—major exposure to something pigging up his hemoglobin, but without an identifiable source. Another few hours without medical intervention and he'd have been just as dead as Britta and Marguerite.

Armed with that knowledge—and a phalanx of unanswered questions—Micah spent his downtime in the infirmary mapping out a series of tests to run on his strange archaea colonies. He had suspicions, but needed facts before he presented them to Jack DeVoe, the man in charge of McMurdo operations. If he went to him now, Jack, who had a Ph.D. in biochemistry, would laugh him right out of his office. And there would go Micah's hopes of earning his chops, so he could go on to something more prestigious than working at McMurdo Station.

ICY PASSAGE, CHAPTER TWO

Jack DeVoe sat behind his desk staring at his computer monitor. He snagged a bottle of whiskey from a drawer and belted back a slug, but it didn't make the news any more palatable. Russia and the U.S. were at it again, arguing over Ukraine like a pack of feral dogs battling each other for a juicy bone. The U.S. threatened to send troops, and the Russian president was screaming threats over network news. Unfortunately, Jack was fluent in Russian, and the barrage of words sounded like much more than posturing.

He'd been in Antarctica for years. Maybe now was a good time to go for early retirement—before World War III stranded him at this remote outpost. The more he thought about it, the better he liked the idea, especially in light of the two dead women who'd shown up in the micro lab the other night. Despite him harassing maintenance until they ran the other way every time they saw him, they hadn't come up with a goddamned thing.

He straightened in his chair and rolled his shoulder blades to loosen the tension making his neck hurt. How in the fucking hell could two women die from carbon monoxide poisoning with no leaks? Not just two women, either. The young microbiologist would've been just as dead—but he got lucky. Jack ground his jaws until his teeth ached. He'd figure out what was killing his people. No matter what it took.

Then he'd leave Antarctica.

His phone buzzed and he picked it up, growling, "What?"

"Hey, boss. Micah here." He hesitated. "Is this an okay time? You seem miffed about something."

Nothing much. The world's imploding and a mystery gas leak is on the loose.

"Nah, I'm fine, Greenwich. You still feeling all right? What do you need? It's ten at night."

Micah cleared his throat. "Thanks for asking, but I made a good recovery." He paused a beat. "I suppose in a backhanded way, I owe my life to Britta and Marguerite. If it weren't for them, I'd be dead too."

"Get on with it." Jack rolled his eyes. "You didn't call to swap philosophies."

"Right, sir. Sorry. I know it's been a while since you did much with your biochem background, but I'd appreciate it if you could stop by the lab."

"Now?" Jack straightened in his chair and screwed the top back on the liquor bottle. "Is the lab on fire or something?" He shoved too-long blond hair out of his face and listened intently.

Micah laughed, but it sounded strained. "I've been running tests on my single-celled samples, but I keep coming up with odd results." He hesitated. "The other problem is a critical mass issue. Something bizarre happens when the colonies reach a certain size."

Jack squeezed his eyes shut. "Bizarre, how? Did you run it past the other microbiologists?" When Micah didn't answer, Jack prodded, "Well, did you?"

"Yeah. They're so freaked out by this, they don't want anything to do with it. They'd rather chalk it up to me being nuts."

Jack clicked away from Yahoo! News. He couldn't do a

damned thing about bad decisions on either side of the political fence. Or dead staff, apparently. Focusing on the phone in his hand, he said, "I still don't understand exactly why you need me," and followed up with, "Can it wait until morning?"

"I really think you should come see this, sir. If you tell me I've spent too much time at this Godforsaken outpost, I'll pick up my marbles, and no one will ever hear another word about my concerns."

Breath hissed from between Jack's teeth. "Fine. Be there in ten."

He dropped the phone into its cradle before the other man said goodbye and pushed heavily to his feet. The cold and isolation of Antarctica did things to people's minds. Maybe Micah had fallen prey to what Jack labeled the, "Aw shit, I'm stuck at the ass end of the world," syndrome.

He flexed his fingers, stretching them after long hours at the keyboard. Maybe a side trip to the lab wasn't a bad idea. He'd worked as a senior researcher in biochemistry at the National Institutes of Health before accepting the job running McMurdo, and he missed being in a lab teasing out thorny problems.

Besides, if he retreated to his quarters, he'd polish off the whiskey. A wry grin split his face. Compared with a lot of McMurdo residents, he was practically a teetotaler. The base went through buckets of booze, but it kept other problems at bay. He booted down his terminal, told the base operator he'd be on the sat phone if anyone needed him, and left his office.

The halls bustled with activity. Between the times when they had twenty-four hours of daylight, and the months of twenty-four hour darkness, no one kept much of a regular schedule. He nodded to a few folk as he passed them, clapping a shoulder here and punching an arm there as he made his way to the microbiology laboratories.

Located near the end of one of McMurdo's many wings, the labs housed state of the art equipment for studying the rich array of unicellular life forms that inhabited the Antarctic. He pushed the door open and strode inside. Not seeing Micah in the outer room, he yelled, "Greenwich!"

"In here, boss."

Following Micah's voice, Jack walked into one of four smaller rooms that shot off from the main one like wagon spokes.

The other man straightened from where he'd been bent over a binocular microscope. Tall and lanky, he wore hazmat gloves. Blond hair stuck out at crazy angles around the mask perched over a full beard. Bright blue eyes regarded Jack. "Thanks for coming."

Jack grunted and grabbed a mask and gloves of his own. "What's got you so fired up, son? And why the major hand coverings?"

Micah shook his head and twisted his stool to face Jack. "Should I start at the beginning?"

"Just hit the high points and let me ask questions." Jack hooked his foot around a stool and dropped into it.

Micah pulled his mask aside. "Okay. I've been here four months. Because I was youngest and new kid on the block, the others stuck me with archaea, you know the prokaryote colonies."

Jack snorted. "Yeah, no one's ever very interested in proks, probably because their structure's so simple." He narrowed his eyes. "You never answered me about the fancy hand coverings. Did the little bastards get away from you?"

Color stained Micah's face above his beard. "Now that you mention it, yes. Things were fine until the colonies developed a certain mass, but then things shifted."

"Are you talking about quorum sensing?" Jack asked, referring to a bacterial mechanism of population control based on density and several other factors.

"That's exactly what I'm talking about." Micah exhaled softly, fogging the lab glasses perched atop his nose. "Before we go further, come look at this." He got to his feet and pulled a sample bin across the table. Beige plastic, it was about eighteen inches long and a foot wide.

Jack got to his feet, frowning. The bin was large for bacterial colonies, which grew just fine on agar plates. Micah removed the lid, and Jack's mouth fell open when he stared at towers of cell colonies growing up the sides and along the bottom of the bin. Instead of the gray-green he'd expected, the colonies were violet, blue, red, and bright green.

"Holy crap!" He grabbed a sterile instrument off Micah's tray, pulled the plastic protector off, and gently prodded the mass in the bin. The tower nearest the tip of his instrument recoiled and flowed into a nearby glob of cells.

"I wouldn't get my hands too close," Micah cautioned.

Jack dropped the spatula back on the tray and motioned for Micah to put the lid back on the colony bin. "So instead of limiting their growth in response to quorum sensing, they're going nuts?" he asked.

"That's what it seems like to me," Micah replied. "But it gets worse. You asked about my gloves. I started feeling bad last week —a few days before I came in here and found Britta and Marguerite. Because of them, Dr. Stewart and Ariana caught my downhill slide in time to save me." He shrugged sheepishly. "The symptoms of carbon monoxide poisoning are subtle, and I'm a guy. I probably wouldn't have ever thought to turn myself in to the medics."

He shook his head. "During my stint in the infirmary, I had a lot of time to think, and I figured out what might've happened. It was pretty off-the-wall, though, and I needed to run some tests, first—"

"Cut to the chase. I'm all ears." Jack sat back on his stool. His stomach tightened, and he wished he'd either laid off the booze— or finished it.

"This will sound farfetched—"

"You already said that. Skip the fucking caveats. Just spit whatever it is out."

Micah inhaled sharply, exhaling in a rush before words tumbled past his lips. "You know how some proks have an affinity for iron?" At Jack's nod, he continued, "My best guess is I got sloppy with my gloves, and the proks worked their way through my skin, latched onto my red blood cells, and displaced their ability to bond to oxygen. It's the same mechanism carbon monoxide—and any other toxic gas—uses to kill you. Basically, you suffocate."

Jack felt like someone had sucker punched him. Before he could stop himself, a long, low whistle escaped. "I can see why the other researchers would want to discredit your theory. Distance themselves."

Micah colored again and studied his hands. "Sorry to bother you, sir. Like I said, you'll never hear another word—"

"Shut up," Jack snapped. "I didn't say I didn't believe you. Did you experiment with mice?"

The color mottling Micah's face deepened. "Er, yes. I know I'm supposed to requisition—"

"I don't give a flying fuck about that. What'd you find?"

Micah straightened his shoulders. "I introduced normal proks into a bin with two mice and these proks into a bin with two others. The mice with the normal proks are fine. The others are dead. When I examined their tissues, they died from oxygen starvation. Just like Britta and Marguerite." He stared hard at Jack. "Since maintenance couldn't find any gas leaks, my best guess is the women looked in the sample bins, were fascinated, and touched the colonies."

Jack felt old when he got to his feet and went to look into the bin with the crazily growing bacterial colonies. Micah's theory made a whole lot of sense. Plus it explained why maintenance had come up dry. After he replaced the lid, he gestured to the microscope. "What's under there is stained samples from this bin?"

"Yes."

"What's unique about them?"

"It's why I called you, sir. We finally made it to where I need your biochem background. These don't exactly look like proks anymore."

Jack strode to the microscope, adjusted it, and peered through the eyepieces. What he saw gave him pause. The prok structure was there, but these had more to them—lots more. He straightened slowly. "What happens if you separate the colonies?"

"Funny you should ask, since I already did. After a day or two, they revert to regular proks. My assumption is they'll stay that way until they divide enough to reach whatever critical mass spurs them to shift into that." He pointed at the sample bin.

"Mmph. Let's limit access to this lab to just you and me. For now, keep the colonies small, even if you have to jettison some material."

Micah shook his head. "I don't think tossing anything is smart. These guys thrive in almost any environment including extreme cold and salt water, but I'll do my best to keep the colonies under critical mass."

"Douse the ones you want to get rid of with ethyl alcohol and see how they like it." Jack stripped off his mask and gloves. "I'm going to call a friend of mine, Brynn McMichaels. He's a microbiologist I worked with at NIH. Just so happens he's stationed at South Georgia Island. Proks were a big interest of his."

"What's he doing with them?" Micah perked up, the flat, worried expression leaving his face.

"Building boutique antibiotics or some such thing. It's been a while since we've talked, so I'm not totally certain. Anyway, his contract must be close to up. If he hasn't signed on for another stint on South Georgia, maybe I can talk him into coming here.

We might be onto something fascinating with these mutant proks."

Micah smiled for the first time since Jack had entered the lab. "Thanks, sir. I appreciate it."

"Hang onto your gratitude. Let's see if we can get Brynn to come here, first. At the very least, I'm sure he'd be willing to bat ideas around on the phone or via email."

Jack headed out the door before Micah could thank him again. He remembered what it was like to have ideas no one else endorsed. The scientific community could be pretty shitty to researchers they viewed as renegades.

As he walked McMurdo's corridors, he rolled Micah's idea around in his head. Whiskey sloshed in his belly, and for the first time in years, he wished he had a pack of cigarettes. To quell his craving for tobacco, he scrolled through the contacts list on his sat phone on the way to his quarters. He had no idea if Brynn would be up yet, but it was morning on South Georgia, so he punched the buttons to put the call through.

After three rings, a sleepy-sounding Brynn said, "Hello?"

"Hey, old buddy. Jack here."

Sputtering blasted through the phone. "What the blazes are you doing calling at this hour? Must be the middle of the night there. Did McMurdo implode?"

"No, but the world might. Are you following the news?"

"Yeah, sure, but that's not what you woke me up for. Or is it? Hang on." Something clinked against the phone—probably a glass. "Damn. It's past eight. Time for me to get up anyway. Back to why you called. You speak Russian. Do I need to beat a path home?"

Jack grunted. "I was actually considering that earlier tonight, but no one's declared war—not yet, anyway. The reason I'm calling is we've got an unusual situation in the lab here with proks that've gone wild—"

"Aw, shit!" Brynn cut in. "You're kidding, right?"

"Wish I were." Jack pushed open the door to his small suite of rooms and kicked it shut behind him. Instincts working overtime, he asked, "You having the same problem?"

"Not exactly, but my colonies are acting oddly. Growing like mad. For some reason quorum sensing isn't slowing them down one whit, and once the colonies get to be a certain size, they almost demonstrate a group intelligence."

Air left Jack's lungs in a whoosh. Brynn had always been the most level-headed of researchers. "Are you certain?"

"Of course I'm certain," Brynn snapped. "What I haven't figured out is what to do about it."

"Be very careful while you're figuring it out. It's likely the proks here killed two women."

"What?" Brynn screeched. "They're single-celled life forms. How could they possibly harm a human?"

"This batch has an affinity for iron. Once they drill through the skin and get into the bloodstream, they have a heyday." Jack paused. "I've read about that phenomenon, but never come across it before."

Time dripped by before Brynn spoke again, still sounding agitated. "Maybe mine have a different problem. If they were going to get me, they've had lots of opportunity, and I feel fine."

"When's your contract with that Brit bio firm up?"

Brynn snorted. "Very soon. I already gave notice. I've had it with the southern ocean. Two years was plenty."

"Would you consider coming here and bringing your colonies with you?" Jack forged on before Brynn could protest. "It's good science to look at both mutating colonies side by side. Maybe we'll learn something critical."

A low rumble—maybe compressed frustration—preceded Brynn's next words. "I don't know, Jack. If I don't charter a flight back to Argentina, I might be stuck here if the political mess heats further."

"You could catch a plane from here to Christchurch," Jack

pointed out, not bothering to mention he'd be on it right along with Brynn.

"How would I get there? We're heading into winter, and the weather's unpredictable."

"Does that mean you'll come if I can figure out the logistics?" Jack pressed.

After a lengthy pause, Brynn said, "Yeah, I guess that's what it means, but I'll be damned if I know why I just said yes."

"Because we go back a long way, buddy."

"Yeah, we do. Keep me posted. If I don't hear from you in a few days, I'll make arrangements to get to Ushuaia or Buenos Aires."

"Fair enough. One more small favor."

"Hard to imagine it could be any bigger than what you just asked. What?"

"Can I give one of the microbiology staff your number? He'd love to have a blood brother to talk with, and the other three here have pretty much blown him off."

"Sure, Jack. No problem. As long as he waits until a little later this morning to call."

"I won't even tell him how to reach you before tomorrow morning here—and I'll remind him about the fifteen hour time difference. My admin staff will figure out how to transport you and your cultures to McMurdo. Stay tuned."

"Gosh, guess I'll make myself some breakfast now that you've given me something to look forward to. A reason to get out of bed and all that."

"Spare the sarcasm. Talk to you soon." Jack disconnected and booted up the computer in his quarters to check the weather window.

As his fingers flashed over the keys, he kept seeing the bacterial colony with its multi-hued towers of one-celled organisms. It seemed absurd, beyond the pale, that they'd attacked Micah and the two women. Regardless, Jack felt certain that if the young researcher hadn't stumbled over the lab cleaning staff, he'd be just as dead as them—and the mice in his experiment.

An uncomfortable sensation tracked down Jack's spine. It took a moment before he recognized it as fear. Thank Christ he'd warned Brynn.

www.ingramcontent.com/pod-product-compliance
Lightning Source LLC
Chambersburg PA
CBHW071236190726
48292CB00007B/2321